The *Kreya* shipped another huge wave, and as she began to roll back Mouritzen looked up, half expecting that Carling would have been swept away. But he still stood there, and standing, pointed down into the gulf of the hold. In a brief slackening of the wind, his voice roared out, harsh and apocalyptic:

'The third sign – look! The horses that swim like fishes!'

Mouritzen, with the others, was drawn to look down. The canvas flapped against the sides of the hold, in which water now lapped high up against the crumpled metal. And in the water, two of the horses threshed and struggled. They had been torn free of their stalls and now were fighting for their lives against the rising water.

'What did I tell you?' cried Carling. 'The third sign. Now the ship is doomed!'

Also by John Christopher in Sphere Books:

THE DEATH OF GRASS
A WRINKLE IN THE SKIN
THE YEAR OF THE COMET
THE POSSESSORS
THE WORLD IN WINTER
THE LITTLE PEOPLE
THE CAVES OF NIGHT

The Long Voyage

JOHN CHRISTOPHER

SPHERE BOOKS LIMITED
London and Sydney

First published in Great Britain by
Hodder & Stoughton Ltd 1960
Copyright © 1960 by John Christopher
Published by Sphere Books Ltd 1984
30–32 Gray's Inn Road, London WC1X 8JL
Reprinted 1986

TRADE
MARK

Set in Plantin

Printed and bound in Great Britain by
Cox & Wyman Ltd, Reading

Chapter One

There was a ragged sky over the city, the clouds grey-black, laced here and there with silver by an invisible sun, scudding away to the south-east. Up to and beyond O'Connell Bridge the Liffey was in motion, its usually placid oily surface whipped into waves that licked against the side of a Guinness barge going empty upstream. It had stopped raining, but the streets were wet and water ran along the gutters. The flanks of the dray-horses steamed in the mild, damp air.

Carling, striding along the quay, had the look of a man going to a trysting place – his demeanour was at once eager and furtive. He was a big man, tall and broad-chested, and but for the grey in his hair and beard might have been taken for someone in his middle thirties. He was forty-six. For forty-five of those years he had accepted life without question or complaint; strength and appetite had been enough. Now the questions were rampant in his mind, and he sought for answers with the simple childlike directness that was characteristic of him, and with a savage unbending brutality that was equally so.

He stopped by a door that stood between a seedy tobacconist's shop and another, as dingy, selling bicycle parts. There were three bell-pushes; by the second a card, protected by yellowed and air-bubbled Scotch tape, announced the Church of Holy Light. Carling pressed the button, holding his large thumb on it for perhaps half a minute. He released it when a window slammed open above his head. A woman looked out. She had long red hair, which must once have been beautiful. Her face was white and had a shapeless look, as though the bones were melting away beneath the flesh. She called down, in a soft, hoarse voice:

'Ah, is it you, then? You can come up. The door's not fastened. Come on up.'

Carling climbed dirty, crumbling stairs to the first floor. The dirt offended him, but in a way he felt that it was reasonable. He had lived in cleanliness and neatness and order, and had found

1

there only frustration and despair. It did not surprise him that hope had its lair in a noisome country.

He went through the tiny kitchen into the parlour. The smell of stewed bacon and cabbage was less pungent, but it still pervaded the room. He was aware of it more strongly again when he sat down, at Mrs Guire's direction, on the sagging red plush sofa; the cloth breathed out vapours received over thirty of forty years, and this, clearly, was the prevailing one. There were only four others in the room: he recognized them as the hard core of the faithful – Mrs O'Donovan, Mrs Walsh, Miss Pettigrew and old Gentrey. Sometimes there had been as many as a dozen, cramped and crowded together among the aspidistras and the coloured vases.

'We were only just after starting,' said Mrs Guire. 'We hadn't even sung the hymn. Is it this morning you've docked?'

'Only just now,' Carling said. 'I came straight here.'

'It will be terrible seas you've had,' Mrs Walsh said, 'with the kind of weather it's been the last week.'

Carling nodded. 'Yes.'

'I was listening on the wireless only yesterday,' Mrs Guire said, 'to them telling of ships in distress all round the coasts of England, and I thought of you, Mr Carling, I prayed for the spirits to watch over you.'

'That was kind,' Carling said.

They looked at him with pleasure and respect; he was so large a man, handsome, in the prime of his life, and his presence enhanced and justified theirs. The hard gleam of determination in his eye sparked their own drifting dampness of spirit.

'When I was a young man,' Gentrey said, 'I sailed to America. Ah, that was a crossing. I've feared the sea since. And you meet it in all its conditions, year in, year out. It takes courage for that.'

'I had a brother,' Mrs O'Donovan said, 'who drowned off the coast of Spain, God rest his holy soul. He was a lad of twenty, and I was two years younger. I mourned him greatly. For a time I thought of taking the veil. But I met O'Donovan and was married instead.'

'It's the priests,' Mrs Walsh said. She was a thin, dark woman, who had been bitter until life defeated her. 'They'd talk a young girl into that kind of thing. God, is there a nation in the world as beset with priests as Ireland!'

Mrs O'Donovan had a reminiscent look on her round, slightly whiskered face.

2

'Not that time it wasn't,' she said. 'It was Father Green, a young fellow not ten years older than myself, who counselled me. He told me to have a good look at the world, before I gave it up. There was a sadness in him. I've wondered since what became of him. He had the makings of a Cardinal, or a renegade.'

'Renegade's the word they use,' Gentrey said, 'for such as open their eyes and use the minds God gave them.'

Carling said restlessly: 'I have delayed you – but we can begin now?'

'Sure we can,' Mrs Guire said. She spoke soothingly. 'Let me just get to the piano.'

She sat down at the upright piano, with brass candlesticks at either end and faded red silk cloth in front. She struck a note and went straight into the hymn, *Lead Kindly Light*. Carling heard the voices quavering and scraping about him for a few bars before he permitted his own deep, heavily accented baritone to join in. They sang the usual two verses and then Mrs Guire turned round from the piano to face them.

'Jesus Christ Almighty,' she said, 'bless our gathering this day. Grant us, Lord Jesus, the knowledge we seek, the power and the wisdom. Remembering Thy conquest of Death and the Powers of Evil, grant us that Thy Spirits may come to us as they have done before. In the name of the Sacred Holy Cross, look down on us and pity us. Amen.'

While the other voices were echoing the response, she moved briskly back to her armchair and sat down. Her arms rested along the threadbare plush, her fists clenching and then relaxing. Her eyes closed and she began to moan.

Gentrey said: 'It's quick today.'

'And it's in need of the words of comfort I am,' said Mrs O'Donovan, 'with the hard times we're having.'

The moan became articulate. 'The sailor,' said Mrs Guire. She spoke through her teeth. 'The sailor!'

'Is it my brother, then,' Mrs O'Donovan said, 'that I've prayed to hear from since the first day I came here? Is it little Paulie?'

Her eyes still closed, Mrs Guire turned her face fully in Carling's direction.

'Great peril,' she said, '– the wind like a thousand banshees, and the great green waves that would pull a man down into the deeps.'

'Is it she?' Carling asked. There was sweat on his forehead. 'Is it she that warns?'

She appeared to strain for words, at first finding none.

'I see horses . . . and a savage brute beast in a cage . . . and the waves and the water and the peril of death . . .'

Carling leaned forward. 'Does she say it?'

'A wave like a wall of doom, like a hammer of Hell. I see death, death. Death for the horses, death for the brute beast that stands as a man stands . . . death for men in the deeps of the sea . . .'

'Glory be to God,' whispered Mrs O'Donovan. 'I haven't heard the power of that in the five years I've been coming here.'

'It is she I would speak to,' Carling said. 'Let me speak to her!'

'Death for some – but not for all . . . a ship doomed, but not all doomed who sail in her. There are three signs. The first is when the beast walks free. The second is when water breaks iron and breaks a man. The third is when horses swim like fishes. Then comes the moment of peril. Then some will die and some will live . . . Death in the savage waters . . .'

'Is she there?' Carling demanded. 'Tell me that!'

Mrs Guire's head sank down on her breast. She moaned two or three times, and opened her eyes. She tossed back her hair and looked at Carling.

'The kettle's on,' she said. 'I'll make the tea.'

Mrs Walsh asked her: 'Is it all, then Maeve? Is there no word for the rest of us?'

Mrs Guire shook her head. 'If there is, I've no strength for it. When I've had a drop of tea, maybe. The power has gone out of me.'

Carling followed her into the kitchen. He watched as she tipped tea from the painted tin caddy into the teapot, and poured on the boiling water from the kettle.

'There will be no more for me,' he said. 'She will not speak today?'

'No.' She looked at him. In the look there was desire, and curiosity, and some fear. 'Jesus in Mercy, I have a headache from it. Can you come round tomorrow? There might be something then.'

'We sail tonight. The storm delayed us; we should have come yesterday, but we are late.'

They were standing close together in the tiny kitchen. She put her hand out and touched his brown, muscled wrist.

'There's truth in it,' she said. 'Danger from the sea, and not so far off either. Don't go back.' She shook her head. 'I saw it – I wouldn't believe it, but I saw it.' Her hand tightened on his wrist. 'Stay behind this trip. You can put up at the Mission.' Her fingers moved lightly. 'Or I could put you up on the sofa next door.'

'I have to go,' Carling said.

'Ah, there's no sense in risking your neck for no good cause.'

'I will come back,' Carling said. He took a note from his wallet and placed it on the table. Mrs Guire did not look at it.

'You'll stay for a cup of tea, anyway.'

'No. Thank you. There is much to do on the ship. I ought not to have left, but I thought . . . In the end, I will speak to her? That is certain, is it not?'

'Ah God, and how can I tell?' She turned from the look in his eye. 'Yes, yes, you'll speak to her.'

'She had a little voice,' he said. 'Like a small bird.'

'Will you not have a cup of tea now? It's ready to pour.'

Carling shook his head. 'Good-bye. I must go now.'

Chapter Two

The m.v. *Kreya* was berthed on the more sheltered northern side of the quay, but even so she rocked a little on the swell and her anchor chain creaked in monotonous rhythm. Captain Erik Olsen stood on the bridge, beside his First Officer, and watched the loading. He was a small man, with a small, handsome head, and eyes that, much of the time, surveyed the world with bleak amusement. Niels Mouritzen, the First Officer, was on a different scale: handsome in a more virile fashion, an inch or two over six feet in height, blue-eyed and fair-haired, with a slightly bent nose. He was deep-voiced, and spoke with a hesitance that was not quite an impediment.

He said: 'We are getting through it faster than I had expected. There's not much this time, is there?'

Olsen looked at his watch. 'Not fast enough.'

'We will be ready by eight.'

'Eight is not six.'

'We've gained a day. The men were hoping we would miss the tide. They could have done with a night ashore.'

Olsen did not bother to answer this. After a time, Mouritzen said:

'She will be riding light – nothing in the forward hold except the horses and the caravan.'

'How many horses now?'

'Ninety-five. Sixty for Dieppe, thirty-five for Amsterdam.'

'If they don't start loading soon we shall not be clear by eight even. When are the passengers coming on?'

'After five o'clock, I told the office.'

'Six here, and the other two at Fishguard?'

'Yes.'

'Poles, Irish and English?' He switched into English from Danish. 'We speak English then on this voyage.' Pointing to a figure that approached the gang-plank, he reverted to his native tongue. 'I didn't know Carling had gone ashore?'

'He asked me if he could, just for an hour.'

'With what reason?'

'Some kind of spiritualists he's picked up with here. They were meeting this afternoon and he wanted to go.'

'You thought that reason sufficient?'

'He's a good man. It isn't the reason that matters, surely.'

'I don't like it,' Olsen said, 'when a man of his type becomes mixed up in that kind of thing.'

'There are circumstances to explain it.'

'That does not interest me. And it was a year ago. By now he should have returned to normal. Instead, he gets worse.'

'It doesn't affect his seamanship.'

'No? The man is more important than the skill. Religion is like drinking; you should develop a head for it when young or leave it alone altogether.'

'Some begin late.'

'Then it's bad.'

Mouritzen put his hands on one of the spokes, and rocked the wheel to and fro.

'Did you ever meet her?' he asked.

'Who? Carling's wife? No.'

'Twenty-five years younger than he. She looked like a child, too. Small and pretty – a nice figure, what there was of it. A happy little innocent soul, one would have thought.'

'And wasn't she?' Olsen made a gesture of dismissal and distaste.

6

'You are a moralist, Niels. You should learn to judge no actions but your own.'

Mouritzen shrugged. 'It's not I who objects to Carling going ashore to listen to the stories the spirits tell him.'

'But you should! This is a matter of the ship. I condemn no man or woman, however savage and enormous their sins, as long as they do not touch the *Kreya*. But anything that touches the ship is different. In this small world, I am God. I judge, I punish, and I need not give my reasons.'

Mouritzen grinned. 'Perhaps you would have been happier on a strictly cargo ship. You cannot play God to passengers.'

'A different God – a modern, liberal God, who exists but does not act.' He pointed his finger at the First Officer. 'Action I leave to my angels – to you and to Thorsen. One can argue with angels. God is in the background, unchallengeable, unarguable-with.'

Mouritzen was looking down towards the quay. The loading crane was aft, taking on steel rails. A woman and child stood to one side of it, looking, with some hesitation, in the direction of the gang-plank.

'That will be Mrs Cleary and daughter,' Mouritzen said. 'The clerk should have come with her. I suppose Thorsen and the boy are below. I think I must go down and see her aboard.'

Olsen said sardonically: 'Can you see from here that she is pretty? Go on, then. But you are a working angel, remember, not a fallen one.'

'Yes,' Mouritzen said. He smiled. 'My respects to God.'

The couple were still hesitating by the gang-plank when he walked down it to greet them. The woman was certainly pretty, he noticed with satisfaction; she had an attractive, compact figure, with silky blonde hair, brown eyes, and a pink and white complexion. She was young, also – not far into her twenties. The child was a small copy, and about six years old. The mother was neatly dressed, but in a coat and shoes that had seen better days. The child's clothes were newer and looked more expensive. She had a wine-red coat lined with white fur, and a white muff.

He said: 'Mrs Cleary? I am Niels Mouritzen, First Officer of the *Kreya*. May I show you on board?'

'Thank you.' She looked at him, with some nervousness but with a pleasant frankness. 'I was wondering if it would be all right. I think we're early.'

7

Mouritzen bent down to the little girl. 'And what is your name?' he asked.

'Annabel.'

'That is a nice name.'

'You speak English very well,' the mother said. 'I was wondering about that, since it's a Danish boat.'

Mouritzen smiled. 'We Danes have become civilized since we first came to Dublin. Most of us speak English. Do you have your baggage with you?'

'It's over there.' She pointed. 'Where the taxi put us down.'

There was one large suitcase and one small, both made of pressed fibre material and secured by cheap yellow leather straps.

'It will be all right there for a few minutes,' Mouritzen said, 'I will tell the steward and he will bring the cases on board. We will go on first. Shall I carry you, little Annabel?'

She looked at him gravely, coldly. 'Thank you, but I can walk by myself.'

'Good, good!' He helped them on to the gang-plank in turn. 'Welcome to the *Kreya*. I hope you will both enjoy your trip.'

Thorsen came out of the lounge as he showed them in. He was much shorter than Mouritzen, with dark curly hair, and features that were marred only by a heaviness of jaw. In repose his face was sullen, but he smiled often. He was conscious of his appearance as part of his stock-in-trade and, aware that his own seemingly natural charm was studied, not spontaneous, mistrusted natural-ness in others. Suspicion of human motives came easily to him.

'Ah,' Mouritzen said, 'this is our Chief Steward, Mr Thorsen. He will look after you. Jorgen, is the boy at hand? Mrs Cleary has two cases to be brought on.'

'How do you do, Mrs Cleary?' Thorsen said. He gave the child a quick smile. 'I'll show you to your cabin right away. Your cases will be here directly.'

From the deck the door gave on to a tiny lobby, with a steep flight of stairs on one side, a service door facing this and the main doors to the lounge directly in front. Thorsen opened the service door; the little room beyond it was a combination of bar and kitchenette, and a boy of fifteen was washing up plates at the sink. Thorsen spoke to him rapidly in Danish, and he nodded in reply. He was tall for his age, fair-haired, with a long face and rimless spectacles that gave him a studious look.

'Then I will leave you in Mr Thorsen's hands,' Mouritzen said.

8

'I shall see you later, Mrs Cleary. Good-bye till then.'

Thorsen gestured towards the stairs, and the woman and child climbed them. At their head there was a T-shaped corridor, with cabin doors ranged along the top of the T: a second flight of stairs led to the officers' quarters. There were four cabins, and he led her to No. 1. It had a built-in settee, covered in grey leather, on one side, and two bunks on the other. Between, there was a small, asymmetrical dressing-table and writing-desk. This was of white wood, contrasting with the light mahogany of the bunks. The floor was covered, wall to wall, with pale blue carpeting.

Thorsen opened a door to the left of the settee.

'This is the toilet – shower, wash-basin and so on.'

She looked round the cabin. 'It's very nice. More – more modern than I expected.'

'The *Kreya* is only three years old,' Thorsen told her. 'Your bags are here now.' He made a sign to the boy to set them down. 'Is there anything else you require just now?'

'I can't think of anything.'

'The Customs Officer will be coming on board in about an hour. Would you like me to take your passport for him?'

She said, a little quickly: 'Can't I keep it and show it to him myself?'

Thorsen nodded, smiling. 'Of course. Some people prefer me to have the documents; then, sometimes, it is not necessary for them to be bothered.'

'I'll keep mine,' she said.

'Of course.' He backed out of the cabin. 'Dinner is served at seven o'clock.'

The Simanyi family came on board a few minutes before six, father and son carrying cameras and the mother carrying a shopping bag laden with fruit, biscuits and chocolate. The daughter, Nadya, carried only a small handbag, from which, as they stood on deck waiting for Thorsen, she took out compact and lipstick to make up her face. She was a fairly tall girl, with straight black hair, strong but good-looking features, and a curved and well-muscled figure. At close quarters she would attract a man who liked powerful women with a promise of temperament, perhaps to the point of violence. In her proper place – seen from a distance in the arc-light's glare as she climbed the twisting ladder towards the

9

trapezes, sequins gleaming against white flesh, she would be irresistible.

The mother was smaller, and had never been as handsome, but she had kept her figure well and still rode a horse in the Grand Parade and the Cowboys-and-Indians tableau; sometimes she featured in the knife- and hatchet-throwing acts when the usual girl was ill. She had an alert, smiling, heavily wrinkled face, fixed in a disposition of curiosity and expectancy towards an ever-changing world.

Josef Simanyi, the head of the family, was not tall either; measured against his daughter he might have had an advantage of half an inch, but no more. He was square in build, inclined to be squat, and although, at fifty-five, his shoulders were beginning to be bowed, he was exceptionally strong. In the ring, apart from bareback riding, he bent iron bars, tore up telephone books and otherwise demonstrated his strength. He had also, at one time, been a fire-eater and sword-swallower, but had more or less abandoned these practices.

His son, Stefan, shared the trapeze act with Nadya. He had a white face and thick black hair which he kept combed back in a hard, glossy shell. His appearance otherwise was nondescript. He had small, uneven teeth and a small moustache.

When Thorsen came out, Stefan and the parents greeted him with enthusiasm.

'So we are back, you see!' Josef said. 'As promised. We said we come back on the *Kreya*. So here we are.'

'Did you have a good summer?' Thorsen asked.

He shook hands with them in turn until he came to Nadya. She nodded at him and smiled briefly, her hands still engaged with the compact.

'Not bad,' Josef said. 'In this country there is more money hidden away than one thinks at first. And not much television.'

'And Katerina? Is she well also?'

'For a time, in the west country, she was ill. I think she ate something bad, you know. But she is fine right now. She comes aboard soon?'

'I suppose so. That is not my job. Will I show you to your cabins?'

'Tell us the numbers and we find them,' Josef said. 'We know the way, remember.'

'All the same, I'll show you.'

He made way for them to enter and climb the stairs. The women went first. Stefan, waiting at the bottom, clutched Thorsen's arm.

'The weather – it will be bad, eh?'

'Not very bad, I think. The glass is rising again.'

Stefan nodded in resignation. 'I will be sick.'

'Perhaps not. Last week it was very bad but it is better now. Maybe you will not be sick.'

'I am always sick,' Stefan said.

Thorsen followed them along the corridor. 'No. 2 and No. 4,' he said. 'This, and the one at the end.'

Mrs Simanyi turned to him in surprise and consternation.

'But they are not together!'

'The other two had been allotted when your booking came in,' Thorsen explained. 'But they are all separate cabins, you know. They do not connect together.'

'We had cabins side by side in April,' she said. 'I could knock on the wall to Papa, and he knocked back to me. I am not happy if there is another cabin between us.'

Josef pointed to the door of No. 3. 'This one is empty. Maybe they are not coming. It is past six o'clock.'

'They are coming on early tomorrow morning at Fishguard. Perhaps they would change then.' Thorsen shrugged. 'But perhaps not. They are English.'

'And the other cabin?' Mrs Symanyi asked.

'A mother and little girl. Would you like me to ask if they will change with you?'

'Yes. No, I will ask myself. She is inside?'

Mary Cleary came to the door in answer to the knock. She had taken off her coat and was wearing a blue wool dress. Behind her Annabel was sitting on the top bunk, her legs swinging. Mrs Simanyi explained her request.

'Of course,' Mary said. 'It makes no difference to us. We'll move over now.'

Mrs Simanyi took her hand in both hers. 'You are most kind,' she said. 'You know how it is that a woman wishes to feel her husband is close at hand.'

Mary looked at her steadily. 'Yes.'

'Stefan!' Mrs Simanyi called. 'Carry the lady's cases to the other cabin. She is like you, your daughter. A beauty.' She fished in her shopping bag. 'Can she have chocolate?'

'Thank you – but not before supper.'

'Then she will eat it after supper, or tomorrow, maybe.'

Annabel climbed down and came for the chocolate. Mrs Simanyi embraced her.

'A beauty,' she repeated. 'Take an apple also. Eat the apple after the chocolate. That makes your teeth strong and white, eh?'

She went with Mary and Annabel to the No. 4 cabin, and looked round it appraisingly.

'It is as good as the other, you think?' she asked.

'Yes,' Mary said. 'Just as good.'

'I am glad. You travel also to Copenhagen?'

Mary shook her head. 'No. Only as far as Amsterdam.'

'You take a trip – just you and the little one?'

'Yes.'

'And your husband stays behind in Ireland?'

Mary said: 'I'm a widow.'

'I am sorry.'

The two women looked at one another, the older offering, the younger warily refusing.

'You want to be alone now,' said Mrs Simanyi.

The horses were brought up for loading about half past six. They were in lines of ten, loosely roped together, each attended by a groom. Mouritzen stood by the open forward hatch and watched them being slung over, two at a time, in the horse-box. One or two whinnied in anxiety as the box was lifted by the crane, but for the most part they were docile enough. The dock labourers, down in the hold, led them out and secured them in the wooden stalls which ran along either side.

Mary and the child had come on deck to watch. Mouritzen walked along and stood beside them.

'Good evening,' he said. 'The horses are almost the end. Then we sail.'

Another row of ten moved forward from the darkness into the glow of lights.

'Where are the horses going?' she asked. 'To Copenhagen?'

Mouritzen shook his head, grinning. 'In Denmark, we do not eat horse.'

'Eat?'

She bit her lip and looked quickly at Annabel, who had turned from watching the scene in the hold to stare at Mouritzen.

He said softly: 'I am sorry.' In a normal voice, he went on: 'It is a saying. I mean, we do not use horses to work in the fields. We have tractors instead.'

She said gratefully: 'Where will these horses be sent to work?'

'Some will leave us at Dieppe, the rest at Amsterdam. You are not a country woman?'

'No. Why do you say that?'

'They are not young, these horses. Ten years old and more. We think all Irish people have a deep knowledge of horses.'

'I've always lived in Dublin.'

'And now you go far away – to Amsterdam?'

'Yes.'

He waited for her to say something more, but she remained silent. He asked:

'Is it your first visit?'

'Yes.'

'I hope you will like it there.'

She made no comment. Annabel asked:

'Do people eat horses?'

Mouritzen looked at Mary. She said after a moment:

'In some countries they do.'

'Will these horses be eaten?'

'No. Not these.'

The next load went to the No. 2 hatch, and Annabel went along there to look. Mary moved to follow her.

Mouritzen said: 'She is quite safe. You do not wish her to know – about the horses?'

'Why should she?'

'There is death in the world. It cannot be hidden.'

'She will have time enough to find out.'

'So you lie to her? Is that better?'

She looked at him, unsure whether to be angry or not. She had it in mind to tell him that she had not asked for his advice and that he had no right to offer it unasked. But in the seriousness of his face she read his innocence of any wish to give offence.

She said, smiling slightly: 'You aren't married, are you? Or if you are, you have no children.'

'Why?'

'Because you don't understand that children are not the same as adults.'

'So it is a good thing to lie to them?'

'In Denmark,' she asked him, 'do you have Santa Claus?'

13

He nodded. 'Saint Nicholas. That is different, I think.'

'How different?'

'A game, a fancy. But this – you seek to protect her, but there are things we must all learn, and it is better, I think, to learn them early and not later. In that way, one accepts them more easily.'

Annabel was still out of earshot, looking over the side of the hatch.

'I think you're wrong,' she said. 'A child has a right to be protected, a right to innocence.'

'Innocence is tougher than you think. Do not confuse it with ignorance.'

She smiled again. 'Do you always give this kind of advice to passengers?'

He smiled also. 'Not always.'

They were silent for a time. The business of loading went on – the line of horses forward, a couple led into the box, the dizzy arc through the night air, the cries and commands as it was lowered into the hold, and then the empty box swinging back for the cycle to start again.

Mary said: 'A life of hard work, and then to be shipped overseas to a foreign butcher. It doesn't seem fair, does it?'

'I have thought that, too,' he said. 'But a farmer cannot be sentimental.'

'Can a sailor?'

'More easily.'

'Yourself?'

'Sentimental? No, I am a realist.'

'But you said that you have thought how unfair it was.'

'One must be realistic about one's emotions, too. Only an idealist thinks himself rational in all things.'

They were coming to the end; the last batch of horses was brought up. Among them a large dappled grey was restless, jerking its head against the rope. When it was brought forward to the box, it refused to enter; they heard the clatter of its hooves on the stone as it resisted the attempts to get it forward. Finally it was led to one side, and another horse brought up to share the box.

'Will they let it stay?' she asked.

'No. It is just that it will be easier to take by itself.'

This was what happened; when the other horses had been loaded, the grey was urged once more towards the empty box. It made less resistance this time. As it was borne through the air towards them, they could see that it had striking light blue eyes.

'He's beautiful,' Mary said.

'Yes. Beauty does not help any more than courage.'

Annabel ran back to them. 'Will there be any more horses?' she asked.

'No more.' Mouritzen bent down to her. 'But something else. Do you wish to see?'

She nodded, and he lifted her in his arms.

'Look!' he said. 'Over there. Where the men are fastening the net to the iron bars.'

'It's just a box,' Annabel said. 'A big box, painted green.'

'There is something inside. Guess!'

'Another horse?' she looked more dubiously at the crate. 'A pony?'

'No. Guess again.'

'I can't.' The crane began to whir, and the crate lifted from the quay. 'Tell me,' she demanded.

'A bear!' Mouritzen said.

She looked at him, her lips compressed. 'You're joking.'

He wagged his head solemnly from side to side.

'No joke. A bear, a real bear. Tomorrow you will be able to see her. She is called Katerina. She does tricks. She is a circus bear.' In explanation to Mary, he added: 'It belongs to a Polish circus family, who have been with a circus in Ireland. They are passengers, too.'

'I've met them.'

The crate was set down on deck, between the hatch and the forecastle.

'Can the bear get loose?' Annabel asked.

'No, no. There is a cage inside the crate, with thick iron bars. She will not get loose. I promise you that.'

The door from the passengers' quarters opened. A woman's figure was framed against the bright oblong of light. Mouritzen put Annabel down.

'And now I must go back to the bridge,' he said. 'To my work. And it is almost time for you to go for your supper, and then to bed.'

'Will you be at dinner?' Mary asked.

'Not tonight. We are late and there is much to do. Good-bye now.'

He bowed slightly to them and left. They saw him cross to the other side and climb the steps leading to the bridge.

There was light rain falling when the *Kreya* backed out into the main stream of the Liffey. Mouritzen stayed on the bridge, not so much because he was needed as to act as a buffer between Olsen and the Dublin pilot. Olsen resented all pilots, and this man in particular. It was his conviction that, after half a dozen entries and departures, he was capable of taking his ship, unaided, in and out of any port in Europe; and he had once been misguided enough to say something of this to Murray, the pilot in question. Murray, seeming at first, in his soft Dublin brogue, to agree with the thesis, had led Olsen on, step by step, until it became transparently clear that he was mocking him. Since then the terms between them had worsened at each encounter. Mouritzen was relieved that, this time, Olsen contented himself with brusque and icy acknowledgments of the pilot's remarks, and that Murray did not seem disposed to object to this or to provoke anything beyond it.

The siren was sounded for the pilot's cutter, and Mouritzen went down with him to the deck.

'Better weather than when we came in this morning,' he said.

They leaned over the side, watching for the cutter.

'How do you live with him?' Murray asked.

'With whom?'

Murray jerked his thumb. 'That one up there.'

'He's not so bad. You made a fool of him once. He does not like that.'

'I've never taken kindly to little men, but there's some worse than others.'

'He's not so bad,' Mouritzen repeated. 'He has a sense of humour, you know. You have seen the worst of him.'

'I'd be as glad to see the last of him.'

'He is a good captain. The best seaman I have sailed under.'

'Is he now? All the same, I would choose to sail under a man with less pride. Pride's before judgment with his kind.'

The cutter was sweeping round towards them. Murray climbed over the side and shook hands with Mouritzen before climbing down the rope ladder.

'Good luck,' he said.

'And to you.'

He continued to descend as the cutter came alongside and, with a lurch, jumped on board. A seaman began to haul in the ladder.

Mouritzen turned away and saw Thorsen coming along the deck from the direction of the galley.

'Ready for dinner yet?' he asked.

'More than ready,' Mouritzen said. 'But I will wait for the Captain. He'll be down when we clear the Howth lighthouse.'

Thorsen smiled. 'Someone's been looking for you. I told here you were busy with Mrs Cleary.'

'You can keep her amused yourself, can't you?'

'You're the one she wants. And these strong women make me nervous. I went to Stockholm on holiday when I was sixteen and it left a mark on me.'

Mouritzen did not care for the sly obscenity which, from Thorsen's side, pervaded this kind of conversation, but he suffered it as a contribution towards shipboard harmony. At the moment, though, he did not feel up to contributing his share. He merely nodded, with a slight smile.

'She's nice,' Thorsen commented, 'the Irish woman?'

'Yes, she's nice. And the little girl.'

'I offered to take her passport to give to the Customs Officer, but she insisted on keeping it to herself.'

'It's her first time abroad. She's probably nervous of losing it.'

'You think so? I was in her cabin while they were at dinner, seeing to the beds.' He paused. 'Your list is not quite accurate. It's Miss Cleary, not Mrs.'

Mouritzen kept rein on his temper. As he had told himself before, Thorsen was what he was, and nothing could alter that or the fact that, for the time being, they must spend the greater part of their lives together. He merely said coldly:

'How long have you been going through the passengers' belongings?'

'I didn't do that,' Thorsen said quickly. 'There was no need. She had left the passport on her bunk.'

Mouritzen was not sure whether he believed him, but there was no point in expressing his doubt. He said:

'Anyway, it's her own affair.'

'I thought it might be yours,' Thorsen said. 'A tip on form before the big race.'

'You observe a lot, don't you, Jorgen? You are a student of human nature.'

'In this job, one has to be. And there's plenty of opportunity.'

'It's a pity you're not better fitted to take advantage of it. You are like a student of music who can only hear notes in one octave.'

'And you – you read characters by intuition?'

'Yes. By intuition.'

'Does it tell you what success you will have with Miss Cleary?'

Mouritzen turned away. 'I'm going to wash,' he said. 'I'll be down in ten minutes.'

There had been grousing in the mess-room at the quickness of the turn-round after the rough westerly voyage. It was the kind of talk to which, normally, Carling was quick to put a halt: he had always been a strong disciplinarian and the outward show of authority had remained after the narrow spring of purposefulness which originated it had broken and grown slack. And Olsen was not a popular captain: the sardonic quality in his personality would only have been condoned in a man physically bigger. In him it was resented.

But this time Carling left them grumbling and went up on deck. He felt the thrust of wind and rain as he climbed up to the poop-deck. Behind him were the lighted port-holes of the passengers' cabins and higher up the lights of the wheelhouse. He looked over the rail at the ship's wake, fading away into the black night of the river. To his right the line of regular yellow lights marked the road from Howth to the city; opposite lay the scattered points east of Ringsend. Far back in the distance there was the city itself, a glow of brightness touched with the flicker of neon.

Was heaven like that, he thought – a bright ball in the faraway night, a city seen from the sea? There had been a story once, when he was a child, about a man who travelled over a dark desert land and came at last to the heavenly city, a light that grew and grew. But this light dwindled, as the *Kreya* left the Hill of Howth on her port side and drove out to the open waters.

Carling felt a brief despair that was close to anger. If there had been another day, time to go again to Mrs Guire's, she might have spoken. She was there – she was always there – but she would not speak. During their courtship and the short year of their married life she had sometimes exasperated him with her mysteries, her teasing silences, but he had not seriously minded them. She would yield at last, overwhelm him with a torrent of talk and laughter, and that which remained of the enigmatic was always there to be resolved in the future. Each time he had left her with a sharper

18

pang, and on each return the rein of anticipation had been tighter, more compelling.

He thought of their last time together, an afternoon in autumn, with the sunlight falling warmly through the windows of the little flat, and Tove lying on the couch, basking in it like a small cat. He had been collecting his things together; he was due to join the *Kreya* at five.

'Eiler,' she said. She spoke his name slowly, reflectively, as though for the first time.

'I must be going.' He went over to kiss her. 'Don't get up.'

'I've been wondering.'

'Wondering what?'

'Why I married you.'

Carling knelt beside her, holding her soft hand against his cheek, making no reply.

'Strong,' she said. 'Quite handsome. But old, so old. And a sailor, I'm a wife for a few days in each month – no more. I'm not sure that it's worth it.'

'I've been thinking,' Carling said, 'that I might give up the sea.'

She looked at him, brow furrowed, eyes half closed, as though he were a stranger whom she could not be sure of trusting.

'Give it up?'

'I might be able to get a shore job, in the docks. Karl Hansen there might be able to get me taken on.'

She said nothing. A faint smile was on her lips.

'How would you like that?' Carling asked.

He knew what one could expect of a woman; an ordinary woman would have shown him her delight, pulled his head down to her breast, kissed him and fondled him, in gladness and pride that her husband should sacrifice all that had been important in his life for the single joy of being with her continually. But an ordinary woman would not have been worth the sacrifice.

'Well,' he said, 'do you think I should do it?'

'We do what we have to do,' Tove said. The smile faded, and was replaced by graveness, by sadness almost. 'Come back to me soon, Eiler. Don't be long away.'

'Two weeks,' he said.

'So long?'

She spoke in a childish, wondering tone. In annoyance, he said: 'You know how long the trip is. It's no more than usual. I will be

19

here less than half an hour after we dock. I cannot be here sooner.'

He spoke the final sentence with more emphasis. She would never go with him to the ship, or meet him there, as some of the women did. It had been an early disappointment; an affront to the pride with which he had pictured her standing there, for all the world and his shipmates to see. But she was Tove, and her uniqueness enthralled him.

'Be as quick as you can,' she said. 'I don't want to be alone.'

As he had prepared to get up she had suddenly stretched up her arms to him and clung, kissing him with a wild passion.

And that had been the end. Nothing more. Only the stunning, inescapable fact. No letter. No motive. No answer now to any of the questions – to love no requital.

Carling clutched the rail in his agony, feeling the cold, wet metal sting his skin. Nothing made sense unless there was an answer, somewhere, somehow. She could not have left him like that without a reason. The need to know, to understand, had grown instead of lessening in the year that had passed since. It was Tove who had gone, but it was he that was the restless ghost, doomed to walk until his cry was answered. This demand, this urgency, had moved into the centre of his being, and stayed there, like a cancer, devouring all other thoughts and feelings. Once again she had spoken, at Mrs Guire's, but if he had waited . . . The lights of Dublin coalesced into a fading star. Next time, next time she must speak.

And say what?

Carling shook his head. The thought probed deep and struck, touching fear that was an open wound. He swayed to and fro. He heard a thin cry, like a gull's call, against the sounds of wind and water, and the throb of the engines. It was his own voice, naked and involuntary.

Chapter Three

The last two passengers were listed as Mr and Mrs Henry Jones. He was the elder, by perhaps fifteen years, a man in his early forties, with greying hair and a thickening waistline; he wore heavy-sided glasses and had the glib, worried look of an unsuccessful businessman. Mrs Jones was dark and rather thin. She wore a black and white check coat, open since the weather remained mild, and beneath that a red jersey under a navy suit. She carried a sturdy and well-worn leather handbag. Thorsen put her down as the kind of Englishwoman whose dress allowance is what she can save from a barely adequate housekeeping budget.

They stayed on deck to watch the ship sail. It was eleven o'clock and the sun, which had been only lightly filmed by the fast-moving clouds, broke through them at last. They stood on the starboard side, aft of the bridge.

'We're off, then,' she said.

'Yes.'

He looked not at her but at the water bubbling away from the ship's sides beneath them. Heights were inclined to make him dizzy. He had a moment's fear that his glasses would fall off into the sea, and pushed them on more firmly.

'I didn't think the ship would be so big,' she said.

'It isn't very big.'

'It is to me. I've never been on anything bigger than a ferry-boat before, remember.'

He took out a cigarette and lit it, turning away from the wind and cupping the flame between his hands. After he had drawn on it a couple of times, he said:

'When I was a boy, I always looked forward to things up to this point. It was after that it all turned flat.'

'Going out to India, or coming back?'

'Both. It was the journey I looked forward to – the voyage especially.'

'I wish I'd been able to travel.'

'It was always a disappointment. Anyway, you are travelling now. With a long journey ahead.'

'It 's different when you do things as a child.'

'I suppose it is.'

She said: 'If we'd gone by air, we would have been there by now, wouldn't we?'

He heard the anxiety in her voice and put an arm round her shoulders. She was a slight thing, even wearing an overcoat. He thought of the thin back under the layers of clothing, the lines of bone under the white skin, and tightened his hold.

'It's safer this way,' he said.

'I suppose so.' She looked up. 'Which is our cabin?'

21

'The second and third port-holes from that end.'

'Did you lock the door?'

'No.'

'But . . .'

'I locked the case,' he said. 'Stop worrying. Everything is all right.'

She said apologetically: 'I'll try not to fuss. It's just that – I'm more nervous than I thought I would be.'

'It doesn't matter.'

'You have enough, without my being difficult as well. Darling, I think I'll be all right. But back there – you know – I wanted to scream so badly. I had to, well, tighten myself up to prevent it. That's why I turned away.'

'You've done fine,' he said, 'and the worst is over.'

'Really?'

'Yes, really.'

'I feel tired,' she said. 'Could we go up now? I think I'd like to lie down for a while.'

He nodded. 'Of course.'

They met Thorsen coming down from the cabins as they were preparing to climb the stairs. He stood back to let them come first.

'Is there anything I can do for you?' he asked.

'Not just at present,' Jones said. 'What time is lunch?'

'One o'clock, sir.'

The two centre cabins were larger than the outside ones, and had twin beds instead of bunks. Their three suitcases were by the dressing table; with them was a portable typewriter. Jones went to this and examined the lock. Sheila Jones closed the door and stood against it looking at him.

'It's all right, isn't it?' she asked. 'Nothing's been touched.'

'I want to make sure.'

He took a key-ring from his pocket. The key he selected was heavier and more complex than would have been usual for unlocking a typewriter case. He turned the case upside down, unlocked it, and lifted the base.

'Yes,' he said. 'Everything's all right.'

'The bear goes a walk,' Mrs Simanyi said. 'Would the little Annabel wish to see this?'

'I'm sure she would,' Mary said. 'Thank you. Where is it?'

She pointed and smiled. 'On the deck. That way.' She bent

down towards Annabel. 'You must not be frightened. She is a very good bear.'

The front of the crate had been removed, revealed the iron-barred cage within. While several members of the crew watched from a respectful distance, Nadya bent down and slid the heavy bolts that secured it. She was wearing blue jeans and a yellow jersey, and her hair was tied up in a red and yellow silk scarf. She secured a heavy leather lead to the bear's collar, and called her out with endearments. Katerina shambled out, and Nadya led her round the corner of the hatch to a patch of deck that was empty except for a dozen steel lager casks. Katerina put a paw up on to one of the casks and followed it with the other paw. She stood up, leaning forward on the cask and looking out over the level waters.

'Hi, up,' Nadya said. 'Come, my dear one, my love.'

She took one of Katerina's paws and lifted it. The bear swung round and put both paws up to her shoulders. The brown, furry head peered forwards, and she licked Nadya's face.

'A little walk,' Nadya said. 'A little fresh air before dinner, eh?'

Katerina dropped back on all fours and ambled along the deck. The crew parted to give her room. A couple of them went round the other side of the hatch, and started to clean out the cage.

'Do you like her?' Mary asked.

Annabel said: 'I think so.'

'She's quite tame, you know.'

Mouritzen, approaching from behind, put his hand on Annabel's head.

'Very tame,' he agreed. 'She's a fine bear, too, isn't she? Four years old. She is in her prime.'

'They've travelled on the *Kreya* before?' Mary said.

'The Simanyis? They came out with us, in April.'

'They seem nice people. And the girl is very good-looking.'

'Nadya? Yes.'

Nadya led the bear along the deck in their direction. They both had, Mouritzen thought, the same kind of awkward, powerful grace. He lifted Annabel up on top of the hatch cover.

'I'm not frightened,' she said.

'Of course not. But you can see better there.'

Mrs Simanyi was standing on the little promenade deck above and behind them. She called out to Nadya and threw an apple, which Nadya caught with her left hand. She held it in the air above the bear's head, and Katerina rose on her hind legs and took it.

Over her shoulder, Nadya called to Mouritzen:

'Hello, there Lieutenant! I have had no chance to talk with you yet.'

'I was on duty last night,' Mouritzen said. 'This morning, too.'

Nadya let her eyes rest on the woman standing beside him.

'I did not ask for reasons.' She smiled. 'Have you thought of us – me and Katerina – on your voyages?'

'Of course. How could I not?'

'We have thought of you. Katerina was sick, pining for you, I think. She is very faithful, this bear.'

'She may be contented,' Mouritzen said. 'Since she left, there has been no other bear in my life.'

'But you do not even come to embrace her!'

Smiling, Mouritzen advanced towards Nadya and the bear, whose jaws were still working on the apple. Nadya jerked the lead slightly and Katerina turned clumsily round to meet him. She put her paws up to his shoulders, as she had done with Nadya, and reached forward to lick his face. There was laughter and some cheers from the crew members, who had moved up behind them. Mouritzen craned his neck to keep his face away from the wet tongue.

'There!' Nadya said. 'He does not love you. He turns away from your kiss because he has found someone he likes better. It is so with men. Come to me; come to your Nadya, who loves you always!'

She pulled the bear back towards her and leaned forward into an embrace. There was a mock sensuality in the way she pressed her body against the bear's and moved her head in a semblance of ecstasy, rubbing her face against Katerina's jaw. But the mockery had its deeper significance and purpose; Mouritzen felt a quickening of excitement as he watched her. She looked at him over the bear's shoulder again, her eyes now dreamy, half-closed.

Mary said: 'It's a very tame bear, isn't it?'

'Yes,' Mouritzen said. 'But basically still a wild animal, you understand.' He took her arm. 'We must not be misled by the clever tricks.'

Annabel was delighted with the shower, which had great convoluted iron pipes painted white, patches of orange rust showing through, and was enclosed by plastic curtains. Mary had some difficulty in getting her out of it. At last she had the small body clothed in her pyjamas and lying peacefully in her bunk. She read a chapter to her from the book she had brought, *The Little Dutch Boy*. When she had finished, she asked:

'You are going to be a little Dutch girl, you know. Will you like that?'

'I don't know. Why couldn't we have stayed at home?'

'Things were difficult.'

'What was difficult?'

'You couldn't understand if I told you.'

'Tell me. I will understand.'

'You will later – when you're grown up.'

Annabel pressed her head deeper into the pillow. 'If I'm going to be a little Dutch girl, then I shall grow up into a Dutch woman. Shan't I?'

'Yes. I suppose you will.'

'I would rather be like you.'

'I shall be a Dutch woman, too.'

'I don't want you to be.'

'Think of all the fun there'll be,' Mary said. 'Skating along the canals in the winter – sailing on them in summer. And in the spring going out into the tulip fields. We'll have a great time.'

'Better than in Phoenix Park?'

'Much better. And I shan't be out working during the day. I'll be with you all the time, except when you're at school. Won't you like that?'

'Yes,' Annabel said. 'I'll like that.'

'Turn over now, and go to sleep. I'm just going downstairs to the place where we had supper. I'll leave this little light on, and if you're frightened or you want anything, you only have to press the little button beside it. Will you go to sleep now?'

'Yes, Mamma.'

Mouritzen welcomed her into the lounge, where the extension half of the dining-table had been closed up and the kitchen serving hatch had become a bar.

'What will have to drink?' he asked her.

'An orange juice, please.'

'With a little gin? If you are going to Holland, you must learn to drink gin.'

She smiled. 'No thank you. Just orange.'

Thorsen was behind the bar. Mouritzen called to him:

'Jorgen! An orange juice and another Tuborg.'

The lounge was roughly oval in shape, one end being lined with

25

bench seats. The Simanyis were there, and so was the Chief Engineer, Bernard Møller. He was a raw-boned, red-haired man, generally taciturn but occasionally given to outbursts of articulation. Tonight he was sitting opposite Nadya, and expressing himself more in looks than words. Nadya, for her part, was in a withdrawn, apparently sullen mood. She paid little attention to Møller, none to Mouritzen and Mary.

Captain Olsen came in about ten minutes later. Mr and Mrs Jones came with him; he held open the door for them to enter. The three of them sat together at one of the small tables. Jones asked:

'What will you drink, Captain?'

'Milk,' said Olsen.

'Milk?'

'I always drink milk. Perhaps I will grow, hm?'

Josef Simanyi called to him: 'I do not think you have grown much since we last sailed with you, Captain.'

Olsen shrugged. 'Maybe I don't want to.' He stretched out his feet and showed that he was wearing slippers. 'When I need shoes I go into the children's part of the shop – good shoes and cheaper. I can get my clothes there, too. I save a lot of money since I am small.'

Stefan Simanyi got to his feet, made some excuses and went out.

'He is always sick,' Josef said. 'Even when all is calm, like this.'

'Then he should travel by aeroplane,' said Olsen.

'Too expensive. And what of the bear?'

'He could go by himself.'

'No,' Josef said. 'We go together. We always go together. He would be more unhappy by himself than with being sick.'

Jones said: 'You're very generous, Captain – recommending a rival form of transport.'

'Eight passengers or none,' Olsen said, 'my pay is the same. I would travel by aeroplane myself, you know, if I were to travel. It is quicker, more efficient.'

'Mr Jones, Mrs Jones,' Josef said, 'did you see the bear at her walks this morning?'

Sheila said: 'No. We missed it. We were sorry we did. We would have liked to take some photographs.'

Josef nodded, smiling. 'There is tomorrow morning.'

'No,' Olsen said. 'Not tomorrow morning.'

'Why not? Katerina must have air.'

'She can wait till we berth in Dieppe. Not a stroke of work was done on the ship while she was out this morning. Tomorrow she stays in, till we dock.'

'You are cruel, Captain,' Nadya said. She seemed to wake suddenly out of her apathy. She laughed, showing her teeth, strong and white with a single gold tooth at the side. 'Will the ship sink if poor Katerina strolls on deck?'

Olsen laughed, too. 'I will make sure of that!'

'I guard her well while she takes her walk.'

'We see it. So do the crew. There is more than the bear to look at.'

She grinned and stood up; she was at her most attractive, Mouritzen thought, when she looked like this – a coquette who might break a man's arm almost without thinking.

'I will go and tell Katerina what you say, Captain,' she said. 'Maybe she will come and eat you.'

She was wearing a full, silky, red dress and she went out of the lounge with a flare of skirt.

Jones said: 'I was looking at the plaque upstairs, Captain. So this is the second *Kreya*.'

Olsen shook his head. 'No.'

'But it spoke of the first *Kreya* being sunk during the war.'

'That was the second *Kreya*. She was torpedoed by the Germans, twenty years ago, and sank with all hands. Eighteen years before that, the first *Kreya* was sunk in a storm, in the Irish Sea – she too went down with all hands.'

Sheila said: 'That sounds ominous, doesn't it? What's going to happen to the third *Kreya*?'

'You wish to know?' Olsen produced a pipe and began to fill it. 'I will tell you. I personally will conduct her to the breaker's yards – in another twenty years.'

Jones said: 'That's encouraging.'

'That is a fact, Mr Jones. Leave me your address, and I will send you an invitation for this event.'

Sheila looked at him. He said:

'I'm afraid I can't be certain what my address will be in twenty years' time.'

'In any case,' Mouritzen said, 'the company will probably sell her off, somewhere in South America, maybe.'

'But she will not sink,' Olsen said. 'Not while I am in command. This you may rely on.'

'We rely on it,' Simanyi said. 'A strong ship, a strong captain.'

Olsen smiled. 'And you, Mr Simanyi – how was the fishing in Ireland?'

'Plenty of trout, some roach and carp – a conger once.'

'Salmon?'

Josef shook his head. 'No salmon.'

'You fish in Ireland, and catch no salmon? What kind of fishing is that?'

'It was a bad year for salmon. Everywhere they told us that. I had one on the line once, but he got away.'

'It takes skill to play salmon,' Olsen said. 'Next time I will go with you, and we will catch salmon together.'

'Will you be going back to Ireland?' Mouritzen asked.

'Maybe. I think so. One must go where one can. In so much of Europe now there is no time for the circus. In Germany, the circus is dead. The circus is for children, and there are no children in Germany.'

Mouritzen felt a slight draught and looked round. The door had opened noiselessly and Nadya had crept in. She had a bear skin thrown over her. She made her way without a sound to the table where Olsen was sitting and suddenly thrust the muzzle against his knee, at the same time emitting a throaty roar.

Without looking down at her, Olsen said casually:

'Mr Møller, I give you the responsibility to put this animal back in her cage. See to it.'

Nadya rose to her feet and leaned over Olsen, embracing him and laughing. He bore with it with no loss of composure. She sat down at last, the bear skin across her knees. Josef came over and picked it up.

'You have not seen this, I think,' he said. 'This was Alexander. We had him before Katerina.'

'He died?' Jones asked.

Josef grinned. 'Yes, he died. One day, when he was five years old, he became nasty – he turned on Stefan when Stefan was cleaning out his cage. Stefan called, and I was near with a small rifle.' He brushed back the fur that covered the head. 'You see – there? Just above the eyes. With one shot.'

'A good one,' Jones agreed.

'I tell you something else,' Josef said. 'So we had the body. It is something, burying a full grown bear – you must dig a big hole. Instead we skinned him; and then we ate him. What we could not eat at once we put in salt. All winter we ate Alexander.'

'Was he good?' Olsen asked with interest.

'I have never tasted such fine meat. When people called, we would say they should stay for supper and they would ask, do you eat your bear? When we said yes, they would say no, shaking their heads. But when they had tried one little morsel, they were ready to eat their bellies full.'

'It is what the bear eats,' Mrs Simanyi explained. 'Fruit and nuts and honey – carrots and things like that. That is how they have sweet flesh.'

'And Katerina?' Mouritzen asked. 'Will you one day eat Katerina?'

'Ah, no!' Mrs Simanyi said.

'She is a wonderful bear,' Josef said. 'She is like a daughter. One would not eat a daughter.'

'I give you a riddle,' Olsen said suddenly. 'It is black. It has eight wheels. But it is no vehicle. What is it?'

His penetrating, slightly protuberant eyes surveyed them as they shook their heads.

'What is it?' he repeated.

'We shall not find that,' Josef said.

Olsen gave a short laugh. 'A priest, on roller skates. I give you another riddle. It is greater than the universe. It is less than a grain of sand. The dead eat it. If we eat it, we too shall be dead. What is it?'

'We shall not guess that, either,' Josef said.

'We give up,' Sheila said.

'Greater than the universe,' Olsen said. 'Smaller than a grain of sand. The dead eat it. If we eat it, we die also. What is it?'

'You will have to tell us again, I'm afraid,' Jones said.

'No. Think of it. If you cannot guess I will tell you another night. But now you can think.'

Mouritzen heard Mary draw a deep, almost gasping breath. He turned to her.

'You are all right?'

'It's only that it's a little stuffy in here.'

'Let me take you to some fresh air.' She looked at him for a moment, and then nodded. 'There is a little deck, right at the top. It is fresh up there. But cold also – you will need your coat.'

'All right. I can see if Annabel's sleeping, on the way.'

They had to go through the wheelhouse to get to the deck. The helmsman nodded respectfully to Mary; when he was out of her line of vision he gave Mouritzen a quick grin.

There was a stiff breeze blowing up here, but the night was clear. Above their heads the radar scanner half-circled to and fro against the stars. There was no moon. They stood together by the rail, their arms not quite touching.

'Fresh here,' Mouritzen said.

'Yes.'

Mary drew her coat more tightly round her.

'Is it, perhaps, too cold?'

'No,' she said. 'I like the wind.'

'I, too. Annabel – is she asleep?'

'Yes. She was very tired. The sea air, I suppose.'

'She is a beautiful child. You must be very proud of her, Mrs Cleary.' He paused. 'May I say Mary?'

'Yes, of course.'

'And you will call me Niels?'

'If you like.' She paused. 'You lead a very – social life, as an officer on a ship like this, don't you?'

'Yes, I suppose so.'

'Meeting new people all the time – getting to know them very quickly. Not very well, though, I should think.'

'Whom does one know well?' Mouritzen asked. 'Parents, children, a wife? It is best to take people as they seem to be, I think.'

'Is it?'

'You do not agree?'

'As long as one doesn't have any illusions, I suppose it's all right.'

'What illusions?'

'That what they are has anything to do with what they seem to be.'

'You are bitter, I think,' Mouritzen said. 'That is a mistake, always. Most people, for the most part, are pleasant. It does not help to look all the time for the unpleasant people, or for the unpleasant parts of the pleasant ones.'

'Different philosophies,' she said, 'suit different people. I should think yours works well for you.'

'But yours,' he said, '– does that work well for you?'

'Well enough.'

She shivered slightly. Mouritzen put his arm on her shoulders. She suffered it to remain there for a moment, and then drew away.

'This journey to Amsterdam,' she said. 'It has a purpose. I am going there to be married.'

The disappointment was something more than was to be expected from the fact of an attractive woman making such a remark at such a time. Mouritzen said:

'My congratulations. Then your fiancé is already in Holland?'

'Yes.'

'He is working there? Has he been there long?'

'All his life,' she said. 'He is Dutch.'

'And he came to Ireland on a visit, and met the beautiful colleen, and now draws her across the sea to the dull and heavy Netherlands as a wife? That is not much like a Dutchman. He is exceptional.'

She did not answer. Mouritzen went on:

'Is that how it was? Have I guessed rightly?'

'Something like that,' she said.

'And his profession? Might I know that?'

'You are very curious.'

He jerked his head. 'It does no harm. Does it?'

'He's a shopkeeper. Hardware. He has stores in Amsterdam and Rotterdam.'

'That is interesting. Then it is unlikely that he went to Ireland on business. On holiday, perhaps? That is still unusual. Not many Hollanders go to Ireland except on business or to visit friends.'

Mary said, after a short silence: 'He hasn't been to Ireland. In fact, we haven't met. I advertised in a newspaper, saying that I wanted to meet a man that I might marry. It was an English newspaper. He saw it because he was thinking of marrying an English wife. He wrote to me.'

'How old is he?'

With some defiance, she said: 'Forty-three.'

'That is a waste,' Mouritzen said.

'Waste?'

'For a young and beautiful woman to become the wife of a Dutchman twenty years older than she. Even though he has hardware shops in Amsterdam and Rotterdam.'

She said coldly: 'Are you criticizing me?'

'No. Nor your Dutchman, either. If I criticize anything, it is life that permits such things to happen.'

She was still angry. 'I suppose in an ideal world, all young women would remain free and available for the pleasure of young bachelors?'

'No. Only the young and beautiful ones.' He took her arm, but in an entirely friendly manner, and she did not pull away. 'I have no right to talk like this about your life and what you wish to do with it. I am sorry, Mary. The world is hard on women.'

'With men like you about, it is.'

'Why do you say that?'

'You had a romance with the Simanyi girl last April, didn't you? And you would have started one with me, if I'd allowed you to.'

'Is there much harm in that? We are all free to choose what we do.'

'It's all fun for you, isn't it?'

'No. Not all fun. There is frustration also.'

With heavy irony, she said: 'I'm sorry that you should be frustrated occasionally.'

Mouritzen took his hand from her arm, and grasped the rail. He said:

'When I first asked you about your husband-to-be, you told me a lie – only a little one, but a lie. And then a little later you told me the truth. You did not need to do this. Why did you do it?'

'It wasn't a lie. You suggested something, and I said: "Something like that."'

'Not a lie, then. But a deception? Yet afterwards you told me the truth.'

She said: 'I don't like deceiving people, even when it doesn't matter.'

'That is what I thought,' Mouritzen said. 'A man does not often meet a woman like you. That is the frustration – to find her already married, or promised in marriage.'

'I think I'll go down now.' She stopped; Mouritzen stood by waiting for her. 'Go back to Nadya. You don't like waste, and you are wasting your time.'

'Must you talk like that?'

'I don't mind charm,' she said. 'It's the pretence of sincerity I don't like.'

'It is not a pretence.'

'I don't want to argue. We aren't going to convince each other, you know.'

'If there were time,' Mouritzen said, 'I would convince you.'

'I don't think so.'

Chapter Four

The *Kreya* followed the winding Arques into the heart of Dieppe, and tied up at an inner wharf soon after two in the afternoon. Meeting Captain Olsen as he came down from the bridge, Jones said:

'Do we stay here long?'

'We sail at midnight. But you cannot go ashore yet. We must wait for the Customs Officer to come.'

'We may not go ashore.'

Olsen nodded indifferently. 'Inform the steward if you are staying on board, so that he can make arrangements for dinner tonight.'

He gave Jones a quick mechanical smile and went on. On the deck, by the forward hatch, Josef Simanyi was setting up a fishing rod. Olsen came up behind and tapped him on the shoulder.

'What are you doing, do you think?'

Josef glanced over his shoulder. 'Fishing.'

'Forbidden,' Olsen said. 'Three thousand francs' fine for any who fish within the harbour.'

'Truly?'

'Truly. Give me the rod. If anyone sees you, it is my rod and you are holding it for me.'

'Then you pay the fine.'

Olsen smiled. 'No one can fine a captain who casts a line from his own ship. What bait do you have? Liver? From our kitchens. Let us see what we shall catch with it.'

There was a small floating dock opposite the *Kreya*, holding a battered fishing smack. Olsen cast a line well out in that direction. It struck the oily water, covered with floating refuse, and sank out of sight. A few moments later the float began to jerk as the line was taken down below.

'Ho, there!' Olsen said. 'We have it.'

He began to wind in. A long, threshing shape came into view at the end of the line.

'We have you, Mr Eel,' Olsen said.

But as the eel broke water a convulsive jerk freed it from the hook. It sank back into the depths and the line came up uselessly.

'You have bad luck, Captain,' Josef said.

'Next time we get him,' Olsen said.

He re-baited the hook and cast again. Josef looked after the rod with disappointment and longing.

Stefan came out from the lounge and stood near them.

He said: 'She has stopped rolling. At least I will eat something tonight.'

'And tomorrow morning,' Olsen said, 'you give it to the fishes. It is of small value.'

'Maybe not,' Stefan said. 'After two days, generally I am less sick.'

'Tomorrow,' Olsen told him, 'you will be sick. The weather forecast is for storms. The *Kreya* will roll like a porpoise, all the way from here to Amsterdam.'

'That is a joke?' Stefan suggested uneasily.

'Ask Mr Mouritzen if you do not believe me.' Mouritzen was approaching them from the direction of the forecastle. 'Is it not so, Niels?'

'He has taken your rod, has he?' Mouritzen asked Josef. 'Yes, the forecast is bad, but forecasts are not always accurate. On the outward trip we were promised good weather, and we had storms all the way to Dublin.'

'My appetite has gone,' Stefan said, 'before I could regain it.'

Mouritzen grinned and went on. He called back over his shoulder:

'Give him back his rod, Captain. You will catch nothing.'

'I will catch something,' Olsen said. 'If I must stand here until we sail, I will have something.'

'Shall I hold the rod for a time?' Josef asked.

'I will give it back to you with a fish on the end,' Olsen said. 'That is a promise, and where I promise, I perform.'

Josef gazed disconsolately at the sluggish dirty water. Mrs Simanyi and Nadya came out to join them.

'Now we have docked,' Nadya said, 'can Katerina be exercised?'

Olsen shook his head. 'Not yet.'

'Why not?'

'They begin to unload the horses very soon. She must wait until that has been done. It will not take long. One hour here, two hours

34

in Dublin, three in Amsterdam. The Hollanders are frightened of horses.'

'And the fish are frightened of you?' Nadya said.

'Frightened or not, I will lure them.'

The three Simanyis remained watching him. Thorsen came out with them, and Mr and Mrs Jones were on the small promenade deck, looking down. There was no bite. For ten or fifteen minutes. Olsen waited without success, from time to time reeling in and re-casting. Then as the French dock labourers came aboard and the mobile crane moved along and picked up the horse-box, the watchers turned their attention to the other side.

Olsen called Thorsen to him. He gave him instructions in Danish and Thorsen, grinning, went off to the forecastle. A few minutes later, Olsen called out to Josef:

'Here you are! I said I would give back the rod when there was a fish on the line. Come now, and take it.'

The onlookers turned back. Josef came across and took the rod. The float was three-quarters submerged. He began to reel in. Olsen stood beside him, watching with interest.

'There it is,' he cried, as a flat shape was drawn up to the surface. 'There is your fish, Simanyi!'

Simanyi was the first to see it. 'Ah, you scoundrel!' he said, but he continued to reel in. Nadya began to laugh, and the others joined in. The fish which Josef unhooked from the end of his line was headless and gutted, and still brick-hard from its sojourn in the ship's cold-store.

'Where I promise, I perform,' Olsen said. He grinned. 'Good fishing, Simanyi.'

As they went back to their cabin, Jones said:

'He's a cool one, that Olsen.'

Sheila said: 'Yes.'

She went to the dressing-table and began making up. Her movements were jerky and nervous. He noticed it, and went to stand behind her. He put his hands on her shoulders.

'Half the voyage behind us,' he said. 'Time is going on.'

'Very slowly. Do we have to stay on board all afternoon and evening? Can't we go ashore?'

'There's nothing to stop you going.'

'Not without you.'

'There wouldn't be any pleasure in it. I know really that nothing could go wrong, but I'd be jumpy all the same.'

'You're not likely to bump into anyone who knows you in Dieppe, in November, surely?'

'No.' He nodded in the direction of the typewriter case. 'It's that.'

'It's locked,' she said, 'and you can surely lock the cabin too if you're going ashore. There would be nothing odd about that.'

'Thorsen would have to come in here to see to the beds. He might decide to borrow the typewriter. When he found it locked he might be struck by the fact that the lock isn't an ordinary typewriter lock. I had to put a new lock on because a child could have picked the other. But it makes it unusual.'

'Would it matter, as long as he couldn't open it?'

'I don't know.' He put his hands up to his face and rubbed his eyes with the finger tips. 'He might find a way of opening it. I suppose he could even break it open and tell some story of having dropped the case when he was cleaning the cabin. There are a dozen things that could happen. I just don't want to give anyone the chance of a couple of hours here undisturbed. You understand that?'

She asked: 'Is this the way it's going to be?'

'Only for a few more days – a week at the outside. Things will be different after that.'

'Will they?'

He kicked the typewriter case with the side of his foot.

'We can have the little ceremony of getting rid of it, if you like. Take it out on the lake and watch it drown. My love, we knew this part wasn't going to be easy.'

Sheila stared at the case. 'It's like an interloper, sitting with us all the time, watching and listening. I didn't know one could hate an inanimate object so much.'

'Be fair,' he said. 'We depend on it. All our future is in there.'

She nodded. 'That's what makes me afraid.'

'Are you sure that's all? You're not beginning to have regrets?'

'For what?'

'I had no alternative,' he said, 'but you did. You're so much younger, and you haven't been beaten by life.'

She got up and kissed him.

'What are you talking about?' she said. 'Darling, what are you talking about? How could I have let you go by yourself?' She strained herself against him. 'It was my idea as much as yours. I think I talked you into it. Everything you say is right. Too much depends on the next few days. We can't take chances. After that . . .' She kissed him again, sighing. 'I can't really believe it – I suppose that's the trouble.'

He stroked her head for a few moments, without talking. Then he said:

'We mustn't let ourselves get too much under strain, though. Perhaps you were right in the first place. Thorsen wouldn't have the nerve to open the case, even if he did notice the lock. Let's go ashore, have a few drinks and a decent meal somewhere – forget the whole thing for a few hours. Well?'

'No.' She left him and bent down beside the typewriter case. She put her arms round it, touching it with fascination and loathing. 'No, we'll stay.'

Mouritzen saw Mary and Annabel on deck and hurried after them. He caught up with them just as they reached the gang-plank.

'Going ashore?' he asked.

Mary gave him a small formal smile. 'Yes.'

'May I come with you?'

'No, thank you. You will have things of your own to do.'

He looked down towards Annabel.

'What do you say, Annabel? shall I come with you? I know a place where we can play games, and a place where we can buy lemonade. Would you like that?'

'I like Coca-Cola,' Annabel said.

'That, too! Well, may I come?'

'Yes,' Annabel said. 'What kind of games?'

Mouritzen assisted them down the gang-plank. 'You will see.'

'I feel sure that your time could be better occupied,' said Mary. 'But thank you.'

He fell into step beside them. 'No thanks. There is not much that one can find to do, in a strange port in a foreign country, when one is alone.'

They came to the end of the sheds and crossed the railway lines towards the road leading into the town.

'It's not a complaint I would have expected to hear,' Mary said. 'I thought sailors were more resourceful.'

'Sailors can be as lonely as other men. Perhaps they are more lonely.'

She made no answer to that. They walked on into the town, and he found a café, after rejecting one that had no Coca-Cola. He consulted gravely with Annabel on these matters; and she replied with matching gravity and courtesy. The two of them got on well together. When they were finally sitting at a table together, Mary felt that they had the look of a family party, and the thought pleased and disturbed her. There was nothing to regret, she told herself, and nothing now to pine for. In two days she would be meeting Jan Volkmar, and he – dark and solid in the photograph he had sent her, with a heavy chin and worried, serious eyes – would give them both all the security they could want.

She drank her tea, smiling, thinking that at last Annabel would have a home like other children, a chance to be more child-like. Watching her, Mouritzen said:

'What makes you smile?'

She shook her head. 'Nothing.'

'If I knew,' he said, 'I would strive to repeat it. I like to see you smile.'

With sudden conscious cruelty, she said: 'I suppose I was smiling out of happiness – that the journey will be over so soon.'

'Yes,' Mouritzen said. He picked up his glass of beer. 'You are right.'

He took them into a pin-table arcade, and played a game of mechanical football with Annabel, manipulating the rows of metal players with enthusiasm. After allowing himself to be beaten, he insisted on another game, with Annabel and he on one side and Mary on the other. The two of them scored an overwhelming victory.

Afterwards they walked down to the beach, and Mouritzen showed Annabel how to build the pebbles into cairns and fortifications. They were still engaged in this as it began to grow dark. Mary looked at her watch.

'We must be going back now, Niels,' she said.

'First we find something to eat.' He prodded Annabel in the ribs. 'Shall we not?'

'I think we'd better go back to the ship,' Mary said. 'There's absolutely no need for you to come. We can find our way quite easily. It will be Annabel's bed time soon.'

'Just as soon,' Mouritzen argued, 'wherever she eats her dinner. Come, I know a good place, where they will have ice-cream as well. Will we like that?'

Annabel's reply was an emphatic one. Mary smiled at Mouritzen over her head.

'All right. Thank you – we'd love to.'

Thorsen was waiting for Nadya when she had finished exercising Katerina. He barred her way to the cabins.

'Shall we go into Dieppe together?' he suggested.

She looked at him with a faint smile. 'No. Thank you.'

The last two words were so drawled as to sound insulting.

Thorsen said: 'Niels has taken the Cleary woman and the child. They went twenty minutes ago.'

Nadya stopped smiling. 'I saw them.'

'You don't want to go by yourself,' Thorsen said.

'There are others.'

'Not with your brother, either.'

'Bernard is taking me.'

Thorsen made a gesture of contempt. 'He is no good to you.'

'What do you mean – no good to me?'

'You're a girl of passion,' Thorsen said. 'So Niels told me.'

She said in a low, even voice: 'You're a liar.'

'That night in his cabin – was it just after two o'clock that you came out or just before?'

'Niels told you that?'

'Who else?'

Nadya laughed, her strong, white teeth gleaming. 'You liar! You were spying on us. I heard the door of your cabin snick, and saw the light under the door. You think Bernard is not man enough for me? What would you say you are, little Jorgen? I would call you a schoolboy.'

He said warningly: 'Don't make me angry.'

She reached forward and rumpled his hair; she was still wearing pullover and jeans and her clothes carried the animal smell of the bear.

'Should I fear little Jorgen?' she asked. Her fingers suddenly tightened in his hair, and she pulled his head back savagely. Tears came into Thorsen's eyes. 'Go back to school,' Nadya said. 'Or to Mama, and ask her to wipe your pretty little eyes.'

She went inside. Thorsen looked round, making sure that no one had seen the incident. Then, after quickly combing his hair, he called to the boy, Ib, to tell him he was going, and hurried off the ship.

He went to a back street, not far from the railway station. The houses were tall and mean and smelled of garbage. Thorsen rang a bell on the ground floor and stepped back into the street. A window opened and a woman looked out, silently. She nodded her head, and he went back into the house.

There was a double bed in the room to which she admitted him, covered with a tattered silk counterpane, of faded gold patterned with faded roses. The only other furniture consisted of a cheap wash-stand and a chest of drawers, and two upright chairs. On the chest of drawers stood a large marble clock, flanked by prancing horses. It had been her mother's, she had told him on a previous visit, and it would fetch nothing anyway.

She was a woman in her forties, who even in her youth could not have claimed anything resembling good looks. Her body was tired and slack, her face fell in sad wrinkles from the dyed blonde hair, and her eyes were dulled and unhappy. She wore a red, woollen wrap; where it was torn at the elbow one could see part of a stained blue nightdress.

She asked Thorsen for two thousand francs, and when he gave her the money she put the notes carefully under the clock. Then, opening the wrap, she went to the bed and sat down wearily.

Thorsen began to curse her, at first gently, feeling his way among the obscenities like a man reluctantly paying out money. He spoke in Danish, and she looked at him, blankly, neither understanding nor caring. He warmed to it by degrees, his voice thickening and growing louder, the obscenities coming more plentifully and with less and less meaning. After a time, he broke into foreign languages – German, English, snatches of French. Although she understood these, she gave no sign of caring or of resenting them. Thorsen grew more violent and less coherent. He shrieked at her, standing close by where she sat. But she showed only indifference, and although he raised his fists as if to strike her, he did not touch her.

At last his voice cracked and broke on the torrent of filth. He stood for a moment staring at her, his eyes wild, his face distorted with rage. Then, suddenly changing, he dropped to his knees beside the bed and put his head down on her knees. He wept, and she soothed him, talking to him in French, monotonously on and on.

Although some of the other men tried to persuade him to go ashore with them, Carling stayed on the *Kreya*. He went down into the forward hold to make sure that everything had been left in order by the French dockers, and stayed down there, resting his arms on one of the wooden stalls from which the horses had been taken, smelling the horses and the hay.

For him it was a childhood smell. He had been born on a farm in Fyn, the eldest of four sons of a small farmer. But it had been the seas that fascinated him, not the land, and when he was fifteen he had left, going first to Odense and then to Copenhagen. There had been no regrets. Even when on account of Tove, he had thought of leaving the sea, he had not thought that he might have been mistaken in giving up farming. Tove would never have been a farmer's wife.

But what would she have been – what had she been? The question, rising all unexpectedly through the quiet melancholy of his mind, pierced him again, and with a new twisting sharpness.

'Tove!' he cried aloud. 'What was it? What should you have told me?'

The horses that were left champed at the straw. In his agony, Carling fled back again to childhood, bridging the years with that smell, those untroubled easy sounds. But his mind played traitor to him: he was in the big kitchen, a boy of five or six, unregarded, listening to the sound of the pot bubbling on the fire, and the slow, quiet talk of his elders.

'Where?'

'In the barn – the little barn.'

'And how, then?'

'With his belt.'

'And with what reason?'

'It's not known. Her, maybe.'

'In Hell – for her?'

'No man knows another's mind.'

'But in Hell,' his mother said. Her voice had in it wonder and dread. 'We know that.'

Carling spoke aloud again, to the present, to the world where torment was ever at hand and hope a thin fugitive.

'No!' he cried. 'That's not true.'

A horse began to kick the planks that held it in, with steady, patient strength. Carling thought of Dublin; the answer was there. Next time she would speak. Next time he would know what it was she had not said to him – the only why that mattered in the world.

41

He would not leave until she had spoken. He would learn the truth and, one way or another, he would find peace.

Chapter Five

The wind rose with the tide. It was Force 5 by the time the *Kreya* was clear of the harbour, and it rose steadily as they beat northwards up the Channel. It came from the south-west but there was no warmth nor softness about it. Cold squalls of rain soaked across the seas from time to time. The night was black, and apart from their radar eye they drove into it blindly.

On the bridge, Mouritzen said to Olsen:

'Nasty enough. And it's going to get worse?'

'So they tell us. At any rate, we're getting a lift from it. We'll save oil on this leg, and a few hours.'

'Yes. Have you had the hatch closed?'

Olsen shook his head, his lips pursed. 'Not necessary. You can keep an eye on things from time to time.'

'Yes, let the poor beasts have some air, while they can.'

Olsen raised his eyebrows. 'It's our job to keep them in the best possible condition for delivery. That's in the contract.'

'Yes,' Mouritzen said. 'So it is.'

'I'm going to get some sleep.' Olsen said. He yawned, and flexed his arms. Mouritzen found himself yawning in sympathy, and Olsen noticed it. 'You should have got your sleep this evening,' he said, with some severity.

'I'm all right.'

'What was it you said to me the other day – that I'd have been better off on an all-cargo ship? That's true of you, Niels. You find passengers too much of a distraction.'

'Not too much, I think.'

'You don't think straight; that's the trouble. Once we've cleared Amsterdam, I suppose it will be the Simanyi girl again?'

'No, no.'

With a grim satisfaction, Olsen said: 'You are not your own master, though. They look at you and smile, and you are as helpless as a little child.'

42

'Lately, I've been considering the advantages of marriage.'

'Marriage? For you, there are no advantages. Only another complication – something else to distract your mind with. Do you think you would stop chasing the others, if you had a wife back in Copenhagen?'

'Why not? When a man has found what he needs, he stops looking for it. Isn't that obvious?'

Olsen paused, his hand on the rail, preparing to go down the stairs.

'And what is it a man needs, Niels? A man like you? When you have solved that problem, you will know more about yourself. Then it will be time to think of taking a wife.'

Mouritzen called to him: 'Tell me what you need yourself, Erik, and then perhaps I will solve my problem.'

'I?' Olsen laughed. 'I have found it already. I need nothing. Nothing!'

They were getting into the Straits as dawn broke, grey and wet on the starboard bow, and the seas were beginning to run very high. Before he went down for breakfast, Mouritzen ordered the hatch battened down over the hold where the horses were stabled. He told Olsen this. Olsen was already at the table, eating bacon and egg.

'Yes,' Olsen said. 'Good. Everything going well?'

'We're still running in front of it,' Mouritzen said. 'The difficulty will lie when we change course.'

'That will not be for a long time.'

'The forecast is for gales strengthening and continuing in all areas.'

'So we save still more time and oil.'

Mouritzen sat down at his place. 'No sign of the passengers for breakfast. I suppose Thorsen is busy?'

'Yes. This is the time when Thorsen earns his pay. I do not envy Thorsen at times like these.'

The door opened and Mouritzen looked, expecting to see either Thorsen or the boy, Ib; but it was Josef Simanyi, and Nadya was close behind him. She was dressed in dove grey slacks with a pink blouse, well open at the neck. She looked very fit.

'Ah,' Olsen said, 'we have visitors! So the storm does not take away your appetites?'

Simanyi grinned. 'My wife stays in bed, and Stefan is praying to

43

the Virgin, but we two are hungry.'

'You should get Thorsen to cook that fish you caught yesterday,' Olsen said. 'Here he is. What are the conditions above stairs, Thorsen?'

Thorsen smiled slightly. 'There will be no more down to breakfast today. I will bring yours for you in a minute.'

Simanyi said: 'She is a stout ship, the *Kreya*.'

Normally they kept the places which Thorsen had given them at the beginning of the voyage, but with Møller and six of the passengers absent to do so now would mean having tracts of empty space between them. Smiling at Nadya with a frank and open friendliness, Thorsen said:

'It will be better if you move in closer, I think. Will you sit beside Mr Mouritzen, Miss Simanyi?'

Nadya smiled in return. 'I am glad to do that,' she said.

'Yes, a stout ship,' Olsen said, echoing Simanyi. 'You need not fear the gale when you are aboard the *Kreya*. Your son may pray to the Virgin for the sake of his stomach, but the rest of his body is in no danger.'

Nadya said: 'You look tired, Niels. You have been on duty?'

'Yes. Soon I am going to bed.'

'Poor Niels. You have a hard time. So much duty, so little sleep.'

She looked at him, her face not quite innocent. Mouritzen smiled at her.

'I am grateful for your sympathy, Nadya.'

Simanyi said: 'Think what it must be like on the little fishing boats in such weather as this.'

Olsen laughed. 'You must keep your fishing for the harbours, Mr Simanyi. A catch is more certain there, too.'

Nadya said to Mouritzen in a low voice: 'I am most sympathetic to you, Niels. Surely you have not forgotten that?'

Mouritzen looked away, embarrassed. 'No,' he said, 'I have not forgotten.'

'I am patient,' Nadya said, 'and I am forgiving. Do you not think I am an excellent woman, Niels?'

He nodded. 'Yes, excellent.'

She smiled. 'Eat your breakfast. You look hungry.'

The gale strengthened during the morning, and the wind grew colder; there were frequent showers of sleet and hail. With the wind in the south-west, the *Kreya* continued to run before it. The

44

heavy seas broke over her stern and bows, but she was fairly dry amidships.

Returning to the bridge at two o'clock, Mouritzen was surprised to find their course still steady on north-east. He mentioned this to Olsen.

Olsen said: 'I tried her on an easterly tack during the morning. She takes a poor grip; we're too light.'

'So?'

'I would sooner beat into a storm like this than cross it. If we change course about seven we can head south to the Wadenzee.'

'What's the forecast?'

'Bad.'

Mouritzen looked at the chart. 'About fifty miles north-west of Hook. We could still make Den Helder.'

'East by north-east,' Olsen said. 'Nearly broadside on to it, and loaded with air instead of ballast. No, we shall do better by staying on our course.'

The ship shuddered, plunging her bows into a high cliff of water. They felt her go down, steady, begin the upward surge.

'When she does turn,' Mouritzen said, 'it will be more than ninety degrees. She will be broadside to it then, all right.'

'For minutes,' Olsen said, 'not for hours. Keep her steady on course, Niels. I think I will take a nap.'

All round the north-west coasts of Europe the winds were ravaging, like packs of hunting wolves. When Olsen took over again, Mouritzen reported to him a still bleaker weather outlook, and three distress signals already picked up.

'Anything near us?'

'One in the Irish Sea, one off the Hebrides, the other north of Bergen.'

'Good.' He smiled with a cold humour. 'This is no weather for rescue operations. Have they made contact?'

'Yes. But the one north of Bergen has little chance, I think. She is taking a lot of water in her engine room. The lifeboats have gone out from Bergen, but they'll be hard put to reach her in time.'

'What is she?'

'The *Firkar*. German – eleven hundred tons.'

'God help them,' Olsen said, 'if there is a God. I would not like to swim in this. We're in a foolish trade, Niels.'

Mouritzen said: 'I've never known you admit to folly before.'

'Nor do I now. If the trade is foolish, the tradesman need not be a fool.'

'Then why choose the trade?'

'In my case, it was not a choice. My father was a sea captain. He was a big man, and by being small I disappointed him. I did not wish to disappoint him altogether. So I took up his trade.'

'You've done well at it.'

Olsen smiled again. 'I would have been a good doctor, too. A better doctor than a sea captain, maybe.'

Before dinner, Mouritzen went to see Mary and Annabel. He knocked at the door, and she called him in. She had put Annabel into the bottom bunk, and was sitting beside her reading a book. She put it down as Mouritzen entered the cabin. She looked pale, but she smiled at him.

'How does it go?' Mouritzen asked gently.

'I think I'm getting used to it,' Mary said.

'And Annabel?'

Annabel said, in a weak voice: 'I feel sick. I've been sick a lot, and I still feel sick. Will we be in Amsterdam soon?'

'As soon as we can be.'

'How soon is that?'

'If you go to sleep,' Mouritzen told her, 'when you wake up we will be in Amsterdam.'

'I can't *go* to sleep,' she said, 'while I feel sick.'

'Maybe you are trying too hard,' Mouritzen said. 'Sleep is like happiness. It is no good chasing it; it likes to creep up and catch you. I will tell you a story about a troll. Do you know what a troll is?'

She moved her head slightly on the pillow. 'No.'

'A troll is a little man with a hump on his back, who can work magic, and is always playing tricks on human beings. The trolls are cousins to the leprechauns, I think. Now this troll, whose name was Kikkipik, lived beside a lake, in the far north, where in summer the sun shines all day and all night long, and in winter there is no sun at all, but a night-time that goes on for months and months. Now at one time, Kikkipik had lived with his brother, but . . .'

Mouritzen went on telling the story to her. It was one he remembered from his childhood, but seeing that she continued to be wakeful, he embroidered and stretched it, and tagged on other stories, rambling on and on. He must have continued for half an hour, before Mary interrupted him softly.

46

'She's asleep.'

Mary bent over the bed and tucked the child's arm inside the sheet. She straightened up, and said to him:

'That was very kind of you, Niels. You have a lovely drowsy voice. I wasn't sure I wouldn't fall asleep first.'

'I thought perhaps I would!' Mouritzen said. 'But I think she will sleep now.'

'I'll stay with her for a time.'

'But you are coming down to dinner then?'

'Am I? I'm not sure. I thought I would, but it seems to have got so much worse in the last five minutes. I don't think I ought to risk it.'

'We are changing course,' Mouritzen said. 'It will not take too long, and after that it will be better, because we will have our nose into the wind.'

'Should I go on deck for a time – get some fresh air? I haven't been out today.'

Mouritzen shook his head decisively. 'You would be blown away. There is sleet and rain, and a wind of sixty miles an hour behind it.'

'It really is a storm, then?'

'It truly is.'

The cabin heaved as a wave struck the *Kreya*. Mary lost her hold on the stanchion of the bunk and fell forwards; Mouritzen moved and caught her. He held her in his arms for a moment or two, and then released her.

She said: 'Thank you.'

Her voice was not quite steady. He regretted having released her, but was sensible enough to make no new move in her direction.

'I'm glad it is a storm,' Mary said. 'I don't feel quite so weak for staying in my cabin all day. Have the others been down to meals?'

'Only two of them.'

'Who?'

'Two of the Simanyis. The old man, and Nadya.'

She hesitated, and then looked at him. 'I think I will come down for dinner tonight.'

'I'm glad,' Mouritzen said.

There was a constant background of sounds – the creakings, throbbings, metallic groans of a ship at sea, accentuated by the strains of the storm through which the *Kreya* was driving – to which Mouritzen was accustomed. The noises registered, but made no impact. But the unfamiliar excited attention. He sharpened into immobility as he heard it: a jarring crack that vibrated along the ship, a *frisson* of iron. The vibration lived for an instant, and died away.

He said: 'If you'll excuse me, I must go up first to the bridge.'

The difference had not registered on her. She said: 'I'll see you at dinner. Ten minutes?'

Mouritzen nodded. 'Ten minutes.'

Mouritzen found Olsen with his own hands on the wheel. He was staring out beyond the glass into the savage blackness of the night, his gaze fixed like a man suddenly confronted with betrayal of his life's purpose. He did not answer nor look round the first time Mouritzen spoke to him.

'What is it?' Mouritzen repeated, more urgently. 'There's something wrong. What?'

Olsen stood back and let Mouritzen take the wheel. He spun it, immediately conscious of the difference in the feel.

'A linkage gone?' he said.

'You heard it,' Olsen said.

'The shaft,' Mouritzen said. 'My God!'

He moved away from the useless wheel. Olsen came back and put his hands on it again. The *Kreya* heeled over as a wave struck her starboard side. Spray dashed over the glass in front of them. She went deep, deep, before beginning the slow swing back to an even keel.

'Have you sent out a distress call?' Mouritzen asked.

'No. Not yet.'

'Shall I see to that?'

'Yes, you can do that,' Olsen said. He seemed to rouse himself. 'If there is anything near us they can stand by to take off passengers. But no melodrama, Niels. The *Kreya* can ride this out. She is toughly built.' He considered a moment. 'And it helps now that she is so lightly loaded.'

'No chance of rigging a jury-rudder, I suppose?'

Mouritzen recognized the futility of the idea before he had finished saying it. Olsen grinned tightly, pointing out into the storm.

'In this?'

'I'll go down to the wireless room,' Mouritzen said. 'With Lauring it is a good idea to stand over him.'

It was possible on the *Kreya* to reach the wireless room and the engine room from the bridge without going outside, but Mouritzen took the outside steps deliberately, to get the feel of the storm. For the present it was not raining, but the wind was carrying spray that served the same purpose, except when the ship rolled and lifted and the huge surge of water crashed down across her, swamping and blinding everything. It was a strange, two-edged element, striking with the force of rock, and then breaking and ebbing away into salty streams across the *Kreya*'s deck. It was worse than it had been; the waves were higher. Still there was reassurance in the way in which, after each new vicious blow, the waves splintered and drained away. She should be able to ride things out till the storm abated and the sea grew calmer. It would mean a tow into Amsterdam; a humiliation for Olsen, but no more than that.

Closing the heavy metal door behind him he was conscious of the cutting off of so much of the noise – the wind's howling, the smashing thunder of the sea. Almost at once it became quieter still. He went into the wireless room and found Lauring struggling up into a sitting position from his bunk. His set was on broadcast; a stream of steady, Budd-keyed morse issued from the speaker.

'At this time of day and in this weather, Lauring, you're supposed to be on constant watch. You don't need telling that, do you?'

Lauring was fair-haired, slight, a neat, lazy young man with a quick mind and tongue, chiefly devoted to complaints about his conditions.

He said now: 'What's that, sir? That was the engines stopping, wasn't it?'

'Yes. Get in your chair while I write out a message for you to send. It's urgent.'

'Why have the engines stopped?'

'It's a new fuel economy drive.' Glancing up, he saw Lauring's face, the lines of bewilderment and fear, and remembered that joking, especially with someone like Lauring, could be dangerous. 'We've got steering trouble,' he added.

'What kind?'

Mouritzen handed him the message pad. He said:

'There's nothing to worry about. Captain Olsen will have stopped the engines while he tries to get a sea-anchor out, to see if we can get her nose into the wind. Get this off right away. Do you know who's near us, offhand?'

'There's nothing!' Lauring said. 'Nothing within fifty miles, anyway. There was the *Astrida*, but she was running for Borkum.'

'How long ago was that?'

'Half an hour, maybe three-quarters.'

'Try and raise her. Send this out as a CQ first. I'm going back up to the bridge. Let us know as soon as you have anything.'

Lauring picked up his earphones, but stared at them instead of putting them on.

'If we can't steer,' he said, 'we're helpless.'

'As helpless as a cork. We may get a shaking, but that's the worst that can happen.'

Lauring put on the earphones. 'I'll try to raise someone,' he said.

'Yes,' Mouritzen said, 'I'm sure you will.'

He ran into a work-party on deck; under Carling's direction they were, as he had expected, rigging a sea-anchor. He stopped to see how things were going. They were proceeding with as much calmness and efficiency as was possible on the deck of a small ship swept by waves thirty and forty feet high, with a wind at Force 8 or 9. But Carling, he thought, looked strange – stranger than the conditions justified. In emergencies, Carling normally exceeded himself, cursing and encouraging with a zest that appeared to be the greater for the difficulties or danger encountered. Now he was shouting his orders to the men with a curtness that made it seem his mind was on something other than the task in hand.

Mouritzen stayed to endeavour to give some kind of encouragement himself, but after a time he abandoned the attempt. He felt it was making Carling's withdrawal more conspicuous. In any case, the work was proceeding well enough. He went back up to the bridge, but did not immediately remove his oilskins. He stood by the door, water dripping from him to form a pool. Olsen had abandoned the wheel and was watching the radar screen.

'Anything from Lauring yet?' Mouritzen asked.

'A Swedish freighter, the *Västervik* – about seventy miles west of Esbjerg.'

Mouritzen glanced at the chart. 'Getting on for a hundred miles. What's she making?'

'Seven or eight knots. That's good, against this.'

'Nothing else?'

'Borkum are ready to send out a lifeboat. I've told them there's no need.'

'No need yet. Are you sure it was wise?'

'They could be here no sooner than the *Västervik*. It would be a needless risk. In any case, we are in good shape.'

A wave broke up against the glass.

'We are taking a hammering,' Mouritzen said. 'I wonder what shape we shall be in by morning?'

'The same as now – with a few bruises, perhaps.'

'Have the passengers been told anything?'

'There is no need. It would be stupid to tell them, from their point of view as well as from ours.'

'Yes, you are right. It's a pity, Erik.'

'What is a pity?'

'You would have made a fine doctor.'

Olsen looked at him coldly for a moment, and then smiled. 'So I would. And I manage well enough as a sea captain, do I not?'

'Yes. The sea-anchor – you will not pull her round with seas like these.'

'I think not, also. It was the only thing to try.'

Mouritzen nodded. 'I'll go down again, and see how it goes.'

The hours went by while the *Kreya* lay helpless under the savage fingers of the giant. The gale veered to southerly, and then fractionally into the eastern quarter, but it showed no abatement. The *Västervik*, on the report that all was still well and that the *Kreya* was being carried north-east, into the path of British coastal shipping, abandoned the attempt to come up with her, and resumed her own original course for Amsterdam. Help was now being offered by a Scottish cargo ship, but there was little chance of her being on the scene before dawn.

About one o'clock, with a noise as rending as though the ship itself were being torn in two, the foremast splintered and crashed. Mouritzen drained the coffee which Thorsen had just brought up, burning his tongue, and went forward to look at the damage. Although he went by the relatively sheltered port side, he had to hold the rail as the waves crashed over, and once, misjudging the roll, he was thrown against the hatch cover.

The mast had crashed down across the forecastle. The result was untidy but did not seem serious. Carling was there with a couple of hands. Mouritzen spoke to Carling but he did not seem to hear. He cupped his hands over his mouth and shouted.

'Nothing we can do about this just now. It will have to wait till things are quieter.'

Carling made no answer. He stared at Mouritzen, his face wet and bewildered in the light of the torch. Mouritzen heard a shout behind him, and turned to see another of the hands coming up from the direction of the forward hatch. Whatever he was saying was carried away by the wind.

Mouritzen shouted: 'What was that?'

He came up to them. 'The bear?'

'What about the bear?'

'The bear's loose!'

'Are you sure?' Mouritzen demanded.

'She's down there, on the deck.'

Carling spoke then, his voice trumpeting over the massed violins of the storm.

'The first sign!'

'What are you talking about?'

'The first sign . . .' Carling roared again, '– the beast walks free!'

Mouritzen considered, as clearly and rapidly as he could, the two new factors. Of the two, a crazy C.P.O. seemed to him to constitute the greater nuisance.

He shouted: 'Get Carling below, and look after him. And send Herning up to the bridge for orders.'

He saw the men clustering round Carling, talking to him, and raced down to the well-deck, getting down the steps during the ship's slow roll to port and hanging on at the bottom while the next wave smashed across. Then he made his way to the bear's crate. The securing ropes had broken and the crate had been thrown up against the forecastle. In doing so it had shattered, and the door of the iron cage within had sprung. In the light of his torch, Mouritzen saw it gaping open, and empty. He flashed the light around, but there was no sign of the bear.

He kept a look-out on his way to the bridge, but found nothing. Olsen looked up from the chart as he came in. Fatigue and strain had made his face pale, giving him the appearance of an intelligent child under pressure. The deepness of his voice, when he spoke, was incongruous.

'Well? How is it!'

'The port rail is smashed. Nothing serious and nothing one can do now. But there's another complication. The bear's loose. Her cage has been cracked open and she's wandering free.'

Olsen asked sharply: 'Where?'

Mouritzen shook his head. 'No sign of her, but I've not made a thorough search.'

Olsen made a gesture of despair. 'Animals are worse than passengers! I've got two men down below seeing to those cursed horses as it is – both very reluctantly.'

The door opened with an inrush of wind and spray, and Herning entered. He ranked next to Carling and was a quiet, earnest man, with prematurely white hair and a slight limp, from an injury to his knee when his ship was torpedoed during the war. He had stood for years in Carling's shadow, and during the latter's increasing moroseness and withdrawal of the past year had shown no signs of being able to step out of it.

'Reporting, sir,' he said to Olsen.

Mouritzen explained quickly: 'Carling's having some kind of a brainstorm. I got some of the men to take him below and asked them to send Herning up here.'

'A brainstorm?' Olsen looked incisively from Mouritzen to Herring. 'Where is he now? How is he?'

'He's below, sir,' Herning said.

'In his cabin?'

'They're persuading him to go there.' Herning looked uneasy. 'He's not dangerous, but he's rambling a bit.'

Mouritzen said: 'He was shouting something about the bear and the first sign.'

'It's a bit queer,' said Herning. 'It's these spiritualists he goes to in Dublin. They told him there was going to be trouble on this trip, and they said that the beast would go free. It's queer, sir. They weren't to know we'd be carrying a bear.'

'Perhaps they weren't to know,' Olsen said, 'but Carling knew. He probably told them about it.'

'He says he didn't.'

'And is he to be believed, the state he's in? He's probably invented the whole thing. Are you fool enough to give any credence to a man who's raving?'

'No, sir.'

'He's not dangerous?'

Herning shook his head. 'No violence at all. They got him down quite easily. He's just talking a lot, about signs and all that.'

'In that case we can concentrate on the bear. Do you think it might have got washed overboard?'

The question was addressed to Mouritzen. He said:

'No way of knowing. I should think the odds are against it, though.'

'So should I,' Olsen said. 'Well, we have enough to contend with, without that.' He left the bridge to go to his cabin, and came back shortly afterwards with his automatic pistol. He threw it to Herning. 'Take a party, find the bear, and shoot it. All right?'

'Yes, sir.'

When Herning had gone, Mouritzen said: 'It seems a pity. It's not the bear's fault.'

'Fault,' Olsen said, 'fault! What has fault to do with it? Do you suggest that in conditions like this I can accept responsibility for a bear running loose?'

'No, of course not. Shouldn't we notify the Simanyis, though?'

'You can, if you want to. If you think it's worth while waking them up.'

Mouritzen hung on to a support as the *Kreya* rolled to a new impact.

'I doubt if they will be sleeping very heavily,' he said.

He left his oilskins on the bridge, and went down the inside stairs to the cabins. He knocked at the door of the cabin which the two male Simanyis shared and was answered by an inconclusive groan. Opening the door, he found Stefan lying in his bunk, his face buried in the pillow and a bowl beside him. The other bunk was empty.

Mouritzen asked him: 'Your father – where is he?'

His mouth muffled by the pillow, not looking up, Stefan said: 'They are downstairs – in the saloon.'

Mouritzen found all the rest of the family down there, fully dressed, sitting in the end alcove, in front of a table that held a half-empty bottle of whisky and a number of ginger ale bottles, some empty and some still unbroached. Josef waved to him.

'You have time for a drink, Mr Mouritzen? Can you get a glass?'

Mouritzen shook his head. 'Not just now. I have some bad news for you. Katerina's cage has been torn loose by the waves.'

'Torn loose?' Josef said. 'She is not drowned?'

'She has got out of the cage,' Mouritzen explained. 'The Captain has given orders for her to be found and shot. There is nothing else to be done. She cannot be allowed to roam loose on the ship in this storm. It is better for her, too.'

Josef stood up, holding on to the table as the ship rolled.

'No,' he said. 'You cannot shoot that bear.'

'The order's already been given. I am sorry.'

'But they haven't found her yet?' Nadya said. She was wearing jeans and the yellow sweater. She looked tired; her eyes were darkly underlined. 'I will go and find her.'

'There's nothing you can do,' Mouritzen said.

He stood in her way as she came towards the door. Josef, after a moment, followed her. She looked at Mouritzen, shaking her head a little.

'Tell Captain Olsen we will see to the bear.'

'It is no sense your going out there,' Mouritzen said. 'You could not do anything, and you might easily be hurt – killed even. The storm is getting worse all the time.'

Nadya took his arm and pushed him to one side; he was admiringly conscious of her great physical strength, hardly inferior to his own.

'There is no time to waste in talking,' Nadya said.

'At any rate, you must get some kind of waterproofs on,' Mouritzen said. 'In two minutes you will be drenched to the skin.'

She went out of the swing doors without replying, Josef following her. The ship lurched, and by the time Mouritzen had followed them, Josef was going out to the deck. Mouritzen hesitated, undecided as to whether he should go up for his own oilskins. But there was not enough time. He plunged after them, fending the door open as it closed on him, and was soaked immediately by a wave breaking right across the ship.

There was a flash of torchlight from the after deck, and the Simanyis headed for it, with Mouritzen behind them. It was possible to see that there were four of five of the hands at the other side of the hatch. Josef shouted to them, bellowing against the wind. As they got nearer, one of them heard and looked round.

Mouritzen came up with the Simanyis. 'Please go back inside,' he said. 'You must not interfere with the running of the ship.'

Herning was there, carrying the automatic.

'Have you killed it?' Mouritzen shouted at him.

Herning shook his head. 'It's hard to get a proper shot, with the ship rolling as it is. And I did not want to wound the animal.'

Someone flashed a torch. It showed Katerina huddled up beside an oil-drum in the lee of the poop-deck. She was wet and bedraggled. She was shivering and she cowered away from the light.

Nadya, without comment, pushed the men aside and went up to the bear. She knelt down and put her arms round the furry neck, lowered her head and whispered in Katerina's ear.

Herning said helplessly: 'What do we do now, sir?'

'Stand by,' Mouritzen told him. He advanced towards Nadya and the bear. 'Nadya!' he called.

'Keep away,' she said. 'She is all right with me, but she is frightened and does not know what she is doing. It is not safe for you.'

He knelt beside them. 'Be reasonable,' he said. 'There's no way of securing her again, and she can't be allowed to go loose. You will be compensated for the loss.'

'Stand away,' Nadya said. 'Tell those others also to stand away.' She called to Josef: 'Papa, bring the lead for her.' He went, and she spoke again to Mouritzen. 'If you get them to stand clear, no one will be hurt.'

'The cage is broken,' Mouritzen said. 'There is no point in putting her back there.'

'I know that.'

'You cannot stay there, and you cannot walk her round the deck in this storm, and she cannot go in the hold because of the horses. Where do you think you will put her?'

'In our cabin,' Nadya said. 'We can sleep in the lounge.'

'But even if you could get her there,' Mouritzen protested, 'she would wreck it!'

'She is a quiet bear.' She smiled sardonically out of the darkness. 'And we will compensate for the loss.'

Olsen said: 'My God! I have never given you credit for outstanding intelligence, Mouritzen, but I would not have expected you to bungle things like that.'

'What could I do – order the men to put her and her father in irons? They wouldn't have been easy to cope with under ordinary circumstances, but in present conditions it was out of the question.'

'They should not have been allowed to go out on deck in the first place.'

'I couldn't stop them. She's as strong as I am, and he's

considerably stronger. Besides, they were out before I realized what was happening.'

'And you should have had the sense to make sure the job had been done before you told them of it.'

'I didn't expect them to react that way.'

'Damnation to your psychological expectations!'

'Does it matter very much, anyway? She got the bear to the cabin all right and they've locked her in there. Any damage she may do will be less costly than replacing a trained circus bear would be.'

'It matters that when I give an order it should be carried out. All right. There is nothing we can do now. But the report goes into the log in full, with you named as responsible for non-compliance with my instructions. Is that understood? Do you have any objections?'

Mouritzen shook his head. 'No objections.' There was silence for a time, apart from the unending crescendo of the gale, and the groaning counterpoint of the *Kreya*'s resistance to it. 'She was incredible,' Mouritzen added. 'A magnificent woman.'

'Yes,' Olsen said. 'But I haven't much liking for masterful women. When, in school history, I read of Joan of Arc, I detested her. I thought it fitting that she was executed, although I did not approve of the method.'

'What kind of women do you like?'

'Those that can be bought. The purchase removes the possibility of sentiment.'

'So you hated your mother,' Mouritzen said, 'as well as worshipping your father. You are the anti-Oedipus.'

Olsen looked at him with cold anger. He began to say something, but checked the words before they could make sense. A smile came to his face, broadening slowly.

'You are a clever man, Niels. I am fortunate in having you as First Officer. A better officer might well be a more stupid one, and I would not care to have to live with stupidity.'

'Thank you.'

'But it is not true that I hated my mother. Hate is a large thing, and what I felt for her was small.'

'You would call it indifference?' Mouritzen said.

He realized that he had allowed some of his scepticism to manifest itself in his tone of voice. Olsen plainly noticed it, but merely smiled.

'You think I do not know myself, Niels? I am a man without

insight, ruled by his prejudices and obsessions. That is how I appear to you, is it not?'

'Not quite like that.'

'The same brush blackens you,' Olsen said. 'Although you are clever, you have not seen this. Find a seaman and you find a man who, deep down, is indifferent to women. He may pursue them, he may even marry, but that does not alter things. No true lover would tolerate so frequent and such long separation from that which he loves. No woman of sense marries a seaman, except for convenience.'

'You have strong views,' Mouritzen said. 'And you put them well. But they are still nonsense.'

Olsen laughed. 'Does it come too close?'

'It comes nowhere near me. It's a matter...'

He broke off as the telephone bell rang. Olsen picked up the receiver.

'Captain speaking.'

Mouritzen watched him as he listened, observed the slight narrowing of the eyes.

'Mr Mouritzen will be coming down right away,' Olsen said.

'More trouble?' Mouritzen asked.

'Herning sounds nervous,' Olsen said. 'Hold him on a tight rein, Niels.'

'What's happened?'

'He says that the No. 1 hatch has gone.'

'My God!'

'Yes. Better get down there right away.'

Chapter Six

Clinging to the steps as a wave washed over the *Kreya*, Mouritzen thought the wind was even higher. He made his way across a deck running with water towards the cluster of lights above the forward hold. Herning was there, with half a dozen hands; and also, he saw with some disquiet, Carling. But Carling made no attempt to interfere as Herning made his report.

'Smashed open, like a tin box, sir! And every sea we ship cracks it farther open.'

Their torches, cast together, threw a double beam and Mouritzen saw what had happened. Presumably a wave had got under the hatch cover and lifted it. Subsequent seas had crashed the cover down against the hatch, lifted it and crashed it again, in a rhythmic pounding under which, in the end, the heavy steel had twisted and buckled. Now the cover on the starboard side was forced down below the level of its mate, useless, and with each wave water was sucked through into the hold, wrenching it further out of shape.

The *Kreya* heeled and a wave lifted higher and higher above them before thundering down to immerse them, for an instant, in a world of savage water. Holding on to the rail, Mouritzen had a moment's dread that there would be no more solid, that this was the end of things – a roaring in the ears, a choking, liquid coldness. In the apprehension of death, he thought of the sun, of all its lavish fire, and desperately worshipped it.

But the ship rolled back, and they were safe still, on their steel raft, tossed on the heaving waters. Above the howl of the gale, the deeper tumult of the waves, the creak and whine of the *Kreya* herself, he heard another sound: cries of shrill agony, inhuman and forsaken. The horses.

He shouted to Herning: 'Bring the pumps up, and call up all hands.'

Mouritzen fought his way to the forecastle, and reported by telephone to Olsen.

Olsen asked: 'Just how bad is it?'

'Bad enough.'

There was impatience in Olsen's voice.

'Can it be re-secured?'

'No.'

'Are you sure, man?'

'Even in a calm sea, we couldn't fix this. The cover is twisted out of shape, and each wave twists it more.'

'Have we taken much?'

'I can't see yet.'

'Then for God's sake get down to the hold and find out.'

Resentfully dignified, though conscious of the absurdity at such a time, Mouritzen said:

'I'm reporting to you first. I've ordered the pumps up. Now I'm going down to the hold.'

'Move fast,' Olsen said, and hung up.

Only one of the double doors to the hold had been closed, and water had seeped beneath it; the corridor was an inch or two awash. When Mouritzen opened the other door, water flooded past him. Two naked light bulbs were burning in the hold and he saw that water was a couple of feet deep on the port side. As the ship rolled, the water raced across the floor and the horses on the starboard side were fetlock deep in it. The horses kicked and struggled and whinnied their distress. The *Kreya* buried herself still deeper, and from above fresh water poured like a torrent. Mouritzen jerked back as it cascaded on to him. As he did so he heard the jagged, abrasive sound of metal scraping against metal. He directed the beam to tilt the other way. The cover had settled still further; it hung down from the hatch, and there were at least three or four feet of space between it and the top.

One of the men called to him as he went above decks.

'What is it?' he asked.

'Captain wants you, sir, on the telephone.'

It was Felck, a youngster from Langeland who had only been at sea a few months. He was tall, still thin from the burst of adolescent growth, with a long face now white and scared. He needed reassuring, but Mouritzen had neither the time nor the necessary reserve of assurance. He nodded.

'Right.'

Olsen said: 'Niels, did you tell Herning to get the tarpaulins across the hatch?'

'I was just going to.'

'Do it now. Wait. Have you had a look at the hold?'

'Yes. About nine inches, if she were level.'

'Then get that tarpaulin over. The pumps can wait.'

'The cover is giving all the time.'

'Get on with it.'

The tarpaulins were tied up under the poop-deck. It was hard enough getting to them, and still harder to get the stiff, greasy rolls forward. For all the cold of the wind and the bitter onslaught of the waves, Mouritzen found himself sweating. At last they had one of the rolls alongside the No. 1 hatch, and Herning with a couple of the hands clambered up over the adjacent hatch, taking an end with them. Herning had brought up a megaphone, and Mouritzen shouted orders through it, and heard his voice, amplified and distorted, blown back to him on the gale.

The derrick lights had been switched on, and it was possible to see more or less what was taking place. On one side, a couple of the men were pulling the tarpaulin up over the hatch end; on the other, Herning's group was edging its way across the No. 2 hatch. At the foot of the hatch, the tarpaulin was being opened up for them. Mouritzen saw that it was caught up, and that a halt would have to be made while the men freed it.

He bellowed to Herning: 'Hold on! She's caught . . .'

Herning was on the bridge between the two hatches. He was half kneeling, and he turned his head towards Mouritzen, as though to make out more clearly what he was saying. The *Kreya* was rolling deep into a trough. Holding on to a stanchion, Mouritzen saw the dark green crest high above his head before everything dissolved. In the dissolution, he thought he heard a cry. He did hear a savage rending sound, as metal strained and yielded and was torn away. When he could see again, there were only two men on top of the hatch.

The hatch cover had gone completely, fallen into the hold and half blocking it, like a lid fallen into a box. Mouritzen peered down into the depths. The hold lights had gone, but the derrick lights showed enough of the scene. Water bubbled round the edge of the shattered steel. A horse was pinned under it at one end, clearly dead. The huddled figure of Herning lay just beyond the horse. There was no sign of life there either.

He barely had time to take in all this before another wave lashed across the ship. Water rushed down into the hold, with a sucking noise like a titanic drain. Mouritzen called out to one of the men: 'Stövring! You and Elkuus get below and get Herning out of there. Larsen! Get on to that tarpaulin again.'

He saw Carling go with the two men he had ordered down to the hold, but paid no attention. It was a relief, in any case, to have him out of the way. The job now was to concentrate on getting the tarpaulin in place, to minimize the weight of water that would go below. He took an end himself, and they pulled the heavy canvas forward. But when the next wave crashed, the ends were lost as the water savagely dragged the tarpaulin down with it.

With each roll, tons of water were sinking down into the *Kreya*, and one could feel now the sluggishness of her climb back to even keel. They wrestled the tarpaulin up over the yawning hatch, foot by foot, inch by inch, letting the ropes go as the ram of water came down and painfully hauling back the canvas after each shock. They had it over the top before a wave, heavier even than the ones that had gone before, wrenched ropes and all away and down into the hold.

Mouritzen, by now, was alternately bullying and cajoling the men. He reflected when, under each smashing onslaught of the sea, he had time to think, on his own inadequacy in coping with this kind of emergency, and on the fact that, in the twelve years of his life at sea, it was his first experience of it. With Herning dead and Carling living in some remote fantasy world, there was none of the crew on whom he could rely. He did not know them well enough. 'When we get out of his,' he promised himself, 'I shall make a point of knowing every man to the absolute limit of such knowledge.'

They wrestled the tarpaulin up again, and again lost it. The third time, it held at the top but the deck end gave way and young Felck was slammed against the edge of the hatch. His shoulder seemed to be dislocated and Mouritzen sent him below. He could not spare a man to go with him.

Carling had come back on deck, when Stövring reported that Herning's body had been cleared out of the hold. He went from place to place, leaning like a giant against the wind and the seas, neither interfering nor helping. Now Mouritzen saw him stride upright over the sloping cover of the No. 2 hatch and balance on the roof line. He looked magnificent in the derrick lights: he was wearing no oilskins and his wet clothes clung to his large limbs. Lear, Mouritzen thought drunkenly – Lear as a seaman. With any kind of luck he would break a leg and they could get him out of the way.

The *Kreya* shipped another huge wave, and as she began to roll back Mouritzen looked up, half expecting that Carling would have been swept away. But he still stood there, and standing, pointed down into the gulf of the hold. In a brief slackening of the wind, his voice roared out, harsh and apocalyptic:

'The third sign – look! The horses that swim like fishes!'

Mouritzen, with the others, was drawn to look down. The canvas flapped against the sides of the hold, in which water now lapped high up against the crumpled metal. And in the water, two of the horses threshed and struggled. They had been torn free of their stalls and now were fighting for their lives against the rising water.

'What did I tell you?' cried Carling. 'The third sign. Now the ship is doomed!'

Mouritzen felt helplessness wash over him as relentlessly as any wave. The only thing he could think of doing was to get hold of

Olsen. To Stövring, he shouted:

'Carry on with securing the tarpaulin. I'm going up to see the Captain.'

Olsen met him as he came on to the bridge.

'What in hell is happening down there?' he asked.

Mouritzen said wearily: 'I don't know. We can't get it in place. Even if we could I don't think it would do any good. The seas we're shipping would rip it to shreds in no time.'

'Then leave it, and concentrate on the pumps.'

'I don't know what to do about Carling.'

'I thought you'd got him below?'

'He came up again. He wasn't getting in the way, so I thought it didn't matter.'

'Didn't matter! Potentially he's as dangerous as the bear was – more so.'

'He's started raving again,' Mouritzen said. 'You can see the horses struggling in the water down there. He's been shouting something about the third sign – horses that swim like fishes – and the ship being doomed. He's up on the No. 2 hatch. I don't think the men would go up and tackle him.'

'And you don't fancy tackling him yourself? Where's the gun?'

'Gun?'

'My automatic that I gave to Herning when I sent him after the bear. You got if off him, didn't you?'

Mouritzen shook his head. 'I thought he'd handed it back to you.'

Olsen stared at him. 'You got Herning's body out of the hold?'

'Yes.' He hesitated, remembering the scene. 'Carling was down there with them.'

Olsen reached for his oilskins. 'Take over here,' he said quietly. 'I'm going down.'

Carling was no longer on the hatch when Olsen reached it. He was standing among the rest of the crew, his hands raised as though preaching. Olsen cut in sharply:

'Stövring. Take three men and get Carling down below. See that he's locked in, and make sure that he can't get out. Then report back here to me.'

Carling turned slowly to look at him. He said, lifting his voice above the noise of the gale and yet contriving to seem gentle:

'We must abandon ship, Captain. Give the order to abandon ship.'

Olsen ignored him. To the others, he said:

'He's mad. Get him below. And at once – we've got work to do.'

A couple of them made a move forward, but stopped as Carling lifted his hands again.

'There were to be three signs,' Carling said. 'First, the beast, walking free. Second, water breaking iron, and breaking a man. Third, horses that swim like fishes. And after the third sign – death in the savage waters. The ship is doomed. There is no hope for the *Kreya*.'

Olsen walked up to Carling. A wave crashed across, and the ship gulped water like a creature dying of thirst. Steadying himself, Olsen said:

'Give me that gun, Carling.'

'We must leave the ship, Captain, or we all die. And I must not die until she has spoken. I must not die.'

Olsen put his hand out. 'Give me that gun.'

Stövring's voice came from behind him. 'He hasn't got it.'

Olsen turned round. Stövring stood a little in advance of the rest of the hands; he held the automatic in his right hand, pointing down towards Olsen's feet.

He was a large, squat man, and looked still larger and squatter in his oilskins. He had broad, swarthy features and an underlying truculence which made him unreliable and which had prevented his promotion, despite seniority and ability, to the Petty Officer rank. It was bad enough, Olsen thought bitterly, to have to tackle him at any time, but here and now, and having given him the initiative by going first to Carling...

'All right, Stövring,' he said casually, 'I'll have it.'

'What Carling said is true, Captain,' Stövring said. 'After the first sign, he told us about the other two. He's not made it up. He told us about the signs before they happened.'

'Guesses!' Olsen said. 'The kind of guess any maniac might make. All right, we're in trouble. No one's denying that. Horses that swim like fishes! There was always a chance, after the steering went, that we should start taking water in the hold. That's all it amounts to – no more than that.'

'He told us,' Stövring said. 'And after the third sign, death by drowning. We've got to get off this ship, Captain.'

Olsen moved forward across the swinging deck.

'Give me that gun, Stövring. This is an order.'

Stövring brought the gun up. It was only a small movement – the action was still less than threatening – but it was unmistakable.

Stövring said: 'Tell us first, Captain – do we abandon ship?'

In the back of his mind, Olsen knew that it was the moment to temporize. The key to the situation did not lie with Stövring or himself, nor even with the weapon in Stövring's hand; it lay with the men that were grouped around them. In winning or losing them, he would win or lose control of the *Kreya*; and he had only to temporize to win.

The act was beyond him. He shouted:

'This ship is sound, Stövring, and I am its Captain! The *Kreya* will not be abandoned. I will take this ship into Copenhagen harbour and it depends on me whether you go above deck or below deck, in irons.'

'You call Carling a maniac,' Stövring said. 'You are the maniac, Captain Olsen. This ship isn't going to Copenhagen any more. She's going where the first *Kreya* went, and the second. She's going to the bottom. But we're not going with her.'

Olsen had been making his way slowly towards Stövring; the gun now was pointed roughly towards his knees. The *Kreya* listed to starboard again, and the new wave hung over her. As it came down, Olsen half sprang, half flung himself forwards, to wrest the weapon from Stövring's hand. But Stövring was alert to the move, and on balance. He caught Olsen easily, held him with one hand, and then threw him back. Olsen's head hit the edge of the hatch, and he lost consciousness.

Water lapped against the back of Olsen's head; discomfort preceded identity. The sense of pain came afterwards, spreading a cold fire at the base of his skull. The ship rolled, and the water lapped away from him. He struggled to get up. The cold fire sharpened, but he made it.

At the other end of the deck a tall figure was searching in the shadows. Olsen recognized Mouritzen, and called to him. Mouritzen came down to him along the sloping deck.

'I was looking for you,' Mouritzen said. 'I thought they'd pitched you overboard.'

'Where are they?' Olsen asked. 'What's happening?'

'They're launching the No. 2 boat.'

'How many?'

'All the hands. Stövring's in charge. They've rounded them all up. They've taken Ib with them, too.'

'Thorsen? Møller?'

Mouritzen shook his head. 'No.' He paused. 'Bernard is dead.'

'How?'

'He tackled Stövring when he went down to the engine room, I suppose. I found him there with a bullet in him.'

'He was a bigger man than I,' Olsen said. He brooded on this for a moment. 'The passengers?'

'They've left the passengers.'

Olsen roused himself. 'They may not have got her off yet.'

They had not. The davits were swung out, though, and all but two of the men were aboard. One of the two was Stövring. He flourished the automatic as Olsen came up on the launching deck, with Mouritzen behind him.

'Keep away, Captain. You may be less lucky next time.'

Olsen spoke, not to him but to the men in the boat.

'Stövring is guilty of mutiny and murder,' he shouted. 'You still have a chance to disown him. It's that or prison.'

The large figure of Carling stood up in the boat.

'Abandon ship, Captain!' he called. 'The *Kreya* is doomed.'

Olsen had taken a step forward. Stövring lifted the gun.

'Back,' he said. 'Right back. That's better.' He called to his companion. 'Lower her. Steady now. Get aboard. Stand by to cast off at the bottom of the roll. Now . . . now . . . cast off!'

As he spoke, Stövring clambered out on the davit and slid down the rope. As they rushed to the side, Olsen and Mouritzen saw him drop the last few feet into the crowded boat. The *Kreya* was beginning her roll back again to starboard, and they saw the sea and the ship's boat tilt away from them. Carling was standing up, crying something. They saw two of the others trying to pull him down, but he brushed them off without difficulty.

Olsen said, in a detached voice: 'They're not getting away fast enough.'

The boat lay at the foot of the long, sloping cliff that was the side of the *Kreya*, becalmed for all their struggle with the oars. Mouritzen felt a chill of panic as the perspective began to change and the cliff rose up from the boiling sea. He saw some of the men look up, and thought he could read something of the terror in their faces. An eddy spun the boat round until her bows were pointing back towards the *Kreya*; then she was tossed against the downward leaning cliff. The men's cries came up as they were spilled into the cold cauldron that surrounded them. Mouritzen stared down in horror.

He heard Olsen shout something, and when he turned saw that Olsen had hold of a rope and was throwing a line down. Out of the black foam, Mouritzen thought he saw a hand reach up, and fall back defeated. Then the *Kreya* rolled back, and there was nothing to be seen but the swell of the waves.

They turned away together. Mouritzen said:

'After the third sign, death by drowning. Maybe they were spirits that spoke to Carling. But what kind of spirits, do you think?'

Olsen said: 'Get on to the wireless. Get a distress call out. Let them have details.'

'And then,' Mouritzen said '– the No. 4 boat? We can't hope to launch from the starboard side in this.'

'And then the pumps,' Olsen said. 'Even with a skilled boat crew I would not launch into these seas unless there was no alternative. And at present that is not the case.'

'She's taken a lot of water.'

'And can take more. I will find Thorsen and have him assemble the passengers. When you have raised another ship, you may come down also. We have a lot to do, Niels.'

'And how much hope?'

'All that is needed. One does not need much.'

Mouritzen saw Mary going down the stairs in front of him, and called to her. She looked back, her eyes heavy with fatigue.

'How is Annabel?' he asked.

'Asleep now. But she's been awake most of the night.'

'I'm sorry I haven't had a chance to see you.'

She shook her head. 'I understand. You must have had a terrible time. Are things getting worse? Is that why we're being called down?'

Mouritzen hesitated. 'Captain Olsen will explain it all to you.'

The other passengers were already in the lounge, together with Thorsen and the Captain. They were sitting around the long dining table, with Olsen at his usual place at the head. But instead of Mrs Simanyi and Mrs Jones being seated on either side of him, Thorsen was in the seat on his left. That on his right was empty.

As Mouritzen slipped into it, Olsen said:

'I did not expect you so soon, Niels. Have you raised anyone?'

He said in a low voice: 'We will raise no one on that set, Captain.'

'They have wrecked it? Can it be fixed?'

'Not by me. Not by anyone without spares, I think. Lauring knew what he was doing. The valves are smashed.'

Olsen shrugged slightly. He looked away from Mouritzen, his gaze ranging down the table.

'Ladies and gentlemen,' he said, 'I have something to tell you. I have not spoken to you earlier because there was nothing you could do and you might have been worried without reason. That would be senseless. I speak to you now because there are things you must do, to help yourselves and to help the ship.'

Josef Simanyi said: 'She does not steer – that's right? The waves do what they like to her.'

'The main shaft to the rudder went soon after seven o'clock last night,' Olsen said. 'That was our first misfortune. A couple of hours ago, the cover to one of the forward hatches was damaged, and then destroyed by the high seas. We have taken a lot of water in the forward hold, and are still taking water.

'These are the acts of Nature. There is also Man to consider. I have to tell you that the crew of this ship have mutinied and have attempted to abandon ship. Lieutenant Møller has been killed in trying to stop this and I myself' – he put a hand to the back of his head – 'I was injured a little.'

'Then we must abandon her too, eh?' said Josef.

'No. We do not abandon the *Kreya*.'

Stefan Simanyi said: 'But if the men abandoned her – what hope do we have if we stay?'

Olsen said heavily: 'The men panicked. I say this with shame, because this is my ship and these were my ship's company. But of the two senior men, one was killed in trying to cover the hatch, and the other began to rave about doom and death. A crew is a brotherhood, and it needs a head. Without that, it is a mob.'

'But they abandoned ship?' Josef said.

'They attempted. They did not succeed. Their boat was thrown against the side of the *Kreya* and capsized. Not one of them survived.'

The tones were measured and without emphasis; even knowing this already, Mouritzen felt the horror of it sink into his mind afresh. The faces round the table showed that the others were as affected as he was. Olsen was not sparing them. His next words showed that he was not going to spare them anything.

'I told Mr Mouritzen to send out a new distress signal, of more urgency. He has found that, before leaving, someone of the crew – most likely the wireless operator – had damaged the transmitter beyond hope of repair. The reason probably was that they feared the details of their crimes would be wirelessed back – as they would, of course. They thought they were leaving us to die, on a sinking ship.'

Jones said: 'Couldn't we – can't we – launch a boat ourselves?'

'Our chances would be small. And now that we have learned of the smashed transmitter, I think we may find they would be nil.'

Mouritzen started. Jones said:

'You mean – they may have sabotaged the other boats?'

Olsen nodded. 'It is quite probable.'

Mary said: 'And are we on a sinking ship, Captain Olsen?'

'This is how it is,' Olsen said, 'with the *Kreya*. She cannot steer, so she must take what the storm deals to her. She has no crew, and no engineer. She is taking water in her forward hold, and has already taken enough to be down at the bows. There is no sign of the weather improving. We cannot call to other ships for help, and the two that were coming to our aid already, no longer have our signals to guide them. They may find us, but the North Sea is large and our course is as the storm wills us. They may find us; they may not.'

'Distress signals?' Jones asked.

'Yes, of course. But they will not be seen far in this.'

'You haven't said,' Mary reminded him, 'whether or not the ship is sinking.'

Her voice had a tremor, but she showed no visible signs of fear. None of them did, which Mouritzen thought surprising. He was afraid himself, with a fear that, instead of shaking, clutched and squeezed his inmost being: somewhere, deep inside, that which was Niels Mouritzen tightened, concentrated into a core of anguish and terror. It was something else that made his body move, respond. From far away, Mouritzen listened and watched.

Olsen said: 'From the moment she is launched, a ship begins to die.' He moved his head to stare at Mary. 'The *Kreya* is sinking. Each wave we ship brings the moment nearer when she fights no longer and must go down.'

69

Mrs Simanyi said: 'Can we do nothing?'

Olson smiled. His voice changed; he spoke with confidence, loudly and sharply:

'We can do everything! I have told you before – the third *Kreya* does not sink. Personally I will conduct her to the breaker's yards, and then I will retire, and end my days sitting in a café in Copenhagen, drinking coffee and looking at the sea. That is how it will be; you have my assurance on that.'

He leaned forward, his eyes now on the two male Simanyis.

'I have talked a lot, hm? I have told you how bad things are – and that is true – and I have told you the *Kreya* is sinking – and that is true – and I have told you that she will not sink. That is true also. She will not sink because we do not permit it. From now on, you are my ship's company and between us we shall save the *Kreya*. I have talked a lot, because I shall not talk again. After this, I give commands; and you obey them. Is that understood?'

One or two assented; the others nodded. Olsen ranged his glance along them with satisfaction.

'For now, the ladies are not needed on deck. Mr Thorsen will show them where the food store and the galley are, and then Mr Thorsen will report to me. We will have an early breakfast – maybe a warm one. But for power we have only the stand-by generator, and that must first feed the pumps. If the drain is too great, then you will have to manage without the electric cooker. There are paraffin stoves also in the galley, but I think maybe you cannot use them until the sea is quieter.'

Olsen stood up. 'The men will come with me. We get these pumps going right away. Work now – not talk.'

The others began to rise from their seats. Olsen smiled at them, his brow furrowed.

'The riddle,' he said suddenly, '– who has read the riddle?' He raised a hand. 'From the other night.'

They stared, bewildered by the new change of tone. Sheila Jones said:

'We gave it up.'

'Greater than the universe,' said Olsen, 'and smaller than a grain of sand. The dead eat it. If we eat it, we die too. What is it?'

He waited for some moments, looking at them with the self-containing uncompromising amusement of a small boy.

'Nothing!' he said at last. 'Nothing is greater than the universe. Nothing is smaller than a grain of sand. The dead eat nothing. And if we eat nothing, we die also. Ladies, for breakfast we will not have Nothing – we will have Something. It is in your hands.'

To conserve power for the pumps, the derrick lights had been switched off. Throughout the hours of storm and darkness, the little party struggled on with no more light than the occasional ray from Mouritzen's torch. As blackness softened into grey, and they could begin to see the outline of each other's faces, Olsen called a halt while he and Mouritzen clambered out on the No. 2 hatch to inspect progress.

'The wind is less strong,' Mouritzen said. 'And the sea not running so high, I think.'

'Flash your torch down,' Olsen said.

The two beams travelled, searched and crossed.

Mouritzen said: 'My God!'

'What is that?'

'The level. It's a good metre higher than when we started.'

'Yes,' Olsen said. His torch light circled, touching the shattered metal of the hatch cover, and all round it the black, tilting water. 'We have done well.'

'Well?'

'We have done well that the *Kreya* still floats.' He snapped off the torch. 'If the storm abates, soon we may begin to hold our own.'

'And if it doesn't?'

'It will. Otherwise the *Kreya* will go to the bottom.' Mouritzen could see his ironic smile in the light of this grey, wet dawn. 'And I have given my word that she will not.'

Mouritzen jerked his head towards the men on deck behind them, squatting or lying against the No. 2 hatch in evident exhaustion.

'They must have some rest.'

Olsen glanced back. 'They are resting.'

'Real rest. In a bunk.'

'Not today. When we are no longer shipping seas, when the hold is dry and we have a cover on it – that will be the time to talk of rest in a bunk.'

Mouritzen shook his head. 'They will drop.'

'We will see.'

Olsen made his way down to the deck with Mouritzen following him.

'We are making progress,' he said. 'Now we get back to our work.'

Three of them responded, though Jones looked as though each moment cost him agony. Thorsen's face was drawn into the compressed lines of fatigue; and even old Josef looked as though his toughness was under strain. The fourth was Stefan Simanyi. He was lying slumped against the hatch, and did not move even to look up.

'Stefan.' Olsen said. 'We work again.'

The oil-skinned shape stirred, and a voice mumbled, but he did not get up. Josef said:

'Come on, Stefan. We are all tired.'

He roused slightly more this time, and it was possible to make out what he said.

'I'm finished. I have no strength.'

'Mr Jones,' Josef said, '– he is a man who has worked in an office, and he is nearer your father's age than yours. He does not complain. You are a circus man. You are used to hard work.'

'Without food? For days, anything that has gone into my stomach has come out again. All night I have been sick. I cannot work any more.'

'We must work,' Josef said. 'On us depends if the ship will still float. You understand that.'

'I understand, but it makes no difference. If she sinks, she sinks. I can do no more.'

Saying nothing, Olsen went over to Stefan and, bending down, lifted him from the deck. Although Stefan was considerably heavier than himself, he managed it without difficulty, with the almost caressing strength of a mother lifting a child, or a cat her kitten. He propped Stefan against the hatch, in a position from which it would not be easy to slide down again, and untied the strings of his sou'wester. He took it off, and the wind blew spray and rain against Stefan's white face.

'A couple of hours' rest,' Stefan said. 'Then perhaps I am all right.'

Olsen's hand moved very fast. The sound of his open palm cracking against Stefan's cheek was very loud. Almost before it had died away, Olsen hit him again. Either the second blow was harder or the first had knocked Stefan off balance; he crashed to the deck.

Olsen stood over him. In a cold but unforced voice, he said:

'Now, get up.'

Shakily Stefan got to his knees and then, holding on to the hatch, rose to his feet. The blows had brought a faint flush to his left cheek.

'You have more strength now?' Olsen asked. Stefan did not reply. 'I am asking you a question: are you ready to work?'

'Yes,' Stefan said.

'Good. Then we continue. We work until I say that we stop, and I tell you now that will not be for a long time. Mouritzen, go below and check the generator.'

Mouritzen nodded. As he prepared to leave, he saw the forecastle door open, and drew Olsen's attention to it. Two figures emerged, carrying billycans and an aluminium box. Although the oilskins they had found disguised them, they were recognizable as Nadya and Mary.

With evident good humour, Olsen said: 'So we have breakfast! You have done well, ladies.'

'We could only manage soup and sandwiches,' Mary said. 'We've been having to hold the pot on top of the stove, with another two holding the stove itself.'

Olsen took a can and helped himself to a sandwich from the box as she opened it.

'That's a fine breakfast,' he said. 'With this in our bellies we shall work twice as hard.' He nodded to Stefan. 'And you, Stefan – do you eat, too? Will you take the risk that your stomach does not like it?'

Stefan managed a faint grin. 'I will take that risk.'

Olsen crammed the remainder of the sandwich into his mouth, and slapped Stefan rudely but genially on the back.

'We will cure your sea sickness,' he said. 'Before this voyage is over, we will cure it!'

Chapter Seven

The sea grew calmer during the day, and as it wore on the pumps began taking out more water than was coming aboard. In late afternoon, with the seas quieter, though still stormy, and with the *Kreya* riding higher for being free of some of her unaccustomed ballast of water, only the occasional wave was breaking over the gunwale, and the pumps got well ahead. There was half an hour's anxiety when the generator broke down, but Mouritzen, prodded and pestered rather than helped by Olsen, finally got it running again. As dusk closed in on them, the pumps were gulping air each time the roll of the *Kreya* carried the residue of water across to the other side.

After a further inspection, Olsen said:

'That is enough. What is left does not matter for now.'

Mouritzen, in a blur of fatigue, was hanging on to the rail. Josef was leaning back against the hatch. The other three lay slumped on the deck.

'What do you think of?' Olsen asked. 'Something to eat, maybe, hot coffee – and then sleep for a few hours, in your bunks, rocked by these gentle waves?'

They made no answer. Olsen surveyed them through eyes drawn tight for want of sleep.

'All right,' he said. 'But first there is work to do. First we get a tarpaulin across this hatch.'

Jones said, in a croaking voice: 'Can't it wait a bit? Until we've had the coffee, at least.'

'If you rest another five minutes,' Olsen said, 'I will need a whip to get you working again, coffee or no coffee. Up, now. Stefan!'

They roused up to their feet, with jerky marionette movements and, following Olsen's sharp-voiced orders, began the task, which had proved impossible the night before, of hauling the heavy tarred canvas up over the open hatch. It was a slow business, but they made progress and at last had the tarpaulin across and well lashed down at each corner. When the last corner was secured, Mouritzen said, his voice heavy with weariness and relief:

'So that's that.'

'Yes,' Olsen said. 'That's that.' He looked at Mouritzen, his face contorted into an attempt at a smile. 'Now we go and get another tarpaulin to fasten over this one.'

Mouritzen protested: 'This one will hold well enough.'

'You told me last night,' Olsen said, 'that even if you had managed to secure the tarpaulin, the seas would have ripped it to shreds. So we make it a double strength, I think.'

'That was at the height of the storm,' Mouritzen said. 'We were taking waves fifty feet high. By comparison, the sea is harbour calm now.'

'Things are better,' Olsen acknowledged. 'They may go on getting better; but they may get worse.' He called to the others: 'Right! Now we go aft to fetch the second tarpaulin.'

Jones collapsed on the way back, as they heaved the awkward roll along the deck. Olsen and Mouritzen bent over him together.

'It would do you no good to hit him,' Mouritzen said, 'however hard you hit.'

Olsen nodded. 'And I have not much strength now to hit hard.'

'Shall we get him inside?'

Jones was lying on his side, with his head near a pool of water.

'When we have the hatch secured,' Olsen said. 'He does no harm there.' He stood up and spoke to the others. 'We continue.'

Wearily they stooped again to pick up the tarpaulin.

When Olsen was satisfied with the sealing of the No. 1 hatch, he dismissed them to the lounge. Mouritzen and Josef Simanyi picked up Jones and carried him with them. For Mouritzen the burden was almost too much; protecting Jones, he found himself swaying and lurching, his own body cannoning against obstructions as they made their way along the deck. When they set him down on the leather couch, Mouritzen leaned over him for a time, his forearm resting against the couch head, before he could straighten up and turn to the others.

Sheila Jones came out of the kitchen at the far end, saw Jones lying there, and moved towards him. She knelt down by him, and looked up at Mouritzen.

'What happened?'

'The work was too much for him. He will be all right. He needs rest.'

Jones stirred, opening his eyes. 'Rest.' His voice was slurred with weariness. 'Darling, are you all right?'

She lifted his head, and sat down so that it rested in her lap.

'Rest now,' she said. 'Just rest.'

Olsen, coming in through the swing doors, examined the scene. Mouritzen, having yielded place to Sheila, had slumped down in a chair, as the other men had done already. Olsen, impeccably upright, put his hands down to the table's edge, as though he stood to address a public meeting.

'Duty cook,' he said. 'Where is the duty cook?'

Mrs Simanyi put her head out of the hatch between kitchen and lounge.

'It is Sheila and I,' she said.

'Where is our soup?' Olsen demanded. 'We have worked hard, and we must be nourished.'

'Nearly ready,' she said. 'In two, three minutes. We have a lot of trouble with the paraffin cooker.'

Olsen nodded. 'From now you can use the electric cooker. And the other ladies?'

'Mary is upstairs with the child. Nadya sees to Katerina.'

'That bear,' Olsen said, '– she will not interfere with work. Otherwise I myself throw her overboard.'

'She does not interfere,' Mrs Simanyi said. 'You interfere, Captain. I will go back to the soup.'

It was thick, tinned soup, studded with meat and vegetables. They drank and chewed it with relish, and returned their billycans for more. Sheila sat by Jones, holding the can to his lips.

Olsen said to Stefan: 'How is the stomach, Stefan? You have not been sick today?'

Looking up from his can, Stefan said: 'Too tired to be sick.'

'Soon you rest.'

'Soon?'

'When the burials are finished. Have you forgotten we carry two dead men?'

'They are patient,' Stefan said. 'They will wait till morning.'

Olsen shook his head. 'One does not keep corpses on a ship longer than must be. I excuse Jones. Mouritzen, you will take the others and see that the bodies are laid out on the No. 4 hatch, on planks. You can cover each with a sheet. I go now to get my prayer-book. I will see you there.'

They looked at him apathetically, neither consenting nor disputing. To Mrs Simanyi, Olsen said:

'The ladies need not attend this ceremony. When we return, I want all to be present here. You will see to that, Mrs Simanyi.'

The two Simanyis went to bring Herning from the forecastle, and Mouritzen took Thorsen down to the engine room to get Møller. Møller's body lay sprawled, as he had fallen, a few feet from the bottom of the staircase. His arms were flung out, his head turned up as though looking for help. Mouritzen felt ashamed that he had not composed the body or, at least covered it during earlier visits to the engine room. Thorsen curiously lifted an arm, and let it fall again.

'Stiff,' he said. 'It will not be easy.'

Mouritzen went to the stand-by generator and examined it. It seemed to be running all right still. He took a can of diesel and topped the tank up. That would hold it for three or four hours.

'Shall we call for the others?'

'Others?' Mouritzen said. 'Why?'

Thorsen pointed. 'We've got to get him up those stairs.'

'We can manage. I'll get him on my back. You can support him from behind.'

It was a nightmarish, struggling business, holding the cold, bony wrists, feeling the cold dead flesh pressing against his neck. This is one of your quiet times, Bernard, he thought – I have never known you so quiet, nor so intimate. Who hath honour now? He that died of Tuesday. It was a brave thing, a stupid thing; unless he had not known Stövring had a gun. If so, it was an accident. But whether an act was brave or stupid or accidental was itself an accident. God help us, he thought, to deceive ourselves.

When Olsen came down, they had the two bodies on planks, side by side on the hatch, and Thorsen was wrapping a sheet round Møller. The sheet had to go well over his head to cover the arms.

Olsen gestured. 'Untidy.'

'A man cannot always die,' Mouritzen said, 'and leave his body tidy.'

Olsen stared at him. 'That was not what I meant.'

'We could break the arms, perhaps,' Mouritzen suggested, '– tie them down to his sides?'

Olsen looked as though he was considering this. Then he gave his attention to his prayer-book.

'The service for the burial of the dead at sea,' he said.

Standing by him, Mouritzen said in a low voice: 'Do we need the whole service? Neither was a churchgoer – Bernard was an atheist.'

'We will do what is usual.'

Darkness was wellnigh complete; they stood like shadows around the white-sheeted figures that alone had substance and a positive shape. The sea was still running high, but for the most part did not break inboard. The wind remained strong, and howled through every hole and channel as though the ship were honeycombed. Olsen held the book in his left hand, and directed a light on to it with his right.

He reeled off the sonorous Danish phrases in a clear sharp voice. It was not possible, owing to the rolling of the *Kreya*, to hold the planks on the gunwales throughout: at the appropriate moment

Olsen halted his reading and ordered the others to bring the bodies up. They had to time the bestowal to coincide with the bottom of a roll. The sheeted figures slid down to the dark, heaving waters and the *Kreya*, as though in revulsion, rolled away from them.

In the lounge again, Olsen paused for a while and surveyed them all before speaking.

'We have done well,' he said at last. The *Kreya* still floats. She is dry again. The hatch is covered, and the storm is abating. Now it is only necessary to wait until we sight another vessel, or are sighted.'

Nadya said: 'Where are we? Are we near Copenhagen?'

'I do not know where we are, except that we are in the North Sea. The gale has been carrying us to the north-west. If we sight land, I think it will be Scotland.'

'And if we get driven on to the coast?' Josef asked.

'We will face that, if we come to it. For present, we man a ship that is sound, but rudderless and powerless. We cannot call for help. There is nothing we can do but wait. I warn you that the waiting may take longer than you think, because the seas are wide and ships, like men, do not stray far from the paths of their fellows. If we are in, or if the winds drive us into such a path, then we are lucky. If not, we may drift for two days, three days, more, and see nothing. There need be no anxiety. We have plenty of food and water. The hard time is over. Now there is only the waiting.'

'Katerina,' Nadya said.

'What is that?'

'Can we put her in a cabin in the forecastle, until her cage is fixed? Here she may keep people awake, if she is restless in the night.'

Olsen closed his eyes, shutting them tight as though to force tiredness away. When he opened them again, he said:

'I have had enough of the bear. That can wait till morning. Listen. Lieutenant Mouritzen remains my First Officer. He is my deputy, and acts for me when I am not present. Mr Thorsen, as the only other ship's officer, is next in command. When I am not there, gentlemen, you will take orders from one of these or the other. But I do not wish to lay on them the task of controlling the ladies. So, just as Mr Mouritzen is my right-hand man, I will have a right-hand woman. Mrs Simanyi, you are that woman. Under me, you will be responsible for the other ladies, and also for the cooking and cleaning. You are no longer passengers, remember, you are crew.

Mr Thorsen will not have time now to look after you. Is all this clear?'

He stared at them, accepting their silence as consent.

'For the moment you may rest. Get some sleep. Niels, you will come with me.'

Mouritzen followed Olsen to the bridge. There was an uncanny feeling in going up there to find it empty, silent, the useless wheel unattended. He felt as though they were intruders on a derelict.

Olsen said: 'Fortunately we have plenty of oil. We can carry lights and we can put the scanner back in operation.'

Mouritzen said doubtfully: 'The scanner is a heavy load for that generator.'

'We will run it when the ladies are not cooking. Tell them they are to notify me when the cooker is in operation.'

Mouritzen looked out through the glass towards the bow light and the invisible sea.

'Do you think we run a risk of piling up on the Scottish coast?'

'I don't think so. I guess we have been driven well north in the last twenty-four hours. The Shetlands, maybe.'

Mouritzen yawned. Olsen looked at him critically.

'I will not keep you long. I will wake you at midnight. Then you wake me for six o'clock, unless there is an emergency first.'

Mouritzen yawned again. 'Yes.'

'Other matters we can discuss in the morning. Go and sleep now, Niels. Tell the women to bring me up some black coffee.'

Mouritzen emerged to some extent from his cocoon of drowsiness.

'You are taking this watch by yourself?'

With irony, Olsen said: 'Do you want to take it?'

'All I want is sleep.'

'With me, desire is never so simple.' He looked angry for a moment, and then smiled. 'Go and get your sleep, Niels.'

Mouritzen hesitated by the door of his cabin and then, rousing himself, turned away and went down the steps to the passengers' deck. He knocked at the door of Mary's cabin, and she called to him to enter.

Annabel was in the bottom bunk, but not asleep. Mary sat on the edge of the bed, dressed and wearing her overcoat. There was, of course, no heat in the pipes with the engines stopped.

Mouritzen said: 'I have had no chance to speak to you. Are you all right?'

Mary smiled. 'Yes.'

'And little Annabel?'

Annabel said: 'I thought the ship was going to sink, but it didn't.'

Mouritzen smiled at her. 'The ship will not sink.'

She said accusingly: 'You said that when I woke up we would be in Amsterdam.'

'The storm blew us the wrong way.'

'Are we *nearly* in Amsterdam?'

'We were blown a long, long way. It may be a little time before we find our way back.'

Annabel looked at him. 'I know something.'

'What is that?'

'The bear is in the cabin we were in first.'

'That is exciting – to have a bear in a cabin. Do you think she sleeps in the top bunk or the bottom one?'

Disappointed, she said: 'I think you knew already.'

'Why?'

'Because you weren't surprised. I thought you would be surprised.'

'She is a clever bear, that one,' Mouritzen said. 'That is why I am not surprised. Her grandfather was the big bear who decided he would live like a man. I will tell you that story some time.'

Annabel sat up. 'Tell it now.'

Mary said: 'Not now.' She made the child lie down. 'Mr Mouritzen has been working very hard, and he's very, very tired.'

Annabel nodded. To Mouritzen, she said:

'Good night. You can kiss me good night, if you want to.'

'Very much.'

In the extremity of fatigue, movements were dream-like and unreal. He walked to the bunk, bent down, and kissed the child on her forehead, between the darker brows and the silky golden hair.

'Sleep well,' he said.

'You, too.'

He turned from her to see Mary looking at him. With the same sensation of being in a dream, he reached towards her and kissed her on the lips. Her lips were warm, accepting, not responding.

Mouritzen stood away from her.

'There is a compensation,' he said.

'Compensation?'

'For the storm. By now, you should have been in Amsterdam, beginning your new life, already forgetting the *Kreya* and those you met on her.'

She frowned. 'He will be worried for us.'

'Your Dutchman? Not too much, I think; you are nothing to each other.'

'I won't have you talking like that.'

'It is true. One cannot rise above the body – our souls live within us. A touch of the hand means more than a hundred letters of passion. To him, you are an abstract thing, a photograph, as it might be a photograph of a film star. But I have kissed you, and you are the woman I love.'

She smiled then. 'Go to bed, Niels. You are drunk with tiredness.'

He went to the cabin door and opened it. Looking back, he said:

'Yes. With tiredness and love. Good night.'

Jones moved restlessly in his bed, and after a time Sheila got up from her own and sat by him.

'What's the matter?' she asked.

'Nothing. I'm tired, but I can't sleep. Thoughts race round my head.'

'What kind of thoughts?'

'This is a front-page story – do you realize that? A ship lost and drifting in a storm, the crew mutinying and abandoning ship – sensations and murders – wherever we end up the reporters will be waiting for us.'

She nodded. 'I suppose so.'

'Our pictures in the papers – on the television newsreels. Someone is going to recognize us. And when that happens, we're finished.'

'No.'

He looked up at her. 'I promised you a lot, didn't I?'

'Only one thing that mattered.'

'How long will I get? Seven years – ten? I should have looked it up. Or you should have looked it up for me. Part of the secretarial duties.'

'Try to rest.'

'Will you wait for me?'

'If there were need, I'd wait.'

'No need.' He spoke with unhappy conviction. 'She'll be waiting. First she'll try making up the deficiency with her own money again; but she'll realize it's too serious to get away with like that. She'll brief the very best counsel. All through the trial she'll sit in the front row, a brave little figure in sober, elegant clothes. She'll smile courageously at me as sentence is passed – with any luck she'll be worth a couple of years' reduction. And then she'll set about getting things ready for the day when the gates clang shut behind me. A new life, maybe in Canada or Australia.'

'If all that happened, would you go with her?'

'What else? This was my last throw, and I left it late. Even in three or four years' time I couldn't start again.'

'Why not?'

'You're young enough to ask that. You wouldn't understand if I tried to explain.'

She asked him: 'Do I matter to you at all – except as a part of getting away from her?'

'You matter. You matter more than anything.'

'Well?'

'One loses the things that count – strength, youth, faith. And love. It's not that they don't matter. It's just that a time comes when you know you've lost them, and there's no point in going on pretending to yourself.'

'Is that what you've been doing – pretending?'

He stared at the cabin ceiling. 'I suppose I have – about some things anyway.'

'About us?'

'Yes. Pretending it was possible.'

There was silence for a time, except for the sound of wind and waves, and the ship's creaking. Then Sheila said briskly:

'No.'

He looked at her. 'What do you mean?'

'You're with me now, not with her. I won't have you talk like that.'

He lay without speaking. She looked and saw that there were tears in his eyes. She knelt beside the bed.

'Darling, darling. You're tired and miserable now. You'll feel better when you've had some sleep.'

'By yourself,' he said, 'you'd be all right.'

'Hush.'

'She'll have you vilified. In court, in the press. I should have thought of that. I could have made the dash on my own, and you could have followed if it was safe.'

'No.'

'Why not?'

'I wouldn't have let you.'

He began to say something, but stopped. 'It doesn't matter now anyway.'

She put her head against his chest. 'How would you manage without me? Who would do all the planning? Look at you now – ready to give up because there may be some reporters waiting when we get back on dry land.'

'And photographers, and the television people.'

She stroked his chin and pushed her fingers against the bristle so that it crackled.

'You haven't shaved for two days. Another two days and you'll be unrecognizable. I suppose it could be a week before we get back to a port, and by then you'll have a beard. I'll hide your glasses for you – you can say you broke them – and I'll put dark ones on myself. Then let them take what photographs they like.'

He held her hand with his. 'Do you think it would work?'

'Why not?'

'It might,' he said. 'I didn't think of that.'

'We only need a couple of days,' she said. 'We can disappear again, can't we? It isn't as though anyone will be expecting us to be on the *Kreya*. They'll think we went by air to Paris. We can be away long before anyone gets suspicious.'

He pulled her down and kissed her. 'You make me feel better.'

'You fool,' she said, affectionately.

'I know. Middle-aged, bankrupt, a thief, and a fool. Why do you bother?'

'You know why. Look. Something to make you sleep.'

She opened one of the cases and brought out a bottle of brandy.

'How did you come by that?'

'I got it from the steward. I think it goes on our bill at the end, if the ship doesn't go down. Drink it. There. Now go to sleep.'

He still held her hand. 'Sit beside me for a while.'

'All right.'

Olsen, on the bridge, paced to and fro, stamping his feet harder than was necessary against the deck to keep tiredness at bay. There was little that could be done – nothing of practical value before morning – and his thoughts revolved unprofitably about the central fact of his failure.

He accepted no blame as to seamanship. The rudder had failed him and after that the ship had been at the mercy of the storm. He had done all that a man could do, and the *Kreya* was still afloat. If the weather got no worse, and if she didn't finish up on a lee shore, the *Kreya* would come through. The owners could not criticize him for his handling.

Nor would they criticize him for the mutiny. With Carling mad and Herning killed, it was not surprising that there had been panic – someone like Stövring should have taken advantage of it and that, after the attack on himself and the murder of Møller, there should have been no alternative for them but to carry it through. It would not damage him. He would remain skipper of the *Kreya*.

And it did not matter that there would be talk – that he would be known always as the 'Captain of the Mutiny'. Talk made no difference. Talk was for little people, who were afraid to act. He feared neither talk nor the talkers.

But the failure remained, unaffected by the justification or condemnation that might come from others. Always the one thing that counted had been his own judgment of his own acts, and in the judgment now he was found wanting. It could not be explained away – he would have disdained to try.

As far back as he could remember, the deviousness of the acts of other men had surprised him. Life, to him, was a simple matter, conditioned by straightforward rules. A man had needs and appetites, and he satisfied them as the law allowed. There had to be law, for without it there was no security; within it there was all the freedom that a man could want – that a sane man could conceive.

A seaman, in this respect, was the citizen writ large. At sea, the law was paramount, more circumscribed and more evidently tangent than in the outer world. Olsen had served before he had commanded, and of these two forms of conformity, it seemed to him that the former was the easier to follow. Leaving madness on one side, he did not understand how it was that a man could reject allegiance. He recognized that it happened, but he did not understand it.

Now it had happened to him, and he sought as best he could for reasons. There had been the moment in which he had felt sure that, by a lie, a moment's deception, he could have won them back. All had turned there on Stövring and himself, and he had only to

84

dissemble to be victorious. But he felt none of the obvious remorse of the man who looks back and wishes he had done otherwise than what he did. To Olsen it was clear that, given the prescient backward leap into time, given the episode unrolling again towards a variable end, he would have done exactly as he had done before – there was nothing else that was within his powers.

Command and obedience. Wherever there were men these two necessities must rule. And yet, wherever there were men, they were flouted.

Thus I refute God, thought Olsen. I do not need to look for wastefulness and cruelty and riot in the jungle or the sea. In the crown and apex of creation there is confusion, disorder, and that is enough.

Chapter Eight

The depressions continued their majestic chase across the North Atlantic, but their westward tracks were moving to the north. The anti-clockwise gales that accompanied them moved north too, sweeping new and colder seas. Each tossed the *Kreya* to its successor. Day after day the wind blew from the south and east. It dropped at times to Force 4 or 5, but only, it seemed, to gain breath before blowing a gale again. They encountered no other ships and made no landfall. In the second night, Mouritzen thought he saw a light on the port side, and sent up flares. He continued to send them up at halfhourly intervals, but when the dawn came there was nothing to be seen but the grey, heaving sea, stretching all round them.

There was no break in the clouds which would have enabled them to get a fix on their position. All that was certain was that the storms had driven them to the north-west. It was Olsen's guess that they had passed between the Orkneys and the Shetlands, and were being carried on in the direction of the Faroes.

There was plenty to occupy the time of the men. Under Mouritzen's supervision, a crude jury-rudder was constructed; part of the shattered foremast provided a vertical shaft, and planks were sawn and nailed on to make the blade. This took most of a day.

In the late afternoon they tried putting it into action, using a metal pipe, lashed to the stern rails, as a sleeve. The bindings tore away, and the salvage operation, though finally successful, proved difficult and dangerous.

The next morning, a new attempt was made, the sleeve being lashed more firmly and secured with hawsers to the anchor capstan. This time the blade tore loose as it entered the water. Olsen, who had come down from the bridge, watched them as they hauled the mast section up over the rails. The wood showed splintered edges where it had been ripped away.

'You waste time with this,' he commented.

Mouritzen drew noisy breath. 'I think so, too. In a calm sea one might do something. For the present, there is no hope of success.'

Olsen nodded. 'Then we wait for a calm sea.'

Mouritzen straightened his back. 'Good.'

'Instead,' Olsen said, 'there are the horses. I do not like rotting carcases aboard my ship.'

'It will mean opening the hatches.'

Olsen shrugged. 'We are no longer shipping seas.'

Mouritzen thought about it. 'God in Heaven – what a job! Thirty-five of them. And how are we to wrestle dead horses on to a loading mat?'

'I leave you with that problem.'

It was the first time Mouritzen had been down to the hold since the night the hatch shattered. The scene, as he flashed his torch from point to point, had a grotesque and savage eeriness. The broken hatch cover cut off most of the view from the forecastle door – one corner rested on the bottom of the hold and two other corners were wedged against the bulkheads – but when Mouritzen had ducked under the overhang of jagged metal, the horrors were in full view.

Some of the horses had either broken free or been washed free from their stalls, and their bodies lay at various points along the hold. Mouritzen recognized the dappled grey that had at first refused the horse-box at Dublin; its coat was dank and slimy, the bright eyes filmed by death. But the great majority had drowned in their wooden stalls; they lay there in two neat rows, and but for their awkward, distorted attitudes, might have seemed to be asleep.

He moved among them, quickly and with distaste, taking note of the difficulties. The warm smell of horse and hay had given way to the cold scents of death and the sea. Corruption was not yet far advanced, but it pervaded the air. He was very glad to get back above decks. He sought out Josef Simanyi, and told him something of the problem.

'We shall have to open up the No. 2 hatch,' he said. 'The broken cover prevents us getting at the other properly. Most of the horses are in that part of the hold. But I do not see yet how we are to raise them.'

Josef asked: 'Why not?'

'Nearly all are tied in their stalls. It will not be easy to manhandle them on to a loading mat.'

Josef shook his head. 'You need no mat. A rope tying all four hooves together will do, if it is strong enough. Then we get a hook under it and lift with the derrick.'

'Will it hold?'

'If it is well done it will hold.'

Mouritzen clapped him on the shoulder. 'That makes you foreman of the hold party. Take Jorgen and Stefan. I will keep Jones here on deck. You will find rope in the aft hold.'

The others were drinking cocoa in the lounge; Mary was serving it. Mouritzen asked her:

'Where is Annabel?'

'In the cabin, playing.'

'You should go up there, too, I think, to make sure she does not come out.'

'Why?'

He told her, and she nodded slowly.

'How long?'

'We shall not finish it today, I think.'

'I'll keep her away.'

'Tell her I will come tonight and tell her a story.'

Their eyes met. 'Yes.'

By the time the approach of night forced a suspension of operations, twenty-three of the carcases had been lifted and dropped over the side. Apart from one occasion when a rope parted and the body was dropped thirty feet back into the hold, all went smoothly, but the working party that came up from the hold and helped Mouritzen and Jones to batten down the hatch for the night was not a cheerful one.

'I stink of dead horse,' Stefan said with disgust. 'It will take more than a cold shower to wash that smell away.'

'We'll get it finished tomorrow,' Mouritzen said. 'It has to be done. Otherwise the whole ship would soon stink of it.'

Thorsen said: 'There is one crushed under the cover. That will be no easy job. I think I take the derrick tomorrow, Niels. You can have the horses.'

It sounded like a joke and Mouritzen accepted it as such. He said:

'I will see to the thirty-sixth horse.'

'No.' Thorsen spoke more loudly. 'I mean what I say, Niels. You have had it easy today. Tomorrow you can go below and I will stay on deck.'

Mouritzen said sharply: 'You will do as I tell you, Jorgen. And I also mean what I say.'

Thorsen stared at him for a moment in silent hatred. He turned away, and started to walk towards the cabins, but stopped after two or three paces and came back.

'Since you are First Officer, you are entitled to give the orders. Is that right?'

'I was named by Captain Olsen as next in command to you. I am the only other officer of the *Kreya*. Yet you put Simanyi in charge of the hold party.'

Mouritzen nodded. 'That grieves you?'

'If we still act under authority, you cannot put Simanyi above me.'

'Josef has been handling animals, alive and dead, since long before you were born. Do not be stupid, Jorgen. No one is taking away your position. For this one job, the man best qualified must instruct the others.'

'Instruction and command are two things, not one.'

Josef, Mouritzen saw, was watching and listening.

'Josef,' he said. 'Tomorrow Jorgen commands down below. Is that all right?' Josef nodded. 'But you continue to instruct, and Jorgen accepts your instruction.'

Thorsen started to say something, and Mouritzen spoke more loudly:

'That will do, Jorgen. We want no further argument.'

Mrs Simanyi had Mary with her in the main galley, preparing the evening meal. Annabel was with them. She had developed good sea-legs and seemed quite unperturbed by the fact that the *Kreya* was still rolling in heavy seas. Mary had brought her along from the cabins after the hatch had been re-secured; shepherding her along the narrow deck against the wind and pelting rain she had been forced to realize that the child managed considerably better than she did. Now she was helping the two women in a deft competent way that made Mary extremely proud of her.

'She is a fine girl,' Mrs Simanyi said. 'It will be a lucky man that gets such a wife.'

'She's always been good. She's had to be left on her own more than I liked, but she's so sensible it hasn't seemed to matter as much as I thought it would.'

'How old was the child when your man died?'

She hesitated, unable, as always, to force herself to the quick and easy lie.

'Only a baby.'

Mrs Simanyi said, with sympathy: 'That is terrible, to happen to a woman – to be left with a child and no one by. A terrible thing.'

'It wasn't too bad.'

'The mother and the father – they helped, one supposes.'

'I had some help. And I was able to get a job. I thought . . .'

She did not finish. Mrs Simanyi hauled out a lump of beef from the cupboard where it had been thawing during the day and slapped it down on the table. Slicing it down the middle, she said:

'What is it you thought? It is not rude, to ask?'

Mary shook her head. 'It was just that I expected things would get easier as time went by. I thought it would matter less when Annabel was old enough to go to a proper school during the day.'

'But no?'

'Some things were easier. Others not. As she got about more – meeting other children with proper homes – fathers as well as mothers. The more she could understand things, the harder it seemed.'

Mrs Simanyi nodded. 'And now – you go to Holland to start a new life?'

'Yes.'

'That will be hard, too – in a strange country.'

'I suppose it will. You must have had a lot of that – having to live in strange countries.'

'Not so much. We circus people carry our country with us.'

'Yes. I see that.'

Mrs Simanyi sliced and chopped the meat with expert fingers. She said, after a moment:

'He is a good man, I think – Lieutenant Mouritzen.'

Mary said: 'He's been very kind to us.'

'He is fond of you – and Annabel. One sees that.'

'You met him when you came across at the beginning of summer, didn't you?'

'That's right. You know, there are some men are hard when they know a woman is weak, needs help – others are more gentle then. That is Niels. He is gentle.'

There were clamps to hold the cooking pots on top of the stove. Mary flicked one open and took the pot over to the table.

'A woman could trust Niels,' Mrs Simanyi said.

Mary said, in a voice colder than she had planned:

'On that other trip – I take it he and Nadya got on well together?'

Mrs Simanyi sighed, and then laughed. 'She is a fine girl, my Nadya. But she is a wild one. She has the strength of a man; she is stronger than Stefan, and has been since they were little. That is wrong for a woman.'

'Is it?'

'Bring me the carrots, Annabel,' Mrs Simanyi said. 'And you may eat one – they are clean. You are a good girl. My Nadya, when she was little, would not work in the kitchen with me as you do – always she was out with the animals and the acrobats.'

'I don't like animals much, except dogs. I'm going to have a puppy soon.'

'That will be fine. Go bring me a lump of salt, little one. As big as your hand when it is closed.' To Mary she said: 'You think a man who takes one woman lightly is light with all women?'

'Some men can't help themselves.'

Mrs Simanyi shook her head. 'Some women also. The men may make good husbands all the same. The women good wives, too, but that is harder.'

'Until they meet each other again, or someone like each other.'

'A wise woman would not mind too much.'

With some bitterness, Mary said: 'Wise?'

'Does a woman leave her husband because he breaks a leg, or drinks too much sometimes, or is a bit of a coward, maybe? No one marries a saint.'

'You talk about the woman leaving. She might be the one that is left.'

Mrs Simanyi heaped vegetables into the pot.

'Yes,' she said. 'It happens. A young woman left, maybe with a child, children. So she has to work hard and suffer much to keep them. No surprise she gets bitter. But she punishes herself so. And she punishes the child, too.'

'That's not true!' She looked at the older woman. 'It need not be true.'

'For a child to be happy, contented, then the mother must be happy. Choosing what is good for the child is not the answer.'

In a low, tense voice, Mary said: 'Not for the child; for me. I want a husband I can rely on, someone who will care for and look after us both. Nothing romantic, exciting. Just someone solid and dependable.'

Mrs Simanyi surveyed her, smiling. 'I think you will be lucky. I think you will be luckier than you expect.'

The storms drove the *Kreya* north and west, slackening only long enough for the hope of calm to flare up and then once more be snuffed out. The hold was cleared of the dead horses, although they sweated a couple of hours on the carcase pinned under the shattered hatch cover. After that Olsen had them concentrate on rigging a more dependable rudder, for use when the seas moderated sufficiently. Meanwhile, there was nothing to do but plot an increasingly unreliable north-westerly course on the chart.

'Iceland?' Mouritzen asked.

Olsen nodded, pursing his lips. 'Iceland. Or Spitzbergen. Or Murmansk. We are North of Sixty, I think, and South of Seventy. And somewhere West of Greenwich.'

'There is a lot of sea in these parts.'

'And not many ships. We are seven days out of Dieppe. By now we are counted as lost.'

'I don't think they have looked very hard for us.'

'We have heard aeroplanes a couple of times, even if we have seen none. What do you expect? As you say, there is a lot of sea here. We are lucky – we have no one mourning us.'

'Your mother is alive still, isn't she?'

'Yes.' Olsen produced one of the little Dutch cigars he was fond of smoking. 'Nearly eighty. A strong woman.'

'I have both parents,' Mouritzen said. 'But three brothers and two sisters. In some things a big family is good. I would not like to have so much hang on one heart, one pair of lungs.'

'So you will have a big family. But first you must find a wife. Isn't that how it goes?'

Mouritzen did not reply immediately. He said:

'Maybe I will not have far to look.'

'No,' Olsen said, 'maybe you won't. She is a fine woman. Pretty, healthy – I think you could be confident of a big family from her. She will make a good wife, providing you can get over the fact of her previous commitments.'

'I think I can do that.'

'Yes.' Olsen grinned. 'If not, you can join the circus yourself, eh? You can help her tame the bear, and maybe learn to swing together from the high trapeze. That breeds great trust between husband and wife, I fancy.'

Mouritzen grinned in return. 'Make jokes, if you like. Nadya is a fine girl, but not for me. I leave her to you. We will have a double wedding; perhaps a double christening.'

Olsen shook his head. 'I think I would sooner marry the bear.'

Katerina had been moved from the cabins to the forecastle, and installed there in the cabin that had once belonged to Carling. Mouritzen had approved this; Olsen knew of it but had not recognized it officially. The cage, it had turned out, had been smashed beyond hope of repair on board ship.

The cabin was at the forward end of the forecastle, well away from the galley and abutting on the lower foredeck. Nadya went there with food for the bear; the supplies that had been brought for the animal's special use were now used up, and she was being fed out of the general ration store. Nadya brought her carrots and potatoes, a few apples, and some wheaten biscuits, smeared with syrup. She fed these to her, bit by bit, talking to her and brushing her with a stiff brush.

'It is too stormy yet, my love,' she said, 'for you to promenade – cold and wet, weather that does not suit a bear. But when the rain stops and the wind goes down, we will go a small walk together. There is a deck here where you can stroll and no one will trouble you. And then we will get your cabin cleaned and made fresh and nice for a bear.'

She had left the cabin door wide open, and would have heard the noise of anyone approaching down the corridor. She was surprised, hearing a sound and looking over her shoulder, to see Thorsen standing beyond the open doorway, watching her.

'How did you get here?' she asked him.

'From the upper deck.'

'It will be longer, coming that way.'

Thorsen nodded. 'But no one knows I am here.'

Nadya stared at him for a moment, and then smiled.

'Is that to make me tremble? Will you rape me, little Jorgen?'

'I wanted to see you, to talk to you, and I wanted you to see that I can be discreet.'

'Yes.' She smiled again. 'I think you can be discreet.' She left the cabin, and closed and locked the door behind her. Thorsen stood beside her. He put his hands on her arms, beseeching rather than demanding.

'Even in oilskins?' Nadya said. 'There is much romance in you, little Jorgen.'

'Don't call me that,' he said. 'I am as tall as you are.'

'Yes.' She surveyed him critically. 'But a woman wishes a man to be taller. Go put on stilts, little Jorgen, and then come back and perhaps I will love you.'

He clutched her arm more urgently. 'Come into the next cabin. I have cleaned it up, made it all nice. There is drink there, and some glasses. We can sit and drink together.'

'You have been drinking already. Your breath stinks of whisky.'

'Have a glass yourself and you will not notice that.'

'Little Jorgen is persistent,' Nadya said. 'Perhaps I will let him give me one little drink.'

He opened the door of the cabin and stood aside for her to enter. It held two sets of double bunks, but the top bunks were retractable and had been fastened back. Thorsen had cleared away traces of the crew members who had formerly bunked here, and had brought in cushions and rugs. He had also wired up a small electric fire, and he now switched this on. Then he removed his oilskins and hung them up behind the door. Nadya looked round thoughtfully.

'You have feathered a nice little nest here,' she said.

'You like it? I am glad.'

'And the whisky?'

Thorsen went to a locker and produced a bottle and two tumblers. He poured a fairly stiff drink into each glass.

'I do not drink raw whisky,' Nadya said. 'I will have water also.'

Thorsen reached into the locker again, and produced a soda siphon. He squirted some into the glasses.

'I have everything you want, Nadya,' he said. 'And I am patient, and I understand women. Maybe you would like to have Niels here instead of me, but Niels likes better to chase the Irish woman. It is right for both of us to be honest with ourselves. You thought that when she went ashore at Amsterdam, you would have him to yourself the rest of the voyage. But things have changed. We will not get to Copenhagen unless we are towed, and if that happens she will be there too. You must admit you have lost Niels.'

He gave her one of the glasses, and she sipped it. Her dark, slanting eyes watched him, with an expression that was not easily to be read.

'I am not so tall and handsome,' Thorsen said, 'but I am virile, and it is virility that you want.'

'Is it?'

'I notice these things,' Thorsen said. 'I have had practice in noticing them. Love is important to a woman like you. Especially confined so long on a boat like this, you grow restless.'

'Yes,' Nadya said. 'I grow restless.'

'I will quieten your restlessness,' Thorsen said. He went to her, where she stood by one of the bunks. 'Sit down.' He put an arm round her waist and she did not resist the action. 'You will find you can rely on me.'

His voice had a cajoling but confident note. She felt it play over her. A man whose pride was on the surface was easy to handle; where, as with this one, the pride was deeply buried under humility, a willingness to swallow insults, it was more difficult. It was ludicrous that he should make an attempt like this, after Dieppe and with the ship still lurching blindly through stormy waters, but the absurdity of it did nothing to release her from her mounting tension. As he went on talking to her in a low, steady tone, she felt that the words were strumming her nerves, driving her forward to find a release. She set her jaws together, and felt her teeth grating against each other. He touched her hand, and she had to tense herself still further to prevent shivering.

'Niels is a fool,' Thorsen said, 'going after a woman like that when he might have had you. You have the kind of fire a man needs.'

She gripped his arm.

'Yes,' Thorsen said, 'that's what you want, isn't it!'

He bent towards her. She had heard the difference in his voice, the cajoling note replaced by contemptuous certainty of triumph, but could do nothing about it. It was only when he laughed against her ear that her need was transmuted into cold rage. Swinging her body over, she pinned him down against the bunk. He struggled, and she hit him hard with her right hand, rocking his head back against the bulkhead. Again and again she slapped him, while he tried to dodge the blows. He cried out to her, but she was too engaged with cursing him to take any note of what he said.

The keen edge of her urgency wore off. Taking his wrists, she pinioned them with her left hand, holding them against his chest. Thorsen struggled again.

'Be quiet,' she said. 'Do you want more slapping, little Jorgen?'

He lay there, watching her with hatred. With her right hand, she reached for the bottle of whisky.

'Now I give you a drink,' she said. 'Open your mouth and take your drink, like a good boy.'

He tried to move his face away as she brought the bottle towards it. Putting the bottle down, she hit him again, four times, with deliberation.

'Drink,' she said, 'when I tell you.'

She lifted the bottle again, and held it to his mouth. He drank in convulsive gulps, each time spilling whisky down his chin and over his chest.

'No more!' he gasped. 'I cannot drink more.'

'The party isn't over,' Nadya said. 'I will tell you when you are finished.'

The bottle had been nearly three-quarters full; when she put it down for the last time, it was empty. Nadya looked down at the helpless Thorsen and, shaking him, released his hands.

'Poor little Jorgen,' she said. 'He is disgusting. I think he will be sick.'

She got up from the bunk and went to the door. He still lay there, his eyes closed.

'I forgot something,' Nadya said. She came back to the bunk. 'I forgot the soda water.'

Taking the siphon, she squirted the jet into the pit of his stomach and then, as he jerked upright, directed it against his face and head.

'That does not wash you clean,' she said, 'but it washes you a bit. Good-bye, my little Jorgen.'

The storms went on, and the *Kreya* continued to roll in their path. But neither wind nor seas rose as high as they had in the North Sea, and fears that the *Kreya* might founder lessened with each day and night that she rode the waves and took no harm. It was surprising but, as the new routines became more familiar, there was time for boredom, and the beginning of monotony. Olsen and Mouritzen continued to search the skylines for possible landfalls or another ship, but the others grew accustomed to the continuing empty waste of grey all round them, to the howl of the wind and the sea's buffeting. At the same time, confident now that they would eventually be saved, they grew impatient as day after day drifted past, as featureless as the rough seas by which they were surrounded.

The Joneses, one afternoon, went up together to the poop-deck, to get some fresh air and a greater sense of privacy: from there they could look the length of the ship and see anyone approaching. The rain had stopped, but grey, tattered clouds trailed low overhead, and the *Kreya* lurched with every new wave that struck her. They wore their oilskins. Sheila's made her look tiny, child-like, Jones thought. He put an arm round her, and she pressed close to him.

She said: 'I suppose we can call ourselves real sailors now. Especially with your beard.'

'It's not looking too bad, is it?'

She shook her head. 'I don't think I would recognize you if I hadn't been watching it grow.'

'Rescue has held off long enough. It can come as soon as it likes now. I don't even mind if we're taken to a British port. We can get clear again.'

'No more worries?'

'I have a feeling that everything is going to be all right,' he said. 'For the first time since we started, there are no doubts at all. It really is going to work.'

She did not speak at once. She said:

'So you really are mine – for the rest of our lives?'

'For the rest of mine.'

'Thanks to a beard,' she said, 'and a typewriter case, full of money. I couldn't have you without those, could I? Without deception and – and theft, there's no future for us.'

'Things haven't changed. It was like that before.'

'I had a dream,' she said, 'early this morning. I dreamt the ship drifted into a lagoon – somewhere in the South Seas, I suppose – late at evening, with the sea blue and the sky purple.'

He looked at the cold, grey, heaving waters. 'We're a long way from the South Seas, I'm afraid.'

'The sun had just gone down,' she said, 'and they came out across the lagoon in canoes, covered with flowers, singing the kind of song that makes you sad and happy at the same time. Somehow we got down into the canoes with them.'

'And the Captain and the others,' he said, '– what about them? And the bear?'

'It was our dream. I don't know what they did. They rowed us back across the lagoon to a beach. The sand was almost white and there was some kind of village – huts thatched with leaves – palm leaves, I suppose – up against the forest. They brought food for us, and wine, and the girls and young men sang songs. They seemed glad to have us.'

'It sounds wonderful. I should think you were sorry to wake up.'

She leaned against him again. 'You'd brought the typewriter case with you. When the feast was over, you opened it, and took out some notes, and gave them to the one we thought was the chief. He looked at them and smiled and shook his head. You tried to insist on him taking them, and he shook his head again, and we realized that they had no use for money – that they were glad to have us, as long as we wanted to stay with them, that there was nothing to pay, and nothing to hide.'

'What did we do with it all,' he asked her, '– make paper boats with the money and set them sailing on the lagoon?'

'I don't know.' He felt her shaking her head against his chest. 'The money just wasn't there after that. And I woke up soon after.'

'That must have been hard.'

'No. I heard you breathing, and knew you were still there.'

'No flowers, though – no lagoon, no songs. Just ordinary life, with the ordinary problems.'

'I don't mind those.'

She was silent for a moment. Then, speaking more quickly, she said:

'We could manage without it, couldn't we? You could find work – I could get a job. I could always get a job as a secretary. We could manage.'

'What are you suggesting?' His tone was neutral. 'That we bring it up here and drop it over the side?'

'Couldn't we? Why not?'

He laughed unhappily. 'It wouldn't knock anything off the sentence, you know. Probably it would add a year or so on. They would think I'd salted it away somewhere.'

She said: 'It's us I'm thinking about. I don't care about the rest of the world.'

'Nothing's changed.'

'No. But some things get worse the longer one lives with them. That little box does.'

'We get rid of it,' he said. 'I get a job – a clerk in the kind of firm where they don't bother about references – and you work all day and clean and cook and mend in the evening.'

'We could do it.'

'You remember what you said – about Carol and not having children? How long would it be before we could have children, living like that? Ours wouldn't be a real marriage either. Scraping along in some miserable English suburb – that's a long way from the lagoon, too.'

'It needn't be England. There must be places in the world where we could live quietly – with just enough for us, and for children later.'

'I suppose there are. But we would have to get there. Before we sink it, shall we take a few notes out, for the fares? And a few more so that we can manage till we find those jobs? Jobs might not be so easy in a foreign country.'

She was silent again.

'How much shall we take out,' he asked her, 'before we make the grand gesture? Five hundred? A thousand?'

She said, in a flat voice: 'We're tied to it. Without it we can't exist – that's what you're saying, isn't it? Not together, at least. We can live separately, but it's the money that binds us together. That's our wedding ring. It has to stay with us, as long as we both live. There's no way out of that.'

He put his arm more tightly round her. 'Now it seems bad,' he said, 'because we find ourselves trapped between our old lives and the new. This was only meant to last a few days. Once it's over, everything will be different.'

'Will it?'

'Everything. First Zürich – then South America. Nothing to fear, and too many things to do for you to brood over the past.'

'Do you think so? Perhaps.'

'And we've got to go through this to get to it. Like going to the dentist to get the trip to the Zoo or the theatre or Madame Tussaud's.'

She shook her head. 'When I was a child it wasn't like that. There was only the dentist's. At the corner of Histon Street – a shop with the window painted over and his name on it in black.'

'Never mind. This time there is going to be a trip. And this time we go home to a different place.'

She looked up, and smiled, and he kissed her. On the bridge, Thorsen, who had been watching them, jerked Mouritzen's arm.

'The English couple,' he commented. 'Not married long. Not married at all, maybe. What do you think?'

Preoccupied, Mouritzen said: 'I don't know.'

'These days you brood too much. If they honeymoon, why has he grown a beard? The wrong time for such an exercise.'

Mouritzen did not reply. Thorsen said:

'Maybe his wife will be waiting for him when we come to port. Perhaps he grows a beard so she won't know him.'

After Annabel had gone to sleep, they sat together on the sofa opposite the bunks, watching her. It was not very big; they were not pressed together but their bodies touched comfortably. They had the single light on over the dressing-table. It dimmed, as though about to go out, and then picked up again.

'I am not happy,' Mouritzen said, 'over that generator. She has had heavy work – heavier than is right. If it fails things will be harder. There is none of us can mend it.'

Mary said: 'It's strange.'

'What is strange?'

'That things are so nearly normal.'

'The *Kreya* is a good ship. On others, one might not have been so well placed.'

'And yet we are lost, drifting. There must be an end to it, mustn't there? What happens when the food runs out?'

'You need not worry over that. She is well stocked. None of us will starve. I do not think we shall even have to eat Katerina.'

She smiled with him, but grew serious again.

'But there must be some end to it all. Day after day, and we still sight no ships.'

'Of course there is an end.' Mouritzen took her hand, moved it forward in a horizontal plane, and then made it dip down. 'We go on and on, and then, one day, we come to the edge of the world, and over we go. Down the great cataract, for ever and ever.'

'No, seriously.'

'Seriously, there is nothing to worry about. We have had storm after storm, but storms do not go on without stopping some time. When we come into calmer seas, we try again with the rudder. We will fix it, and when we have fixed it we can see to the engines. Then we limp quietly to the south, into the shipping lanes. With clear skies, we can fix our position. Even if we do not sight a ship, we can make a port.'

'What port?'

'Maybe Reykjavik – Iceland, that is.'

'I know. We've been blown so far north?'

'Farther, maybe.'

'And then – I suppose the *Kreya* will be in port for some time, while the rudder is mended?'

Mouritzen laughed. 'Truly, for some time!'

'And us – the passengers?'

'You will be taken to your destinations. By air, I guess.'

'I see.'

'And all the bells of Amsterdam will ring for the marrying.'

Her hand, which he still held, was drawn away.

She said: 'Please, Niels. Please don't make fun of me.'

'I make fun of you,' he said, 'because I love you. Don't turn away from me, Mary. You are listening? I love you. I will always love you.'

Her voice stifled, she said: 'Don't say that.'

'Why not?'

'Because I've heard it before. Because it doesn't mean anything, except loneliness and misery.'

'Words can be good or bad, true or false. What do you think I want of you?'

'The same. It's always the same.'

'Listen. You will not go to Amsterdam, you and Annabel. You will go to Copenhagen, where my mother and my two sisters and my two sisters-in-law will look after you both until the *Kreya* can come back. And when the *Kreya* comes back, there will be a wedding, and much talk and laughing and drinking, and afterwards I will take you to bed. And not until then will I even kiss you on the mouth. Not even though you beg for it.'

Mary looked at him. She said:

'Now I think you mean it. But people change. They think they're strong, constant, but they're not.'

'I am not strong,' Mouritzen said. 'I cannot say you will be getting a strong husband. But constant is something else. A weak person can be constant.'

'It's easier if they've had practice. Harder if the practice has been in something else.'

'All right,' he protested. 'I have known a lot of women. That gives me firmer judgment. I have searched the world for an honest woman. At last, I have found one.'

Her face showed pain. 'Honest?'

'That before anything else.'

She got up from the sofa and went to the dressing table where her handbag lay. She opened it, and took out her passport. Coming back, she gave it to Mouritzen.

'Something you should see.'

He held the passport without opening it, looking up at her and smiling. He said:

'I love you very much when you look grave. When we are married, I must give you lots of troubles, so that you will look sad and serious over them.'

'Open it.'

He did so, and studied the photograph. He shook his head.

'Here you are grave also, but the expression is different. I do not like this one.'

'Read it.'

Instead he looked up. 'To find that little Annabel is a love-child? I knew that.'

'How?'

'At the beginning. Thorsen is a creature that pries. Do not waste anger on him. He is a sorry thing. The other day, when he was drunk and soaked in whisky – I think perhaps he tried to make love to Nadya and she poured the whisky over him. I think that from something she said, and the way he looked at her. You will not worry about Thorsen?'

'No. But you . . .'

'For me,' he said, 'I am sorry you have had so much unhappiness. But I am glad he did not marry you, because you would have been a true wife even though he was not worthy of you, and if, somehow, I had met you, you would not have let yourself look at me. And I am glad you were seduced, for otherwise there would not have been an Annabel, and I have always wanted such a daughter.'

She started to sob. Mouritzen drew her down beside him.

'I think you will like Copenhagen,' he said. 'It is better than Amsterdam. Amsterdam smells of stale cigarette ends, and all the men spit in the streets. I think you and Annabel will be happier in Copenhagen.'

She sobbed against his chest.

'Do not cry,' Mouritzen said. 'I do not want you to cry.' He put his hands to her cheeks and lifted her face. 'I would like to ask a question,' he said, 'but since you are an honest woman, I fear the answer.'

She stopped crying. Her eyes were a little red but she looked, he thought, more beautiful than ever.

'You needn't ask,' she said. 'I love you, Niels. I do love you.'

'Then I am entirely happy.' As their faces came together, he raised his lips and kissed her on the forehead. 'As I told you,' he said. 'Not even though you beg for it.'

Chapter Nine

Mouritzen had the night watch. In the evening of the previous day, after a sudden squalling tempest of hail, the winds and seas had moderated, and they continued to lessen throughout the night. About three o'clock the clouds began to break up and, for the first time in weeks, Mouritzen saw the stars. The clouds went quite rapidly, and the seas slackened until there was no more than a long swell astern. On it the *Kreya* rolled at her ease.

So it had come at last, Mouritzen reflected – the end of this over-long symphony with its tyranny of repeated crescendos. In the morning they would be able to rig the jury rudder, and the *Kreya* would have direction and purpose again. It would be good if she could come, under her own steam, into port, for other ships to gape and wonder at. There would be something to make them wonder. By now the company would be looking for the insurance.

A memorable voyage – storm, wreck, mutiny, a ship driven aimlessly by wind and waves for two weeks nearly, and for himself, a wife. Mouritzen smiled. It was good to have a direction, after drifting so long. They would like her at home. It was always easy to know the things the family would like. I will marry before Eiler does, he thought: that will be a surprise for them.

The stars overhead were very bright. The radar scanner revolved, showing an empty screen. There should be a half-moon – no, three-quarter, rising later in the night. When it did, he decided, he would cut the radar. The generator had been running with a very ragged note the last time he had attended to it. Even though they should have the engines working by midday, there was no sense in not continuing to observe reasonable precautions.

The starlit sea was empty; the long swell rolled across it like a dark, dipping shadow that repeated itself again and again. Mouritzen turned from it. He contemplated the new life that lay ahead. Perhaps a little house out towards Virum. Perhaps near Inge; she could look after Mary, help her with all the things that would be hard at the beginning. And Annabel and Viggo would be almost the same age – they would play together. And there would be the holidays at Aarhus, by the sea, in the old house. It would be pleasant to take Mary and Annabel there – and, in time, the other children. It was a wonderful house for children, in the summer. He could see Mary, in the big room, surrounded by children...

The fog came up suddenly, on the port bow, and he was not aware of it until the stars lying lower in that arc of sky were blotted out. After that he could see it advance, a vaulting shadow that moved in over the rippling shadow on the sea, and swallowed it. Soon the poop-light was dimmed and then the fog was all round. It settled on the ship like cold, translucent fur.

Mouritzen thought of calling Olsen, but decided against it. There was nothing to be done, and Olsen was getting little enough sleep these days. The *Kreya* lay at her ease in the middle of nowhere; the fog made little difference to that. They were in calm seas at last; that was what mattered. He glanced at the screen, but there was only emptiness.

After a time he put a heavy coat on and walked out on to the quarter-deck. There was nothing to be seen but the ship's lights and the chilled and thickened air. Mouritzen turned up his coat collar. It was bitterly cold – colder than it had been during the previous evening's hailstorm. The very stillness of the air seemed to make it bite deeper. He stamped the deck energetically to keep warm.

When he went inside again he took the thermos flask and poured himself a mug of coffee. The cold followed him in, and he held his two hands around the mug to warm them. He drank from the mug slowly and poured himself another. It was when he was half-way through this second one that his ears caught the dull, distant roar of surf.

The screen showed nothing, and he could not understand that. A very low foreshore . . . but the noise was distinct, and these were not heavy seas. He would have to call Olsen now. He went to the speaking-tube that led to the Captain's cabin, and blew. There was no immediate reply. That also surprised him. The surprise lasted only a few moments, until he heard footsteps on the ladder. He turned as Olsen put his head above deck-level.

'I was just calling you,' he said. 'That is surf breaking. Listen.'

Olsen nodded. 'I hear it.'

'But the screen is blank.'

'That is not surprising. You do not know these waters, Niels?'

'No.'

'I know them. Is there any coffee left?'

'In the second thermos. I'll get you some.'

Olsen took the coffee and drank it. Hunched against the cold, he looked smaller than ever, an old, wise and wizened man. He nodded towards the windows.

'The moon comes up.'

He was right; the fog was taking on a whiter, pearly look forward. Probably it did not rise very high above the surface of the sea. Olsen walked over to the radar screen and Mouritzen followed him. He pointed.

'There is your foreshore.'

The glowing line was scarcely visible, but it was clear and extensive, covering more than ninety degrees.

'We should not hear the noise of surf so soon from that,' Mouritzen observed. 'Something is wrong with the screen, maybe?'

'You should have wakened me when the seas dropped and the fog came down.'

'I thought of that. But all was clear, and you need the rest.'

'Yes. And we are helpless still – one forgets that. The fog woke me; it always makes me cough.' He cleared his throat, as though to emphasize this. 'And then, feeling the cold, I guessed what it was even before I heard the noise.'

'The surf?'

'Not surf. Pack-ice. The floes grinding against each other on the swell. With these seas you hear it before the screen shows anything. The sound carries far.'

'I thought it might be the coast of Iceland. Pack-ice! Have we come so far north?'

'Before the fog – was the sky clear?'

'Yes.'

'Did you take a fix?'

'No. I thought there was no urgency.'

Olsen stared at him. 'Give up the sea, Niels. You are young still. And if you think there is ever a time at sea when there is no urgency, you are in the wrong profession.'

'Perhaps I am. Perhaps I will find a job on land, and sail a little boat at weekends.'

'If we get back to land. I will take over here. Rouse the men. Get them to work on that rudder.'

'Now?'

'You have never seen pack-ice. You will, soon enough. Right away. We may hold clear until we have time to get steam up and start the engines. Or maybe it is a mirage and will vanish. Go to it. Waste no more time.'

By the time he had them mustered, the mist was whiter yet from the rising moon, and the crackling thunder of the ice sounded nearer and more menacing. The cold was still intense, and all of them found difficulty in handling gear. The business progressed slowly, with many checks and fumblings. The length of piping which they were using to sleeve the shaft presented the major problem; it had to be lashed securely and the metal was burningly cold to the fingers.

From the quarter-deck, Olsen called down to them:

'How does it go?'

Mouritzen called back: 'Nearly ready. But I don't know whether we have enough clearance. It is going to take some pushing to move her, anyway.'

The blade of the home-made rudder dipped in the water as, with the sleeve lashed, Mouritzen released the block on the shaft and they let it down. It was a very rough fit. At first they could not move the tiller but slowly, reluctantly, it swung over. The *Kreya* still drifted through the milky sea of mist. Without power she had no purchase on the water.

He went back to the bridge to report to Olsen, who nodded in silent acknowledgment. Over his shoulder, Mouritzen saw something whiter than the pervading grey appear, take on shape as a raft of ice, and glide past. He drew Olsen's attention to it.

'Yes,' Olsen said, 'I have seen others.'

'If we hit it . . .'

'Such small clumps will do no damage to a ship like this.' He pointed to starboard. 'There is our danger.'

Dimly through the mist it was possible to see a long, unbroken line of white, without beginning or end. From it came the now familiar throbbing roar, louder and heavier.

'My God!' Mouritzen said. 'We must be within a couple of hundred metres of it.'

'A little more, I fancy. Perhaps three hundred. And a current – one knot, maybe. So in ten minutes we make our ice-fall.' He grinned. 'I do not think we shall manage to get a head of steam up in that time.'

'Then what?'

'We trust to luck. And we must hope she will keep her screws clear of the ice.'

The line loomed nearer out of the mist as the minutes passed. There was no break. It appeared to rise no more than a foot or two out of the sea, but the greater bulk, naturally, would be below the water-level. As they approached it, Mouritzen could see individual turrets and blocks of ice rising out of the featureless mass, and could see, too, that the vast plain was in slow, undulant motion, as the tide lifted it and sucked it down again. The sound, also, broke up as it grew louder; one could hear the crashes and grindings of individual encounters.

'I never thought ice would frighten me,' Mouritzen said.

Olsen clutched his arm. It was a rare gesture; he was not physically demonstrative.

'Niels! I think we've made it.'

Forward of the starboard bow, there was a difference. The line of ice curved away; where it should have continued there was the black emptiness of open water.

'We are rounding it!'

'What else?' Olsen clapped his hands together loudly. 'This is good fortune! We shall not clear it by more than twenty metres.'

They cleared it by less; a small, floating outcrop of ice grated harshly against the side of the ship. The current still took the *Kreya* westwards; the mist still clung to the heaving sea.

'She roars as loudly,' Mouritzen said. He peered through the mist. 'Ahead – is that more ice?'

'Where?' Through his glasses, Olsen studied the quarter Mouritzen had indicated. Then he put the glasses down. 'Not so lucky after all,' he said drily.

'It is ice.'

'Yes, ice. We are in a lead, an inlet. The ice lies north and south of us, and the current is taking us farther in.'

'We may get right through to clear water.'

Olsen cocked his head, listening to the noise.

'I do not think so. This is a big field.'

'So?'

'We will hope to back out again,' Olsen said, 'when we have power.'

'Yes,' Mouritzen said, 'of course, we can back out.'

He stared ahead with mingled fear and excitement and awe. Although the fog persisted the air was bright, perhaps as a result of the ice, which could now be seen to stretch away on either side of the ship. It was as though they were making up a fjord, between ice-hung shores.

The fjord narrowed rapidly. On the starboard side, Mouritzen saw a glimmering mountain, a white berg, rising from the surrounding plain; slowly it moved past them and was gone. Then they struck: the *Kreya* shuddered all along her length, and he saw the stump of the after-mast lurch against the background of white. A second, lesser impact followed the first. After that there was no more motion than that of a ship tied up in a quiet harbour.

Olsen and Mouritzen set to work together on the engines, pooling their knowledge, each bridging over, to some extent, the inevitable gaps in the other's understanding of what had been jealously maintained as Møller's preserve. When things appeared to be going fairly smoothly, Olsen left Mouritzen to it. There was no indication that the engines had suffered by their lengthy shut-down.

Mouritzen heard the clatter of feet on the ladder. He glanced at his watch as he looked round; by Central European time, on which the ship was still running, it was a few minutes after nine o'clock. The real time would be seven, or earlier.

It was Olsen who came down into the engine-room. Mouritzen said:

'Nearly full pressure. How are things above decks?'

'There is breakfast for you,' Olsen said. 'Bacon and sausage. I will take over here. You can send Thorsen down and I will instruct him in the controls.'

'I could wait for breakfast. Isn't it more important to back her out of the ice?'

'No,' Olsen said. 'Not now.' He smiled in the sharp, unyielding way which Mouritzen, from experience, knew as a sign that something had gone badly wrong and that Olsen did not wish to discuss it. 'Get your breakfast.'

'What's the matter?' Mouritzen asked.

Olsen turned to the controls, not answering him. Mouritzen stood by the foot of the ladder, waiting. After a while, Olsen said, over his shoulder:

'I want Thorsen down here. Get him.'

Olsen spoke again when Mouritzen was half-way up the ladder. He called:

'You can chart a way out while you're up there, too.'

Mouritzen went out on deck without putting a coat on. Coming from the warmth of the engine-room, the bitter, damp cold was a shock. The air was lighter. It was much too early for dawn in these latitudes; the brightness must be moonlight. A film of condensation was on everything – moisture ran down the ropes and dripped from the gunwales. He took the corridor through the forecastle, and heard the sound of Katerina scratching in her cabin as he went through to the after-deck. He stopped there.

In confusion he thought at first that he had remembered wrongly – that the *Kreya* had backed into the ice instead of ramming it. But she had rammed it, all right. He stared at the heaving ice, unbroken all round the ship's stern. There was a different explanation. The lead no longer existed; the ice had closed around them.

Towards noon the sky grew lighter, and there was a hint of sunlight in the south, but the fog did not clear. Visibility was about four hundred yards; all round the ship, for that distance, one could see the shrouded hummocks of ice, engaged in their slow, drunken, jostling dance on the surface of the waters. The impression was of immutable permanence underlaid by flux, a world poised on the surface of a bubble.

The day, such as it was, did not last long. By five o'clock on the uncorrected time, dusk was closing in, narrowing the confines of their ice-bound world. The long night lay ahead of them.

But the atmosphere on the *Kreya* was one of relief, not apprehension. There was calm, after stormy seas, and the solid shapes of the ice reminded them of land; they could almost imagine being locked in some wintry port. A very great difference was made by the fact that, with the engines running again, there was warmth, and adequate light. They could have hot showers, and Mrs Simanyi was able to prepare meals on stoves that kept their heat, and stayed on a level plane. Lunch, like breakfast, was a scrappy affair, taken as people found opportunity, but for the evening meal they all sat down together, with Olsen at his accustomed place at the head.

During the bad weather, only Olsen, Mouritzen and Josef Simanyi had continued to shave when they could, but now Stefan and Thorsen had greeted the return of easily available hot water by themselves returning to clean-shaven states, and Stefan had carefully trimmed his little moustache. Mouritzen, sitting opposite Jones, was surprised to see that he had retained his beard. He was the more surprised in that it was not a particularly good beard; it was coarse and grey in patches and was of uneven luxuriance. In other respects, Jones was clearly conscious and careful of his appearance, and he was, after all, a man in love with a much younger wife.

It was Mrs Simanyi who commented on it.

'So you keep your beard, Mr Jones? You will be the sailor, or the patriarch, maybe?'

Sheila answered for him. 'I persuaded him to keep it.' She gave a small laugh. 'I've always had an ambition to be married to a bearded man.'

She looked nervous, Mouritzen thought, and Jones himself looked embarrassed. But that was understandable, particularly since they were English. He addressed himself to what was before him.

'This is good soup, Mama,' he said.

During the last week they had all learned to address her, as her family did, by the affectionate diminutive.

'In winter,' she said, 'if the soup is good, everything is good.'

'We will keep you on the *Kreya*,' Olsen said. 'We have never had so good a cook.'

She smiled widely. 'And what do my family do?'

'They can stay also. Even the bear. We will teach her to be a deck-hand. I have trained men with less sense than a bear has.'

Sheila said: 'Perhaps we could all stay. Do we have to sail her back to Copenhagen?'

Olsen lifted his eyebrows. 'Would you stay in an ice-field for ever? What happens when fuel runs out, and food?'

'Not in the ice-field. Sail her round the world, perhaps.'

'The Company,' Olsen said, 'is generous and like a father, but I think they will want their ship.'

'She is lost!' Josef said. 'She was sunk in the storms in the North Sea. Like the other two *Kreyas*, she lies at the bottom of the sea. Captain, I know what we will do! We will make a flag of the skull and bones, and turn pirate.'

'We are well armed for that,' Olsen said drily. 'We have fists, and the bear has claws. We will inspire terror.'

Stefan said to Annabel: 'And you, Annabella – do you wish to be a pirate?'

'No, thank you.' She looked up. 'Girls aren't pirates.'

'Ah, no,' Josef said. 'Better she will be a little Hollander, with wings on her bonnet, and wooden shoes, watching the wind blow the mill.'

Annabel shook her head. 'Mamma says I'm going to be Danish instead.'

There was a ripple of amusement and interest. Mary tried to shush her and then, realizing she was only making matters worse, broke off in some confusion.

Mouritzen said: 'Yes, she will be a little Dane. And I am to be her Pappa. True, Annabel? You will have me for a father?'

'Yes.' She considered him. 'It was Mamma who decided, but I like you, too.'

Mrs Simanyi leaned across to Mary: 'That is good. I am very glad. You will be happy; I know that.'

Olsen said: 'I have lived with Niels for two years. I express my sympathies, Mrs Cleary. But we must celebrate on his account, anyway. Jorgen, is there any champagne?'

Thorsen shook his head. 'No champagne.'

'But there is Schnapps – that is certain. We will all have Schnapps, and Annabel will have Apfelsaft maybe. See to it, Jorgen.'

Nadya said: 'Congratulations, Mary. And you, Niels. I hope it will be a happy marriage.'

Olsen jerked his head up. 'If you are impatient, I will wed you now. It is something I have not done yet. And it will go well in the log, along with the other disasters.'

110

Mrs Simanyi said reprovingly: 'Only the selfish think badly of marriage.'

Olsen raised a finger at her. 'You are a good Catholic, Mama. Were the saints selfish?'

'The saints thought well of marriage for others.'

'I do also.'

'And you are no saint!'

'That does not come in the question. Ah, there we are.' Thorsen was getting out *akvavit* glasses and filling them. 'By custom, I do not drink. But today I have brought the *Kreya* safe into her ice harbour and beyond that there is a betrothal. That is something to drink to. Ladies and gentlemen, to the health and happiness of the Mouritzens all!'

They drank, and Nadya pushed her glass towards Thorsen.

'Fill mine again, Jorgen,' she commanded him. 'That was quickly drunk.'

As usual, Mouritzen was desperately tired when he lay down in his bunk, but for a time he lay awake, listening to the noises outside. There was a difference, he thought, a more purposeful rhythm, and a greater preponderance of the grinding of ice against the metal sides of the ship. Perhaps the ice was breaking up again. Maybe in the morning there would be a way clear for them to back or nose out to the open sea. The screws had been run from time to time so that they should not ice up, and the jury-rudder had been lifted clear. It only needed the ice to break up, and they would be all right.

Olsen woke him at 6 a.m., Icelandic time; he had adopted this the previous day from a rough estimate of the sun's position through the mist. Mouritzen sat up in his bunk. The growling and groaning outside continued.

'No way clear yet?' he asked.

Olsen shook his head. His face was drawn with fatigue and darkly shadowed – his beard grew quickly. The euphoria of the previous day was markedly absent; but tiredness would account for that.

'Nothing yet,' he said. 'See that I am called at ten.'

'You need more sleep than that.'

Olsen smiled, closing one eye. 'Four hours is enough. There is coffee in the thermos.'

Mouritzen drank his coffee and then stepped out on to the

quarter-deck to look around. He felt a breeze from the east, and saw that the mist was beginning to swirl and eddy, instead of lying flat and motionless over the ship. A wind would blow the fog away. And it might help to break up the ice.

By eight most of the mist was gone, and the breeze was strong enough to lift the *Kreya*'s flag from time to time. Several of the others went out on deck to look about them. There was moonlight and faint starlight, and in the south there was the early glow of dawn. All round there was the ice, a landscape of low-lying, jagged shapes, peaked with the more massive outlines of bergs. In this light it was desolate, chilling the heart equally with the flesh. They stared for a time, and talked in whispers, and then, one by one, they went in.

Gradually the glow in the south brightened. When Mouritzen called Olsen at ten, it had turned to sunrise. The two men stood together and watched the red disc lift above the far horizon.

'There is water there, I think,' Mouritzen said.

'Yes.'

'And to the east. A mile, do you think?'

'You are not used to gauging Arctic distances. Three miles more likely.'

'The ice has settled more. It makes less noise.' Olsen nodded. 'If this wind strengthens, will it scatter the ice to the east – open a way?'

'See to the engines, Olsen said. 'I do not trust Thorsen with them.'

When Mouritzen came up again, the sun had lifted clear of the ice. The sky was red all round it, turning to green and blue higher up towards the zenith. The pack-ice was spotted and stained with crimson, and those pools touched by the sun's rays were bright and bleeding red. Where the sun did not penetrate, the water was a deep blue-green. It looked colder and purer than any water Mouritzen had ever seen.

There was some free water on the port side of the *Kreya*. Josef was there, reddened by the sunrise, patiently fishing. Stefan stood near him, whistling through his teeth. He called to Mouritzen:

'This is better, Niels. I think I will go skating on the ice. Is that permitted?'

Mouritzen grinned. 'You must have the Captain's permission to take part in sports. I will ask him for you.'

112

On the bridge, he said to Olsen: 'Stefan wants to go out on the ice. Do you permit it?'

Olsen was preoccupied. He listened for a while, as though making sense of what Mouritzen had said. Then he shook his head.

'No. It would not be safe. If the fool got into trouble, we would have to rescue him.'

Mouritzen looked towards the east. 'No break yet.'

Olsen said: 'Look. The other way.'

To the west the ice-field stretched away with no hint of open sea – but there was something else. At its limits, lifting white crests into the deep blue sky, there were mountains – range on range of them, as far as the eye could see.

'Greenland!' Mouritzen said.

'The Alps of Liverpool Land,' said Olsen. 'They are pretty, are they not?'

'How far? Twenty miles?'

Olsen shook his head. 'You underestimate again. Twice that – three times. I have got a rough calculation of our position. About 72 North by 20 West. We lie west and north of Scoresby. A hundred and twenty miles away, maybe, as the crow flies.' He pressed his hand to his chin. 'Listen, Niels, I am going to talk to them all. I have a plan.'

'What is it?'

'That will emerge. But if they think those mountains are no more than twenty miles away, let them continue to think it. It will be better if they do.'

Mouritzen felt some resentment at the combination of confidence and reticence in Olsen's attitude to him; whatever scheme he had in mind, there was no reason why he should not discuss it with Mouritzen in advance. But this was a part of Olsen – of the inflexibility, the chill, inhuman quality that stamped him. Mouritzen wondered, as he had before, about the crisis point of the mutiny. Olsen had never talked of it. True, they had killed Møller when he tried to stop them, but by that time Olsen had been knocked senseless, and they had been committed to the full completion of the act.

But there would be no point in arguing with Olsen, nor in resenting his attitude. He was almost certainly unconscious of it. Mouritzen said:

'You want to see them? Where? In the lounge?'

'First show them the mountains,' Olsen said. 'I do not think they have noticed them yet. Then, yes, I will talk to them in the lounge. I will come down in ten minutes.'

The noise of chatter died away as Olsen came in through the swinging doors. He had presence, Mouritzen reflected – a mysterious quality. When he required attention, it was given, without hesitation or stinting. Now he stood, looking round the table for a moment before taking his seat. He smiled, almost boyishly.

'Well – you have seen the mountains?'

He allowed the murmur of acquiescence to die down, and continued:

'That is Greenland,' he said, 'our Danish empire! On this side of those mountains lies the settlement of Scoresbysund. After all, the storms have brought us within sight of haven. Now all that remains is we take a little walk over there.'

Despite the obviousness of the implication, Mouritzen was staggered by this. His protest came automatically:

'Across the pack-ice?'

His eyes on the others, Olsen nodded. 'A little walk,' he repeated.

'But the risks!' Mouritzen protested. 'That stuff is moving all the time. At any moment a floe might break up beneath you.'

Olsen turned towards his First Officer. His eyes were narrowed: his face showed something of a sense of betrayal. Mouritzen realized that he had come down prepared to meet and to beat down the objections of the others, but that, despite having failed to take him into his confidence, he had expected blind and unquestioning support from his deputy. The expectation had clearly been so certain that for a moment Mouritzen felt that it must have been justified.

Olsen said: 'I am the Captain of this ship, Niels. I take no unnecessary hazards. You know that.'

But it was not justified, Mouritzen argued. This was merely another sign of Olsen's inability to come to terms with other personalities, other wills.

He said: 'The hazards of a journey over sea-ice are not the same as ordinary sea hazards. They should be discussed. After all, we will no longer be on the *Kreya*.'

'Do you know the Arctic ice?' Olsen asked.

'No.'

Olsen looked down the table. 'Is there any here who does?' The response was negative. 'I have been here before,' he went on simply. 'Twenty years ago I came to Scoresbysund, on the supply ship. It is not much, for experience, but it is something: enough to give my words weight, I think.'

'But the ice is shifting,' Josef Simanyi said. 'One sees that. And we are safe here in the *Kreya*. We can wait here until help comes.'

'What help?' Olsen asked. 'Who seeks us here? As to the ice, it is firmer to the west – one can see that through the glasses.'

Mouritzen said: 'Would it not be better to wait for a time. We might be seen from the air.'

'Since we have lain here,' Olsen said, 'has anyone heard the noise of an aircraft? And they would be flying high, and this ship is a speck in the Arctic Ocean.'

He paused, drawing them into a silence, a measured pause for consideration.

'And there is something else,' he went on. 'Two things. It has been a long voyage, though there are fewer mouths than when we started. We do not have too much food left.'

'There are fish to catch,' Josef said. 'And I think I saw a seal out there.'

Olsen smiled. 'So we live on the fishes that Josef catches. How many so far, Josef?'

'One needs patience.'

'To catch a seal, also. But there is also the other thing. The ice out there – it is *storeis*, the great ice that drifts down from the Pole. It is not of this season, nor last. It is many years old. And it is tough. The *Kreya* is tough, but this is tougher. No ship is safe in the *storeis* unless it is specially built for it. Even then, it can happen that the ship is cracked like a nut.'

Mouritzen said sceptically: 'Would there not be warning?'

Olsen half-closed his eyes. 'This morning, you saw no difference out there? One ridge of ice is like another. But in the night, I saw an ice volcano. Maybe a mile to the north, in the moonlight, I saw ice lift, swell up like a mushroom.'

'I felt the ship shudder,' Mary said, 'Just as I was waking up.'

Olsen nodded. 'Great blocks of ice – a hundred tons, maybe, squeezed up into the sky, pushed up thirty feet or more. What happens to the *Kreya* if such a zone of pressure builds up here, instead of a mile away? And it happens fast – in a few seconds.'

115

'But it might not happen like that,' Mary said.

Olsen shrugged. 'If not, it squeezes more slowly, maybe. Go look over the side. See how the ice is piling up against us. Already I have felt her plates groan from it.'

Mary said apologetically: 'I'm thinking of Annabel. She's very small to make the kind of journey you're talking about.'

'So we put her on a sledge.' Olsen peered at the child, smiling. 'Do you like to ride in a sledge, across the ice?'

'Might it not be best,' Mary said, 'if we stayed behind on the ship? Then when you get to the settlement, you could have them send help.'

'No,' Olsen said, 'we go together. That is the best way.'

Mouritzen said: 'You cannot force this, Erik. You are Captain of the *Kreya*, but we have our rights.'

Olsen said heavily: 'I am the Captain, as you say. You are the First Officer, and not a lawyer. I think you forget that.'

'Human rights come first,' Mouritzen said. 'I think you forget that, Erik.'

Olsen leaned back in his chair, and let his chin sink on his blue jersey. He looked grave and then, unexpectedly, smiled.

'Do I meet a second mutiny, on one voyage? That would be unique for a sea captain, I fancy. Right, we will have democracy, a free choice. I give you the possibilities.'

He raised his hand, clenched except for one finger.

'First, that all stay here on the *Kreya*. In a week, two weeks at most, there is no fuel for the engines, and so no heat, no light. If we are careful, maybe the food lasts three weeks. Then we begin to starve and freeze, if the ice has not crushed us already.'

Olsen released another finger.

'Second. That we form a party to travel across the ice to Scoresbysund. This is my plan. There are risks, but we meet them together.'

The third finger went up.

'Third. Some go, some stay. Those that stay must take the risk of the ice. And they must wait, in patience. If no help comes in a week, they must be patient. In two weeks, even, because in this kind of thing there will always be delays, difficulties. After three weeks, they may guess that the advance party has met disaster. Then they set out in their turn, with less food and with less skill.'

His eyes fastened on Mary. He spoke more slowly.

'If this is the choice, I take the advance party. And since, for the good of all, this party must travel fast and surely, I choose two men to go with me – Niels and Josef.' His gaze darted briefly to Mouritzen and then returned to Mary. 'Josef might refuse this. Niels, as a ship's officer, cannot refuse. He is bound to obey my order.'

Mama Simanyi said: 'I go with Papa, if he goes. That is understood.'

'Those are the choices,' Olsen said. 'Now we vote. My plan first – that all go together to the mainland. In favour, please raise hands.'

Their hands were raised. Mary, shaking her head slightly as she looked at Mouritzen, put hers up.

'Niels?' Olsen said.

'All right,' Mouritzen said, 'you win.'

'Put up your hand, then,' Olsen told him. He smiled faintly. 'That makes the vote unanimous.'

'When do we start?' Jones asked. 'It's too late today, isn't it? Tomorrow morning?'

'We shall not be ready by the morning,' Olsen said. 'First we make our preparations. This is no jaunt. We must make sledges, collect food, prepare clothing. The men will work on the sledges, and the women see to the rest. We start right away.'

Josef and Stefan were Olsen's chief aiders on the sledges; both, by reason of their experience of the nomadic life of the circus, were reasonably skilled in carpentry and its allied crafts. Olsen sketched out for them plans for two six-foot sledges, and they got to work right away.

'Extra sets of runners,' he warned them. 'Two extra sets, if it can be managed, for each. That is where the strain will come.'

'On such a little journey?' asked Josef.

'By the time we have hauled them over a couple of hundred ice-ridges, you will not call it a little journey.'

Stefan said: 'We can be at the foot of those mountains in a day.'

'Yes?' Olsen smiled. 'All the same, we make extra runners.'

He discussed food with Mama Simanyi.

'We will have two hot meals each day – in the morning and at night. In the middle of the day, we eat chocolate and biscuits on the trail. For breakfast, we make porridge, with milk and sugar, and then cocoa with biscuits and butter. Plenty of butter – at least one hundred and fifty grams each person every day. It is fine to keep out the cold.'

She nodded. 'More than a kilo and a half each day.'

'How much have we in store?'

'Seven kilos – perhaps a little more.'

'We take rations for ten days; more would be too much to carry. There is margarine?'

'Enough.'

'Make up with that. A hundred and twenty grams of biscuits per day. We have enough biscuits, I know.'

'They are not very good.'

'They will taste good. For supper, the best thing is a stew. We want plenty of good stew, every night, and those dried potatoes. Then more biscuits and more butter. And more cocoa, sweet and milky. The dried milk is best. The milk in cans may freeze.'

'How do we cook? The paraffin stove? It is a bulky thing to carry.'

'No. There are two Primus stoves in the galley. One may need mending, but only a support to be welded, I think. And there are two pressure cookers. That saves fuel, and there is less condensation inside a tent.'

'Are there tents on the ship?'

Olsen shook his head. 'But there is canvas, and wood. We will make them.'

'There is a tent in our caravan down in the hold, if it has not been washed away. That will take four people.'

'And the child, too? Then that serves for the women. We need only make one for the men.'

Mama Simanyi called to Nadya: 'Go find the tent, in the caravan, Nadya. It will need drying, I guess.'

Nadya said: 'Yes.' She smiled at Olsen. 'When you work it out, do not forget the rations for Katerina.'

Olsen shook his head, his eyes narrowing. 'You must turn the bear loose. She will fend for herself.'

'Then I will see to Katerina's rations,' Nadya said. 'There will be enough left over when you have taken all you need.'

'We carry no extra weight on the sledges – not one ounce more than is needed.'

Nadya smiled again. 'You have not seen Katerina's act, Captain. She wear a harness and carries a sack on her back. She will carry her own rations.'

'She will not carry much.'

'She is a strong bear, and a sensible one. And she goes with us, Captain, or we do not go.'

Olsen stared at her grimly; she continued to smile. Mama Simanyi said:

'She will be no trouble, Captain. We will promise that.'

'She gets no rations from the sledges, and if there is trouble, we turn her loose – that is agreed?'

'But yes, Captain,' Nadya said. 'Now I will go for the tent. I will get Katerina's harness at the same time.'

Grumbling, Olsen said: 'A bear – on such a journey.'

'For the chocolate,' Mama Simanyi said, '– I get that from Jorgen?'

'Yes. A hundred grams as the daily ration.' He paused, considering this. 'You can take a couple of kilos extra. No, better, I will have Jorgen get you the emergency ration from the lifeboats. That takes up less room, though it does not taste so good.'

'For the stews, I take as much as I think will be needed?'

'Yes, but choose what bulks smallest and weighs least.' He smiled. 'We should have pemmican, but the company does not expect us to end our journey by sledge.'

'Can we take coffee as well as cocoa?'

'Cocoa is better, and more easily made. But you can take some coffee, for special treats.'

'And pastes, for the biscuits?'

'Hunger will be the best paste. But there is Gye, in the store. It is made from Guinness – we buy it in Dublin. That will go well on biscuits, and it does not take up too much space.'

'Special treats,' Mama Simanyi said. 'And food for ten days. I guess it is a long little walk we take across the ice.'

'I like to have all well prepared. We will see how we go when the sledges are loaded. If there is room, maybe we can add a little more – cans of fruit and such. But we make room for the essential things first. We will need plenty of blankets. It may be we have to spend a night out on the ice.'

Mama Simanyi shook her head. 'It will be cold out there. We must wear plenty of clothes.'

'That is the next thing. Get the other women to work on that. Boots are most important.'

'We have fur boots, Nadya and I, in our cases.'

'No, listen. We need *mukluks*, but we have not got them. So we must do what we can. In the forecastle, you will find boots, and Jorgen must give you the boots from the store and all the boots of officers and passengers. Then you share them out, giving each person boots one, or even two sizes too big. Inside we wear two pairs of socks; but we need more insulation under the foot, so you must make pads for each boot.'

'Pads? Of cloth?'

'Cloth outside. Inside – we have hay in the stern hold; that is good for insulation. Make pads to fit the inside soles of the boots, and inside the pads put hay – enough for them to be about seven millimetres thick when pressed down hard. Use the softest, driest hay you can find for this.'

Mama Simanyi nodded. 'We can do it.'

'For the other clothes, again we need insulation. It would be good if we had string vests, but we have not. If you can find thin cellular vests to go underneath wool ones, use them. On top, flannel shirts, jerseys, jackets that will best keep out wind and rain and snow. And all must wear trousers – pyjama trousers underneath – and you cut an opening in the seats, and fasten with buttons, eh? – and then two pairs of trousers over them. There are denims in the crew's quarters for the top pair.'

Mama Simanyi said doubtfully: 'It will not be easy to find outfits for ten people. And there is the child. There will be no boots two sizes too big for her.'

'You must do what you can, Mama. We rely on you. For the child's boots, it is not so important – she will not be walking like the rest of us. Take extra woollen socks that can be pulled over her boots from outside. They will keep her warm.'

'And gloves, too.'

'The stoutest you can find, with liners if possible, and wool wristlets sewn on.'

'We cannot do all this by tomorrow morning.' She was apologetic. 'At least, I do not think we can.'

'It makes nothing,' Olsen said. 'The sledges and the tent will not be ready either. We take our time. Better to start later, and better prepared.'

They were alone at this end of the lounge. Mama Simanyi said, in a low voice:

'The little walk. How many days do you think, Captain? It is best you tell me since I am to prepare for housekeeping.'

Olsen looked at her intently. 'If all goes well – a week.'

'And if not?'

He shrugged. 'Who knows, Mama? We will get there as soon as is possible, I guess.'

Jones had cut his hand during the sledge-making. In their cabin at night, Sheila removed the old dressing and put on a new one.

She said: 'It's nasty.'

'The knife slipped.'

'Does it hurt much?'

'Only when the cold gets to it. I'm glad we shan't be ready to go in the morning.'

'Do you think it will be all right the next day?'

'Yes.' He examined the cut. 'It's healing already.'

'Apart from that,' she said, 'it will be good to go, won't it – to get off the ship, to have some purpose in view.'

'I suppose so.'

'Won't it?'

He nodded towards the typewriter case. 'I'm worrying about that.'

In a flat voice, she said: 'What about it?'

'Olsen says we shall only have room for essentials on the sledge. He's right, I suppose.'

'If you leave it, it will be safe here. No one can touch it, can they?'

He laughed, with some harshness. 'And if the ice crushes the ship?'

'Probably it won't. He meant that you couldn't risk human lives to it. We can't be far from the edge of the ice. The steward, Thorsen, was saying they would probably salvage it when the ice breaks in the spring.'

'And we're to wait till then, wondering what's happened to it – and whether one of the salvage crew will get curious about that lock?'

She finished bandaging his hand and put her arms round him to draw him to her on the bed.

'I know! We'll put it inside one of the big cases – there's room with the clothes and things we're taking out. The lock on the blue case is a good one, and that won't make anyone curious. We could even seal the cases; it's a reasonable sort of precaution.'

He showed a brief interest, and then shook his head.

'Four months at the least, perhaps six, perhaps longer. How do we live during that time?'

'We could take enough with us in our pockets to last till then. A few hundred, anyway.'

He was silent for a time. Then he said:

'I'm not going to risk it. I'm taking it with me.'

She thought of arguing with him, but she saw that it was no good. Logic was on his side; once you started something you carried it through to the end.

As though following her thoughts, he said:

'Sheila, darling, are you sorry?'

'Sorry?'

'That you got into all this.'

There was not enough reassurance in words. She put her mouth to his and kissed him, passionately, desperately. Even that reassurance would not last, but for a time it was enough.

Annabel was asleep. The Arctic air tired her, and at night she went to sleep quickly and slept soundly. Mouritzen had looked in on his way to his cabin. Mary smiled and came to him. She was wearing a woollen dressing-gown over a white silk nightdress. The dressing-gown was knotted loosely at the front. He tugged at the knot, and the front fell open.

She said, smiling, wary and welcoming at once:

'Remember your promise.'

'I have not forgotten. I will not kiss you. To look at you in a nightdress is something else.'

'Do you like it?'

He grinned at her. 'Do not tempt me too far! You have told me how weak a man I am.'

'I've been thinking,' she said.

'Hm?'

She drew the dressing-gown round her again, and tied the belt more securely.

'Now, listen. You said before that you would have to stay with the *Kreya* and Annabel and I were to go on ahead. But we're leaving the *Kreya* here. So we can go together!'

'Will you like that?'

She smiled. 'Anyway, I was scared of meeting your family by myself.'

'You need not have been. But you are right – it seems we will meet them together. There is one thing, though.'

'What's that?'

'There is no boat from Copenhagen to Scoresby until July. We have a long wait there first. Unless we are taken by aeroplane. But I think there is no landing place for big aeroplanes, and I am not sure that the little ones can carry fuel to go so far from Iceland.'

'We can wait. We'll be together.'

'Ah, that is the trouble. Together, in the Arctic winter, with no sun for two months . . . I think I would be very weak by the time the sun came back.'

'I'll put a padlock on my igloo.'

'I have a better idea. We will get married at Scoresby. Then in the summer I will take you back to Denmark as a wife. If the boat takes us back in July, perhaps there will just be time.'

'Time? For what?'

He took her hand and kissed the fingers.

'For our first little Dane to be properly born in Denmark.'

The wind died down and the fog returned. The next day it thinned a little, but the sun, in its brief visit, was no more than a red streak in the haze. The work of preparation went on. Olsen found Mouritzen and Josef binding the runners on to one of the sledges with wire. He examined the sledge carefully.

'Good,' he said. 'I think we start tomorrow.'

'Even if the fog is thick?' Josef asked.

'If it is no worse than today, we go. The ice is piling up on the starboard side.'

Josef nodded. 'I saw that. And it gets more noisy, I think.'

'Mama has given us boots,' Mouritzen said. 'With pads filled with hay to go inside. Might not the sea-boots be better?'

'The sea-boots are of rubber. They make you sweat too much, and the sweat becomes ice under your feet. Then it is not pleasant.'

'Weapons, Captain,' Josef said, '– have we weapons?'

Olsen smiled. 'We go for a little walk, not to fight a war.'

'Maybe we kill a seal.'

'We have the flare pistol,' Olsen said, 'but we will need that for flares, maybe. If you wish, you can make some spears – fix sharp knives on the end of sticks. I will leave the weapons to you.'

'Yes, I will make them,' Josef said with satisfaction. 'And maybe I will catch fish, too.'

'I do not think we can stop on the way long enough for that.'

'It will not take long, Captain.'

'I know a quicker way.'

'What is that?'

'Catch a seal and tame it. Then the seal will catch the fish for you.'

Chapter Ten

The wind rose again that night; it was not very strong but savagely cold. It numbed flesh after the first burning brand of its touch. But it dispersed the fog. They had their last breakfast on the *Kreya* at seven in the morning, and at eight, with the first beginning of half light, Olsen began to organize the transfer of the sledges to the surface of the ice, and their loading with equipment, food and blankets.

The sledges were piled high, and tarpaulins were drawn over them and bound tightly with rope: these tarpaulins would also serve as ground-sheets for the tents. A place was left, at the end of one of the sledges, for Annabel, and when all was ready she was carried down the rope ladder by Mouritzen and propped in place.

'Is it well with you, little one?' he asked her.

'It's so cold.'

'Pull the flap across your face. So. And now I wrap the blankets around you and tuck them underneath. And then I must tie this strap, so that you do not fall off if the sledge tilts. It will be a rocky journey. Have you ever ridden on a camel?'

The small, covered head was shaken. Her muffled voice said: 'Only an elephant, at Phoenix Park.'

'Then you can pretend this is a wooden elephant.'

'It doesn't feel like being on an elephant.'

'No? So you must pretend all the harder. Remember Kikkipik, the troll – he was good at pretending things.'

She said: 'Mr Niels?'

'Yes.'

'Is it as cold as this in Denmark?'

He laughed. 'No. We shall not freeze you into an ice-maiden. And in the summer it is hot, much hotter than Ireland. We will have a lot of fun in summer.'

124

He left her with Mary to look after her, and clambered back on board. He heard the throb of the engines stop, and the lights winked off. It was a moment in which the full understanding came home to him that they were abandoning this stout and comfortable refuge for all the hazards and uncertainties of the ice-field. Olsen came up from the engine-room, slipping a torch into his pocket.

'All is done,' he said. 'Now we say good-bye to the *Kreya*.'

Mouritzen said: 'You said you would sail her back into port – that at last you would take her to the breaker's yards.'

Olsen clapped his hand on Mouritzen's arm. 'If the ice does not squeeze the heart out of her, I can still do all that, Niels! And maybe she will still be afloat in the spring. She is a tough one: she has survived much already.'

Mouritzen looked down to the little party on the ice. They had a helpless look in the dark dawn.

'This is an undertaking, Erik,' he said. 'One would not do it for choice.'

Olsen shrugged. 'There are few things one would do for choice. Necessity is better, I think.'

'In what way, better?'

'As an incentive to effort.'

Mouritzen looked at him curiously. 'The incentive is not the same for all.'

'No?'

Mouritzen turned back to watch the waiting group.

'The sledges,' he commented, 'are loaded high.'

'Yes. That cannot be helped.'

'Without those empty oil-drums we could have spread things more. It would have been safer.'

'Yes. But we may need them.'

'For what?'

Olsen stared at him. 'For crossing open water – what else?'

'But we are going towards the shore.'

'Exactly. You will see. Now I think we abandon the *Kreya*. You first, Niels. It is my privilege to go last.'

The two men clambered down the rope ladder and left it swinging against the side of the deserted ship. Olsen mustered the party for final instructions.

'There are two sets of traces on each sledge,' he said, 'and a harness which goes across the chest. It is a bit rough, perhaps, but we could do not better in the short time there was. The men will pull in this harness – an hour's pull, half an hour's rest – and the ladies will take it in turn to help push from behind. Of course, when there are difficulties, all help together.'

Nadya said: 'I could take my turn with the harness. I am as strong as any man here.'

Olsen smiled. 'Then you can push the harder, can you not?' He nodded towards the brown shape of Katerina, squatting on the ice beside her. 'And you have another duty – to control the bear.'

'She needs no controlling.'

'That we all hope.' Olsen patted his pocket. 'I have a charged flare pistol here. If she is naughty, I use it. Even if I do not kill her, I will singe her a little.'

'Katerina will cause no trouble.'

'Good. Then we are ready to start. Jorgen, you pull the first sledge with Niels – Josef with me on the second. After half an hour, you are replaced by Mr Jones and Stefan. And so it goes. Right. We begin.'

The typewriter case had been concealed behind Jones's legs. As Olsen moved towards the second sledge, he picked it up, and Olsen saw him. He stopped.

'A typewriter? Do you think you will write a book of our journey? But is it not better to wait until it is over?'

Jones said: 'I'll carry it, Captain. I've no intention of adding extra weight to the sledge.'

Olsen slowly shook his head. 'You should have left it on the *Kreya*. I said nothing must be taken that was not essential. A typewriter is not essential.'

'All the same, I insist on taking it. It isn't very heavy. I can carry it easily.'

'Give it to me,' Olsen said. 'I will take it back on board and put it in your cabin. We lose a little more time, but it cannot be helped. And it will be safe there until they come to salvage the *Kreya*.'

'I want it with me,' Jones said.

With exasperation, Olsen said: 'I know the English are sentimental, but are they sentimental over a typewriter? Was this a family heirloom – did Lord Wellington write the news of Waterloo on this machine?'

Jones said: 'I have – private reasons for wanting to hang on to it. I don't propose to discuss them.'

'We need no discussion. If it is not taken on board the *Kreya*, it must be left here.'

'There is a further alternative.' Jones spoke stiffly, but as though in embarrassment rather than anger. 'My wife and I can stay on the ship.'

'That is impossible. There is no heat nor light now, and little food. And the dangers do not grow less.'

'We can manage. And there are dangers, I would think, whether one goes or stays. I have had some misgivings over this journey from the beginning. I have more now.'

'Mr Jones, you have already given your agreement.'

'And the Englishman never goes back on his word? You don't know us as well as you think, Captain.'

The others were watching and waiting in silence. The thin, bitter wind keened over the ice, counterpointing the continuous bass grumble of the shifting floes. The scene, in the less than half-light, was melancholy. Although the setting was so vastly different, Olsen was reminded, looking at the watchful figures and the one protagonist, of the scene on the *Kreya* when Stövring had defied him. He had resisted, as he had known he must, and all had gone wrong. Now he was being defied again, and over an absurdity. But the crux of the matter was that it was impossible to force the two English to come with the others if they decided not to. There was no lever he could use against them as he had used the threat to take Mouritzen away against Mary Cleary. And he could not leave them: he was not prepared to divide the party for which he had accepted responsibility – still less was he willing to leave others on the *Kreya*.

He said harshly: 'You are determined in this, Mr Jones?'

The muffled figure of Jones nodded in reply. 'Quite determined.'

'A bear,' Olsen said, 'and a typewriter. I am becoming a connoisseur of human stupidity. You cannot carry the machine, Mr Jones.' He waved down an attempt by Jones to say something. 'If you carry it, you cannot properly do the work I require of you. Put it on the sledge, beside the child.'

'Thank you, Captain,' Jones said.

'In return for this burden which you place on all of us, you will be given more and harder tasks during the journey. Do you accept this?'

'I accept.'

'Then, at last, we go, I think. We have wasted too much time already.'

127

Their route took them almost due west, towards the mountains they had seen two days before. The previous day the mountains had been hidden by the fog and at present, although the sky was clear, there was not enough light to make them visible. There were a few pale stars, and moonlight filtered through the bars of a high bank of cloud.

The going was hard. There was no level surface of ice; in months, even years of jostling, the floes had slid under and over each other to form slanting platforms, separated by hummocks and ridges of ice, and by fissures anything from a few inches to several feet wide. There was a constant jarring motion as the swell lifted the floes and pulled them down again – air hissed in and out of the fissures with each rise and subsidence. But the motion was less pronounced than it had been, and as they moved to the west it became still less noticeable.

As far as possible, they manoeuvred the sledges to take advantage of what favourable contours there were, and after a time Olsen appointed one of the free men as a scout, to go ahead and, climbing an ice hillock to a vantage point, call back the best line to take. All but the smallest fissures had to be avoided; sometimes they widened markedly as they were being crossed. Although it was generally possible to find a gap, or a lower level at which to haul the sledges over, occasionally a ridge several feet high made it necessary for all of them to get under the sledges and manhandle them over the obstacle.

It was a slow business; at the end of two hours they had progressed, Mouritzen guessed, about as many miles. It was his turn out of the harness. He walked beside Olsen, and spoke to him quietly:

'How far, do you think, to the coast?'

'Twenty miles. Perhaps a little more.'

'We can only move during the hours when there is some light – about eight hours each day.'

'Yes.'

'So it will be three or four days before we reach the shore even.'

Olsen heaved on his traces. His face was blue with cold and there was a crust of ice on his eyelashes.

'Maybe. I think it will get better after a time. One would expect the ice to be rougher and more broken up towards the edge of the field.'

'I hope so. Four days of this will not be amusing.'

Olsen put up a gloved hand to his nose.

'No feeling,' he commented. 'There is always something one forgets. Tonight, if there is the material, the women must make nose protectors for us.'

'And tomorrow,' Mouritzen said, 'I think I will have one less vest and only two pairs of trousers.'

'Better too hot than too cold,' Olsen warned him. 'And we cannot stop by day if you want to put another pair of trousers on.'

Away to their left the sky reddened and the sun made its short climb towards the shrunken zenith of its course. They could see the mountains ahead, as white and unbelievable as ever against the dark blue sky.

'We are nearer, Mama,' Josef shouted.

'Nearer to what? To Heaven?'

'To the mountains!'

'That is something,' she said. 'The mountains are nearer to Heaven, and we are nearer to the mountains.' She gasped. 'I am sweating and freezing together.'

Nadya said to her father: 'They look farther away to me.'

'That is because you saw them before from the deck of a ship, high above the ice.'

'Then why do you say they are nearer?'

Josef laughed. 'Not they – we! They are farther, but we are nearer. We have come so far that we must be nearer.'

With the red ball of the sun standing clear of the southern ice, Mama Simanyi brought round packets of chocolate and biscuits, drawn from a haversack which had been left easily accessible on the second sledge. After that she went round with a water bottle. Drinking from it, in his turn, Mouritzen observed:

'The water is almost warm!'

Mama Simanyi pointed to the front of her voluminous wrappings.

'I have a place for it, in there. To keep it from freezing.'

Mouritzen laughed. 'It keeps well there, Mama.'

They struggled on. By the time the sun dipped below the horizon again it had become, as Olsen had prophesied, a little easier: there were stretches of as much as a hundred yards where the sledges could be pulled without having to be lifted or coaxed up or down slopes. But it was hard enough; their muscles were unaccustomed to the tasks they now had, and as the day wore on they were tiring.

Stefan at last said to Olsen: 'It is time to make camp, surely, Captain? It is too dark to see where we go.'

The glow had long faded from the south. Overhead the stars were beginning to wink into vision. The ice all round them was grey, featureless.

'We see well enough,' Olsen said. 'When it is time, I will order the halt.'

Stefan made a sound of melancholy disgust.

'It will be too dark to see what we do. We will pitch tent over a fissure in the ice, and in the night . . .'

He made a grating noise in his throat.

'What of it?' Olsen asked. 'You can swim?'

'No. It is hard to learn to swim when one lives always in a circus.'

'I have seen seals in a circus,' Olsen said. 'They swim.'

But it was true, he reflected, that some care would be needed in selecting their night's resting place, and although they had four torches between them it would be better not to leave the decision until darkness had set in. He called Jones, who had recently been relieved, to take his place in the harness, and went ahead of the party to where Mouritzen was reconnoitring the way. He joined him at the top of a mound of ice, formed by accident into a round hump that reminded one of an igloo.

Guessing his purpose, Mouritzen said: 'What I would like now is a hollow somewhere in the woods above Aarhus. A little stream, and perhaps a fawn drinking. That is where I would like to pitch a tent.'

'You do not like this land?'

'Land! If it were land, I would be happier.'

Olsen pointed. 'Over there. Under the lee of that ridge; the wind is from the north and there will be some shelter. How do you like it?'

'Is it solid, do you think?'

'We must go and see.'

The ridge marked a point of junction, some time in the past, of two fairly large floes. It gave every sign of solidity. Mouritzen jumped up and down on the surface of the ice, but there was no new or nearer note in the distant creaking and groaning.

'This will do,' Olsen said. 'Tell them we pitch our tents here tonight.'

Unloading the sledges took a long time, to start with. All their fingers were numb to varying degrees, and grew more numb as they wrestled with the knotted ropes. The problems of tent erection followed hard on this. Places for the pegs had to be marked out on the ice, and outward-slanting holes chiselled out. The pegs were then set, the chipped fragments of ice packed round them, and water poured round to freeze them in. Full night had fallen long before this was completed; the women stood round with torches, flashing them to different points as directed.

At last the tents were got up and it was possible to prepare the interiors. Each tent had a tarpaulin as a ground-sheet and Olsen had loaded a bag of hay on each sledge. Josef had commented on this: 'So we sleep on mattresses out there, Captain? If so, they will be thin, I think.' Olsen had smiled, without answering. Now his purpose was made clear: he had them spread the hay over the tarpaulins, and then lay bankets on top of the hay.

Stefan objected: 'I would rather have my blankets on me than the floor.'

'You have a lot to learn,' his father said. He added, to Olsen: 'The hay is even thinner this way.'

'It will give some insulation – enough, I hope. We could not have carried more.'

The tents were set up side by side; the one which had belonged to the Simanyi's had an extra flap at one end, and it was possible to use this to form a small covered tunnel between them.

Mouritzen carried Annabel inside as soon as there was a place for her.

'I'm cold,' she said.

'And brave,' he told her. 'A most brave little girl; you have hardly complained all day. Soon you will be warm. See, Mama Simanyi is lighting the Primus stove.'

'I wish we had a proper fire.'

'You will be surprised how quickly it will get warm.'

She looked up at him. Her eyes were like Mary's, but a deeper, smokier blue; as a woman she would be even lovelier, he thought.

'Will we be there tomorrow?'

'Or soon after. Rest now. Then there will be hot stew. That will warm you also.'

Outside, Nadya took the pack off Katerina's back, and gave her some of the food from it.

'It is not much,' she said, 'for a big bear like you, but there is still a long way to go. If we eat all at once, there is no more left. See, a little honey on the biscuits. And then we take a little walk to the ridge here. No water for a bear, but this is snow, which turns into water in your mouth. And here the snow is deep where it has drifted with the wind. You must make your bed here, Katerina. It is not a good bed, but it is better than the hard ice. Sleep here until morning.'

She rubbed the bear's head with her gloved hands.

'If you grow tired of such a supper and such a bed, and leave us in the night, I will not blame you. But if you go, my Katerina, take care of yourself. This is a bad place, for bears as well as men.'

At last, all were inside the tents. A stove had been set going in each tent, and already there was some warmth from them. They took off their outer clothes and their boots. The insoles which the women had made showed a covering of frost underneath, which they brushed off. Socks were taken off and fresh pairs put on. There were tapes running across the top of the tent. Olsen had had these sewn in, and he now instructed them to hang the socks and insoles over them.

'As the heat from the Primus rises, they will dry,' he explained. 'It is important to have dry socks.'

Jones said: 'I'm glad to get those boots off. That sole rucked up underneath – it's been like walking over ribbed rock.'

'Tomorrow,' Olsen said, 'you must take greater care in putting your feet in the boots. I will help you. We cannot afford to have a cripple with us.'

'Tomorrow,' Stefan asked, 'we get off the ice?'

Olsen shrugged. 'Maybe.'

'Last night,' Stefan observed wistfully, 'we slept on bunks, with spring mattresses, as many blankets as one wanted, sheets...'

Josef grunted. 'We are doing well, I think. No trouble, no accidents, and we are snug for the night. All we need is food.' He lifted the flap and called through to the other tent. 'Mama! How long before the stew comes?'

She called back: 'In a few minutes we send you the pot in, ready to put on your stove. After that, it is up to you.'

Josef let the flap fall again. He made a smacking noise with his lips.

'I think I could eat it raw,' he said.

*

Olsen awoke during the night; his watch told him it was nearly three o'clock. About him there was the sound of steady breathing. He found his boots, slipped them on, and quietly made his way outside.

When he had relieved himself, he stood for a while looking around. There was no moon yet, but the stars were sharp and heavy in the sky. Across the northern hemisphere a broad, pale, luminescent band moved slowly – brightening, dimming, always passing across the heavens, always transient and always renewed. The air was intensely bright: the light from stars and Northern Light reflected everywhere from the ice-field – although the field of visibility was quite small, objects shone within it, and it gave the impression of being larger than it was.

Right under the ridge there was a hump of brown in the powdery whiteness of the snow. Katerina, the bear. He was glad now that the girl had insisted on bringing the animal. The strangeness of it, the touch of fantasy, somehow made their position seem less hazardous. He listened for the grinding of the floes. It was quieter and, more distant; because the swell from the east had lessened, perhaps, or because they were in a region of firmer ice. He hoped it was the second. The ice here was steady under foot, with barely a trace of movement.

There would be hazards, no doubt. For the moment, it was enough to be here. Olsen looked at the glory of the sky and nodded: it was enough to be here.

A gust of below-zero wind made him shiver. He went back to the tent and quietly slipped inside.

They made better progress the following day. The ice continued to improve, the wind had dropped again, and they themselves were more accustomed to the work they had to do. They camped for the night on a wide plain of ice, almost featureless for as far as the eye, in the deepening dusk, could see.

They had been over three hours on the trail, on the third day, when they reached open water. The pack-ice ended abruptly, giving way to a channel of water about three hundred yards wide. Beyond the channel there was more ice; farther to the west there were snow-covered hills and the high glacier-decked mountains. Small floes drifted in the dark green water; the sound of the ice now was a tinkling whisper, like little horse bells.

From a slight elevation, twenty or thirty yards from the edge of the ice, they stood and stared at it. The sun, three-quarters of its disc clear of the skyline, streamed sunset on their faces. Mouritzen could see Mary and Nadya standing side by side. Mary's blondeness looked pale, her face tired, but the blackness of Nadya's hair caught crimson tints – her skin was a deep russet bronze.

Thorsen said: 'We'll never get across that. Even if the raft idea works, we'll never get everything over.'

Olsen paid him no attention. With his glasses he swept the course of the channel to north and south. He pointed to the north.

'It narrows, in that direction. About a mile away it is most narrow. We will cross there.'

They changed direction and plodded on across the ice. Mouritzen would have liked to talk to Olsen but at the time they were both in harness on different sledges. When, at Olsen's command, they halted again, he slipped the harness from his shoulders and went over to him.

Olsen said with satisfaction: 'A lot nearer. Not much more than a hundred metres.'

'First we have to strip both sledges,' Mouritzen said. 'Then make the raft. It will not take more than two of us at one time, so that is nine trips. And all the food and gear to be taken across bit by bit. We have only three hours before night falls. I do not think it is enough.'

Olsen beat his gloved hands together.

'Nor do I.'

'Then we camp here for the night, and cross in the morning?'

Olsen shook his head. 'We make a start.'

'And find ourselves half on one side, half on the other, when it becomes too dark to continue?'

'That is right.'

'How, then?'

'It is simple,' Olsen said. 'We have two tents. We get the women across today, the rest of us tomorrow.'

Mouritzen thought about this. 'It will need some organizing.'

Olsen clapped him on the shoulder. 'We do not lack organizers! Niels, that is shore ice over there. Once we are on it, the worst part of our journey is almost over. You are right in saying we could not take everything across today, but what we can take, we will. If we left all until tomorrow, a storm might blow up when the job was half done. As it is – if we work hard today, I think maybe tomorrow night we will sleep with earth beneath us instead of water.'

134

'The storm,' Mouritzen observed, 'might blow up tonight.'

'Then at least half our party is across.'

The sledges were stripped of their contents, and the women put to dividing the material for immediate transport from that which would be left for the next day. There were protests when they realized that Olsen's plan entailed separation from their menfolk; but the ascendancy he had now achieved was such that the protests were not sustained long.

Mama Simanyi said: 'If you say it is the only way, Captain . . . but Papa and I have never been separated.'

Olsen grinned. 'Nor will you be now. You can call to each other across the water. If you wish, we stretch a rope across and tie one end each to the big toe. Then you will know if he goes wandering in the night!'

'You must cook your own supper tonight,' Mama Simanyi said, warningly.

'You make it ready, eh?' Olsen said. 'Put it in the pressure cooker. It will keep there till dark.'

A raft was made by lashing the two empty drums to the underside of one of the sledges and, having secured one end with a rope, they eased it down into the water that gently lapped against the edge of the floe. It floated, but one end was deeper in the water than the other. Olsen stared at it, his brow furrowed.

'I think it would be all right,' Mouritzen said. 'We could distribute weight to make it all right.'

For a moment, Olsen continued his contemplation. Then he said sharply:

'No! We take no chances. Haul her up again. We fix that drum a bit nearer the centre. And maybe we also take the runners off that end. She will balance better if we do that.'

The raft floated more evenly on the next launching. Olsen picked up a shovel and handed it to Mouritzen. He took another for himself.

'First we will go across together, and find a place from which to run our ferry. Then we start the crossings in earnest.'

It was awkward paddling with the shovels, but the water was extremely calm, unruffled by the faintest breeze. They had to manoeuvre out of the path of a small drifting floe, six or seven feet in diameter, but otherwise the journey was uneventful. They climbed up on the ice at the other side, and waved to the watching figures.

'This will do,' Olsen said. 'The ice is firm here. If they put up the tent fifty yards to the west, there will be no danger.'

'It is fortunate you brought the drums,' Mouritzen said.

Olsen shook his head. 'Not fortunate.'

'You knew there would be open water?'

'At this time of year there is always a channel between the shore-ice and the pack-ice. Well, it will not be too difficult. But it is best that we get on with it right away.'

He was a strange man, Mouritzen thought; in him the interplay of confidence and reserve, natural to all human relations, bore an unfathomable, distorted pattern. There was no reason why he should not have told Mouritzen this when, on the *Kreya*, he had queried the value of taking the empty drums. Mouritzen pictured the small boy, an only child, a mother cold and without sympathy, the big sea captain for a father, briefly with them and then away. The roots went deep.

They paddled back, and gear was loaded on the raft for Mouritzen to begin the transportation. On that trip, he found difficulty in getting the stuff unloaded at the other end; as he heaved things up on to the ice, the raft slid away into the channel. There were two requirements: a mooring post and an assistant on the ice at that side. When he got back to the main party, he explained this to Olsen.

'The post is easy,' Olsen said. 'Chisel a hole and fix a runner in it. For the helper . . .'

Nadya said: 'I will go. Since the women are to be on the other side tonight, it is better me than one of the men. It saves a crossing. And while Niels is rowing to and fro I can prepare the camping place.'

It was reasonable. Olsen nodded.

'Yes, we will do that. And we will make a post on this side also.'

Nadya settled herself opposite Mouritzen on the raft. She stretched her hand out.

'I will take the other shovel.' They began to paddle out into the stream. She cried suddenly: 'Katerina!'

The bear was standing on the edge of the ice, watching them. Nadya said:

'She must come, too.' She waved her arm and cried a few words in Polish. In English, she added: 'Come, you stupid bear! Sooner or later you must cross.'

'If she pulls at the raft,' Mouritzen warned her, 'she may turn it over.'

'She will not do that. She is a good bear. Come now, Katerina!'

The bear hesitated a moment and then, squatting down, slid rump first into the water. She swam steadily after the raft. Nadya called in delight:

'Good! A little white paint, and you are a polar bear.'

The crossings went smoothly and with reasonable speed after that. Mouritzen was impressed by the competence with which Nadya helped him. She was as useful as any of the men would have been, and her dark face, catching the rays of the disappearing sun, afforded a satisfaction that had nothing to do with utility. Between trips she staked out the tent. By the time the first of the other women crossed, with the sun lost and the afterglow almost gone, she had it erected.

He took Mary and Annabel together; the child gave little extra weight.

Mary said: 'It seems much wider when you're crossing it. I wish we could all be on the same side tonight.'

Mouritzen nodded. 'Erik is right, though. It is better to get as much over today as we can.'

'I suppose women aren't as practical as men.' Mouritzen threw the mooring rope and Nadya caught it, with a loud cry of 'Right!' 'Most women, anyway.'

They finished while the day was still fairly light, and Mouritzen made his last trip back. The camp had been prepared on that side, too. They hauled up the raft, and dragged it over to the tent.

There was time after that for them to stand and wave at each other across the barrier of water. In the dusk the water turned from green to black, and seemed to be flowing faster. There were more ice chunks, too, floating down from the north. They called their good nights, their voices flat and echoing. Then they trooped away and squeezed into their tents.

During the night Mouritzen was awakened by noises. There was the wind first; it had risen again, and he could hear it howling, cold and angry, over the ice. More ominously there was the distant roaring of the ice itself – louder, more menacing, punctuated by occasional louder cracks, like thunder. Mouritzen roused himself to sit up.

From the other side of the tent, Olsen's voice said:

'You hear it, then?'

'I hear it,' Mouritzen said, 'and I do not like it.'

'I wonder,' Olsen said, 'how it goes with the *Kreya*.'

'How does it go with us? That is more important.'

'We are all right, I think,' Olsen said.

'And the women?'

'They, too. The disturbance is well out to sea.'

They lapsed into silence, but Mouritzen did not go to sleep again; and he fancied that Olsen remained awake also. Olsen began to dress soon after six, and Mouritzen followed suit. They went outside, but it was impossible to see anything outside a radius of about fifty yards.

'Breakfast first,' Olsen said.

Mouritzen pointed to the sky. 'Clouded over.'

'The weather is changing. But it will not change much before breakfast.'

When they went out again, it was light enough to see that there had been a change, during the night, in more than the weather. The channel between the pack-ice and the shore-ice was twice as wide as it had been, and there were still more floes in it. As they looked a berg drifted past, as high above the water as a house.

Mouritzen, astonished, said: 'The whole field must have moved; but we felt nothing.'

'The wind is offshore,' Olsen said, 'from the north-west.' His voice had exultance in it. 'It is as well the crossing is half completed.'

'One of them is coming out,' Mouritzen said. He pointed to the tent on the otherside. 'Nadya, I guess.'

'We will waste no time,' Olsen said. 'I think I smell snow in the wind.'

Crossing now was more difficult, not only because of the greater distance, but also because there were more floes to avoid. They pressed on with it as fast as possible; urgency was given to the operation by the fact that the women, during the night, had felt tremors in the ice on which they were camped, and these tremors increased during the morning. The wind was higher, too; the clouds were high but fast moving. When the last trip brought the second sledge, towed behind the raft, Olsen was insistent that no time be wasted in resuming the journey.

'We shall not need the drums once we are on land,' he said. 'The sledges will travel lighter without them.'

Mama Simanyi said: 'If we are to pack rightly, we need time to make ready – to sort things out.'

'We can do that tonight,' Olsen said. 'When we are on firm land. The important thing now is to get away. As long as they are properly on the sledges, it does not matter how things are packed.'

They moved off soon after midday. There was no sun; the sky was pale grey to the south, dark grey in the remaining quarters. This ice, they found, differed from the pack-ice both in contours and texture; asperities were blockier and more frequent, and it lacked the hardness and toughness of the older ice. It crackled sharply under the sledge runners, and when they were hauling over slopes and ridges it was not unusual for large sections to break away.

Progress was slower again, but it was perceptible. At the same time the ice was becoming less stable. There were cracks in it, which opened and closed with the tide sweeping under the sea. Occasionally rifts formed, up to a score of feet wide. A dyke which they skirted closed while they were alongside it. A small wave of water spurted up as the jaws of ice jarred together. It was not easy, afterwards, to see where the division had been.

There was a tilting slope of ice in front of them. Going round it would involve a fairly wide detour because of the jagged ice on either side. Olsen and Josef, heaving together, hauled their sledge up while the others pushed from behind. Dragging the sledge on to level ice beyond, Olsen shouted:

'We are there! That is the shore.'

He pointed to where, no more than a hundred yards away, a long snow field advanced towards the hills. Behind him Mouritzen and Jones were struggling up with the second sledge. Mouritzen heard the crack of breaking ice before Olsen had finished speaking. At the same time the surface under his feet canted up. He fought for his footing as Jones fell heavily, and managed to twist round so that he could dig his heels in. Thus, looking back, he saw before any of the rest the gap that was opening at the bottom of the slope.

'Behind,' he cried, '– crevasse!'

Some of them looked back; they all, automatically, slackened in the effort they had been making to push the sledge. It tilted farther, crashed on its side and, scattering some of its load as the ropes gave under the strain, slid back down the slope. There was a confusion of cries, and a single frightening shriek of pain. As he bumped to a halt on the ice, Mouritzen heard Mama Simanyi's voice:

'Oh, my God, she is trapped beneath it!'

He flung off the harness and, without waiting to help Jones to get clear, raced round to the other side of the sledge. He looked for Mary and Annabel, and saw them standing clear. The trapped woman was Sheila Jones.

She lay with the rear of the sledge pinning her across the middle. Her head pointed down the slope; her hood had fallen back and her hair lay free against the ice, not more than a foot from the dyke which had opened up. It was three or four feet wide, brimming with grey-green water.

'Quickly,' Mouritzen said, 'we all lift together.'

He got his hands under the edge of the runner and heaved. Mama Simanyi tugged beside him, and he saw Stefan pulling as well. There was a moment's strain, and then the runner lifted clear of the figure pinned under it. She was dragged away, and they let the sledge down and went to tend her.

Jones had her head cradled in his lap. She was silent, apart from an occasional sobbing intake of breath.

Jones bent towards her. 'Are you all right? Darling, are you all right?'

From the top of the slope, Olsen cried something, and Mouritzen looked up. Olsen began to run down towards them.

'The sledge!' he shouted.

As he whirled, Mouritzen heard the slithering of wood on ice. The sledge, still on its side, had begun to slide again. He jumped for it and got a hand to a trailing rope; it pulled through his fingers but he held on. The sledge was still sliding, but he thought everything would be all right until, with an unexpected lurch, it tipped over the edge of the ice into the water. The pull on the rope multiplied as the water took it, and this time he lost it. He saw the front of the sledge rear up, and then the water closed over it. A few bubbles floated up from the cold, dark depths.

Chapter Eleven

Mouritzen stood staring at the water. Olsen, scrambling down the ice, stood beside him.

'You're a fool,' Olsen said. His voice was controlled, coldly bitter. 'And one never fathoms a fool; however often you sound him, there is always more folly on which you may ground.'

Mouritzen assumed Olsen had not seen all that had taken place. He said:

'It was Mrs Jones. She was trapped under it.'

He pointed to where she lay with Jones holding her.

'Two people pulled her clear,' Olsen said. 'They could see to her. The sledge was your responsibility.'

Mouritzen realized the truth of this. He said:

'Yes. I'm sorry. But I could only think of the woman.'

'Even if there was no one to get her out, the sledge still came first. You should have left her there until I came.'

'She might have been dying.'

Olsen turned away from him. 'And through your stupidity, we might all die.'

Josef and Mama Simanyi came to them. Josef said:

'She is all right, I think. The sledge – can we get it back from the water?'

'Get your rod,' Olsen said, 'and fish for it.'

Josef stared down into the depths; the water was like black crystal. It was possible to see several feet down, but there was no sign of the bottom, or the sledge.

Mama Simanyi said: 'The food.'

Olsen turned to her, his face intent. 'What was on that sledge?'

'Before, I packed things equally. But today you said not to waste time with that. There is some food on the other sledge – not much.'

'The tents!' Olsen said. 'How were they packed?'

She nodded towards the dyke. 'One on that.'

'Which?'

'Ours, I think. Yes, I am sure.'

'The smaller one lost,' Olsen said. 'Better than the other – or both. And the Primus stoves?'

'There was one on each sledge. But . . .'

She hesitated. Olsen asked sharply: 'What?'

'The paraffin is all on the one which sank. There was a confusion over that.'

Olsen stayed silent, and his silence seemed to bind them all with it. He walked across to the Joneses.

'How is she now? Can she walk?'

Jones said: 'She can't walk. It hurts when she moves at all.'

'Then we change our plans,' Olsen said. 'She must ride on the other sledge. It will not be very comfortable, because the sledge is loaded already, but it is the only thing possible.' He turned briefly to Mary. 'We will take it in turns to carry the little one on our shoulders.'

Annabel said. 'I can walk. I don't mind walking.'

Olsen smiled slightly. 'But piggy-back is better, is it not?' There was a shifting of the ice again; they all felt it. 'First we get to land,' Olsen went on, 'before worse happens. You and I will carry your wife up to the other sledge.' He called to the others: 'Pick up what is fallen. Not much, I guess, but everything is of value.'

'I'll carry her,' Jones said.

She gave a little cry of pain as he picked her up, and then was silent, her arms round his neck. Olsen went with him up the slope to the remaining sledge. The others salvaged the items that had been scattered on the ice. Mouritzen picked up a shovel and an emergency chocolate ration.

Olsen said: 'We repack this sledge so Mrs Jones can ride on it. But quickly. We must get clear of the ice.'

They began stripping the sledge. Jones lowered Sheila gently and knelt by her, supporting her. Looking at her, he did not see Thorsen who, last of the party, now appeared over the brow of the slope. He was carrying the typewriter case.

'Good news for you,' Thorsen said. Jones looked up, and Thorsen tapped the case. 'This was thrown clear, too. Battered a little, but it is safe.' He smiled. 'You will still be able to write your book, Mr Jones.'

Immediately offshore the ice was badly broken, and Sheila had to be taken off and carried over the obstacles. They ceased quite suddenly. Instead of the hummocks and ridges and jagged pinnacles, untroubled snow curved up in a long, gentle slope to an escarpment with hills behind it.

'Land,' Olsen said. 'We have walked across the Arctic Ocean some of it. Now we are in Greenland.'

'I have known greener,' Josef said.

Jones said: 'Can we camp here for the night?'

The sky was very dark grey, but still held a fair amount of light. Olsen looked at his watch.

'Not yet. It is not yet three.'

Jones said: 'My wife – she's in pain. She must have a rest from the jolting.'

'There will be less jolting now. The sledge will travel easier over snow.'

'She needs complete rest.'

Olsen looked at him. 'I will give her such rest, if I can. But I must think of all. We have lost much of our food, one of the tents, the paraffin. We are on land but a long way from help. And I think snow may come.'

He turned to the others. 'We continue. Now we will make better speed, eh?'

Mouritzen walked beside him. The snow surface was soft in places and Olsen, with his short legs, had difficulty in floundering through these patches.

'Where do you think we are?' he asked him. 'Greenland – that is a lot of territory.'

'There is a fjord system north of Scoresby. A lot of islands – I think we are on one of them.'

'We have to cross water again?'

'They will be frozen – frozen enough to cross, anyway.'

'How far are we from Scoresby?'

' A hundred and fifty kilometres. Maybe a little more.'

'Six days?'

'If we find the way through the hills.' Olsen looked up at the sky. 'And if the weather holds.'

'How much food is left?'

'We will discover that when we make camp tonight.' His face was grim. 'That will be soon enough to think about it.'

The foreshore ran straight for a time, and then began to curve to the west. Olsen called a halt, and peered through the field-glasses into the deepening shadows of the southern sky.

He pointed. 'Our course lies that way.'

Josef shook his head. 'Across the ice again? I think it will be better to stay on land now we are here.'

'There are hills there,' Olsen said, 'and Scoresby is beyond the hills. This is not open sea, but a fjord. But I think we will not cross it today. Tonight we stay here.'

Stefan's voice, itself startled, startled the others.

'Look,' he said, 'over there! There are men on the ice.'

They stared where he was pointing. In the distance, dark figures moved. Half a dozen; perhaps more.

Puzzled, Mama Simanyi asked: 'Are they lying down?'

Olsen laughed. 'Lying down,' he said. 'Diving in the water, catching fish. They do not feel the cold and wet because they wear seal skins.'

The disappointment brought home to them still more strongly their isolation in this barren land. They stood staring across at the seals until Olsen rallied them.

'We will make camp,' he said. 'Tomorrow we cross the fjord. In a few days we will eat *biksemad* in Scoresby.'

There had not been much spare room in the tent for six men; with the addition of the four women and Annabel there was none at all. A little space was made by having them all, except Sheila, huddle together at one end, while Mama Simanyi and Olsen made an inventory of the remaining stock of food.

The result was discouraging. Olsen announced the details in a dry, even tone.

'Oats, four kilos. Chocolate, nine hundred grams. Biscuits, about two and a half kilos. Butter, nil. Cocoa, maybe five hundred grams. Dried milk, three cans. Sugar, three and a half kilos. Two cans of beef, a few onions, a can of potato powder, a can of pineapple in syrup. That is everything.'

Josef said: 'And we cannot cook it either.'

'By the previous standard of ration,' Olsen said, 'there is six day's supply of oats, and no butter or margarine at all. Of other foods, varying quantities, but not much biscuit or chocolate, and very little meat.'

'Two cans,' Stefan said. 'I could eat them myself, right away.'

'Mama,' Olsen said, 'tonight we will open one of the cans, but half you will save for tomorrow. The other half you can divide into eleven pieces. It is not so much, but something. Six biscuits each – they are not very big, I am sorry. And if you melt some snow, you can put a little water with cocoa and sugar and make a paste to go on the biscuits. And some more water can be mixed with the oats and sugar and dried milk. Perhaps not so tasty, but it will nourish.'

'How do we melt the snow?' she inquired.

'I grow stupid,' Olsen said. 'If we bring some in, the heat from our bodies will melt it by morning. But morning is not now. How much water have we?'

She held a flask up and shook it. 'Maybe half a litre here; and as much in the other, I guess.'

'We need that for drinking.' Olsen rubbed his chin. 'And if there is any to spare, I will shave myself. So no paste tonight. We must eat the oats dry, with a little sugar. And you can mix up cocoa, milk and sugar, and we will have two spoonfuls each.'

Stefan said dolefully: 'We will not grow fat on this diet.'

'There will be time to grow fat,' Olsen said. 'Just now it is enough to keep alive.'

Thorsen gestured towards the pile of provisions.

He said: 'There is some more food than you have counted there.'

'Where is it?'

'In the haversack that the bear carried.'

Nadya said angrily: 'That is Katerina's food. She carried it. It is hers, and there is little enough.'

Olsen stretched his hand out. 'Give it to me, Nadya. Jorgen is right.'

She shook her head. 'It is Katerina's.'

His voice deepened slightly. 'Give it to me.' She stared at him in sullen refusal. 'You fool!' he said. 'Do you think this is a game? Do you not understand that, unless the food lasts till we can get help, we must eat the bear itself?'

She had put the haversack just outside the tent. She nodded slowly.

'All right. I will get it.'

She put her boots on and went outside. Already, in so short a time, the tent had become stuffy, and she breathed the fresh night air with relief. A brown hump showed where Katerina had curled up in the snow. Nadya made a whistling sound through her teeth, and the bear sat up, shaking herself. Nadya had given her supper before retiring to the tent; now, tearing open the harversack, she reached inside. She grabbed in haste, and threw an assortment of things across the snow: some carrots, a couple of apples, and a handful of biscuits.

'Eat while you can,' she said. 'The rest they steal.'

Katerina moved in a leisurely fashion to retrieve the items that had been tossed to her. Nadya picked up the haversack and stooped down to get into the tent. She hesitated, straightened up again, and fished once more inside the bag. She took out a can of syrup, prised off the lid, and walked with it to Katerina. She put the open can down on the snow.

'You are a faithful bear,' she said. 'Perhaps too faithful. I think you should not stay longer – they talk of eating you.'

Going back to the tent she saw a face looking out: Thorsen's. She pushed him aside to get in, and threw the haversack to Olsen.

'There you are.'

'She has taken some out,' Thorsen said, 'and given it to the bear. A full can of syrup.'

Nadya smiled mockingly. 'I fatten her for the feast. She will taste better for that can of syrup.'

Olsen emptied out the haversack. 'Carrots, apples, three oranges, biscuits, more oats, a little chocolate,' he said. He held a packet up curiously. 'And these?'

'Dried bananas,' Nadya said.

'I did not find them in the ship's pantry,' Mama Simanyi said.

'I looked first.' Nadya shrugged. 'But Katerina did not like them much.'

Most of the blankets had been on the sledge they still had; crowded into the one tent as they were, they did not, after a time, miss the heat the Primus stoves would have given. Mouritzen, Mary and Annabel were at one end, with Nadya next to them. Mama Simanyi and Jones were on either side of Sheila; beyond Jones lay Thorsen, and then Stefan and Josef. Olsen had the end position on that side.

They lay and talked quietly in the darkness; the awareness of Sheila lying injured had a sobering effect. She had refused to eat anything, despite urging. She seemed to have no bones broken, but was painfully sensitive in the region of the spleen. She said there was very little pain as long as she lay still; watching her face in unguarded moments, Jones had not been sure that he believed that.

The evening that was also night dragged on. Jones held Sheila's hand, and talked to her in a low voice. Mostly he talked about the future: the flat in Rio, high above the city, looking out on the Sugarloaf and the sea, the warmth and gaiety, the golden beaches, the cafés . . . She listened and answered him from time to time. Once, when he paused, she said: 'I love you, I love you,' and their

146

hands pressed together as though for the first time, as though everything was still ahead.

Gradually sleep claimed her, and Jones drifted into sleep in turn. He woke some time later and, in an unreasoning panic, thought she had stopped breathing: her body, against his own, seemed stiff and immobile. He sat up and, in the dark, put his face close to hers; the relief of feeling her breath against his cheek was exhilarating. Punching his coat into a more comfortable pillow, he lay down again.

A moment or two later, Thorsen whispered:

'You awake, Henry?'

He whispered back: 'Yes. What is it?'

Their heads were close together. 'Henry,' Thorsen said. 'Henry what?'

He said: 'I don't understand.' A chill of fear touched him. 'You know my name.'

'Jones,' Thorsen said. 'A good name, Jones. Like Nielsen, in Denmark. The kind of name that does not stand out, that draws no attention.'

Jones made no reply. Thorsen went on:

'Don't go to sleep, Mr Jones. I want to have a little talk. If we whisper quietly, no one will hear us.'

'I'm tired,' Jones said. 'I'll show you my passport in the morning.'

'That's right. Talk quietly. I've already seen your passport, Mr Jones. I look into these things. It tells me something. It tells me you are a clever man, a man who arranges things in advance, who makes plans. It is not too hard to get a new passport in a new name. Maybe you put a new wife on the new passport, too?'

'You're talking nonsense.'

There was silence; long enough for Jones to begin to hope that Thorsen had been bluffing, and that his bluff was called. Then the thin voice said:

'I listened to you and Mrs Jones talking. I heard a little bit of it now and then.'

'However much you eavesdropped,' Jones said, 'you didn't hear anything that it would have mattered if the whole tent heard.'

'Montevideo,' Thorsen said. 'I was there once. That's a great place. I guess you will have a good time with Mrs Jones in Montevideo. You know what – I wouldn't mind going along with you?'

Jones said nothing.

'Don't go to sleep,' Thorsen said. 'I think you will be happy in Montevideo. But I will not come with you. Three is a crowd – that's an English saying, is it not? Anyway, I cannot leave my mother for too long. She is a fine old lady, but strict. If I went to Montevideo, she would come after me. It would spoil the fun.'

He paused. 'I guess I have a lot of commitments in Denmark. Expenses, too. The things I like cost a lot of money. You can understand that, Mr Jones. The cheap stuff is no good when one has a taste for the best. You and I like the same kind of things, Mr Jones.'

'I don't think so.'

They lay face to face, conspiratorial, almost like lovers. Thorsen gave a thin chuckle.

'But we do. You like money, and I like money. Have you looked at your typewriter since it fell off the sledge?'

'No.'

'That was lucky, it falling off like that. At first I thought it had gone down with the rest. I tell you, I felt bad about that. I was curious about that typewriter from the start, having a big new lock on it. And when you insisted to bring it with us, I knew it was a valuable machine. Maybe you are worried in case so valuable a machine got damaged when it was thrown off on the ice?'

Outside the tent the sound of the ice was farther off and muffled, but the wind howled loudly. Jones lay quietly, waiting for his tormentor to continue.

'It got a bit damaged,' Thorsen said. 'I think it hit a hard piece of ice. The lock broke. You don't have to worry, though. It still shuts. And tomorrow I will tie a piece of rope round to make sure it doesn't fly open by accident. I know some good knots. I can tie one no one else will be able to undo.'

He drew in breath and sighed it out. 'I will help you look after that typewriter, Mr Jones. When I saw the lock was broken, I looked inside. That's a good model. I like that model. You and I will take good care of it the rest of the journey.'

Jones said: 'If I choose to carry currency in a typewriter case, that's my affair. It has nothing to do with you.'

'And nothing to do with the Customs Officer, when you came aboard the *Kreya*? I guess the Customs people would be interested to ask you questions over it. Maybe the police would be interested, too. But you are right – that's your business. I will help you look after it till we get to Scoresby. I think you will pay me something for helping.'

'How much?'

Thorsen chuckled again. 'We will think about that. It is hard to decide right now. If it is only the Customs, fifty-fifty might be fair. But if it is the police as well . . . We will talk about that another time, Mr Jones. In the morning. Now we go to sleep. You dream of Montevideo. I will find something to dream about also.'

Mouritzen woke when he was kicked in the stomach by a small foot. The figure that had nestled between him and Mary wriggled. He said:

'What is it, Annabel?'

'I had a pain in my leg. It's better now.'

Mary said softly: 'She had some cramp.'

Annabel snuggled back into her previous position.

'Listen to the wind!' she said.

It was wild and high-pitched; there was an impression of fury, hysteria almost.

Mary asked: 'What time is it?'

Josef's voice answered: 'Soon after six o'clock.'

'Then mine had stopped,' Nadya said. 'It says half past four.'

It was apparent that most, if not all, were awake; there was a general shifting and stirring. Olsen said:

'Niels, before breakfast I think we will see if the tent is properly secured. If this wind gets underneath it, maybe we lose the tent altogether.'

Mouritzen said: 'Right. I am dressing now.'

He had trouble with one of the insoles; it kept rucking up when he put his foot into the boot. Olsen was ready before he was. He flashed a torch and then bent to open the flap at his side.

'Snow!' His voice was muffled by the canvas. 'And falling fast.'

Mouritzen at last made his own exit. He crawled into snow two or three inches deep. The snow was falling in big, whirling flakes, carried on a north-westerly wind. He walked round to the seaward side of the tent and came into its full blast. Putting his head down against it, he pushed forward towards the already snowy figure of Olsen.

'Not good,' he said. 'We cannot travel in this.'

'We need not fear for the tent, at least,' Olsen said. He pointed with the torch and Mouritzen saw that snow had already drifted up against the side of the tent, anchoring it. 'We will keep a roof over our heads.'

Mouritzen flashed his own torch around. The large, bright flakes drove through the beam, coming out of blackness and going into a blackness equally deep.

'Save the battery,' Olsen ordered him. 'The spares were on the other sledge.'

He switched the torch off. 'What do we do?'

'What can we do? Wait till the blizzard stops.'

'How long will that be?'

'I brought no barometer,' Olsen said, 'and I had my corn plucked before the last voyage. For guessing, you are as well equipped as I.'

Inside the tent the news was received with considerable gloom. They did not, Olsen realized, share his own apprehensions: of a delay that could wipe out the already dubious margin between the time their food supplies would last and the time it must take them to reach Scoresby. They were depressed merely by the prospect of having to stay cramped up together in the tent. And that was enough in itself. It was virtually impossible for one person to move without disturbing three or four others. Generally the readjustment affected the whole tent.

They had a meagre and unsatisfying snack for breakfast, chiefly consisting of oats with milk and sugar and water from the melted snow. Sheila could not eat any; she had a little piece of chocolate and drank some water, but otherwise nothing. The others helped to make her as comfortable as possible, but there was not much that could be done. She lay there quietly, and Jones held her hand.

The actual physical gloom was as hard to bear as the cramp and confinement. Even though the blackness outside moderated as a meagre daylight filtered through the blizzard, it remained as pitch dark in the tent. The torches, clearly, could only be used in moments of actual need, such as during the preparation and distribution of food rations. For the rest there was continuous darkness, unbroken even by the glow of a cigarette. The smokers had stocked up with cigarettes and tobacco before leaving the *Kreya*, but Olsen ruled against any smoking inside the tent.

When noon passed with no slackening in the storm, hope of getting away that day was finally abandoned. Somewhat later paths were cut through the drifts that now packed on either end of the tent, to enable people to go outside for the requirements of elimination. After that there was nothing to do but lie in the dark, waiting for an inadequate supper, and for the long night which would be no different from the day.

'In the night,' Josef said, 'it must snow itself out. Tomorrow we find all clear. For now, I have heard sleep is as good as food. We must try it.'

But in the morning, although the wind was less strong, it was still snowing. It snowed all that day, and all the next. They kept the paths from the tent clear, and by the evening of the third day the snow was packed higher than Olsen's head on either side. The tent itself was covered with snow. It had a fairly steep pitch, but Olsen wondered how long it would be before it collapsed under the growing weight.

As to the members of the party, the second day saw a time of savage irritability, and a number of explosions into anger. Stefan and Thorsen quarrelled furiously when Thorsen claimed that Stefan, moving about restlessly, had kicked him. There was trouble of a less precise kind between Thorsen and Jones, and at one point, after he had been singing tunelessly in Polish for some time, both Stefan and Nadya rounded on their father. Olsen himself felt irritation grow in him like lust, with the same drive towards dissipation in some grand orgasmic outburst; but he fought it and controlled it. That the others should so signally fail to do the same was cause for the irritation to rise again out of its damped ashes; he took refuge at last in the cold haven of contempt.

By evening they had grown calmer; during that night and the succeeding day, tension turned into apathy. There was less talk. Blind and helpless, they withdrew into their separate cocoons of memory and desire.

Throughout, Sheila showed little change. She ate practically nothing, but did not complain. There was a period when Jones talked wildly of going out on his own to find help for her, but the obvious impossibility of travelling more than ten yards without getting lost hardly needed pointing out. Sheila quietened him. She asked him to talk to her because it soothed her. He talked of their life together; but always of the future, Olsen noticed, not the past.

It was snowing on the fourth day, too, but the impetus seemed to have declined; the flakes were much smaller and came in gusts. In the early afternoon, the snowfall stopped. Except for Jones and Sheila, they went outside to stretch their legs. They had to break a way up through the drift to the surface.

Olsen and Mouritzen talked together, away from the others.

Mouritzen said: 'My legs feel weak. I had almost forgotten what it is like to walk – or to breathe fresh air.'

Olsen gestured towards the grey sky lying over the white world. 'It still does not look good,' he said.

'Do we break camp? Even if we only travel a kilometre, it would be something to do. We all need that.'

Olsen pointed at the frozen waters of the fjord. Snow lay thick on them, too, rounding and planing the angularities of the ice. Visibility was about a mile.

'That is our direction,' he said. 'Five kilometres will not see us on dry land again if we set out. The risk is too great.'

'So we stay here?'

'We have almost no food,' Olsen said. 'If the blizzard returns, we may have none. If we can find it, I think it is time to kill the bear.'

Mouritzen shook his head. 'The bear has gone. Did you expect it would stay, without food, for nearly four days? I saw Nadya searching for it. I think she was glad not to find it.'

Olsen gazed around at the unbroken surface of the snow, as though expecting to see the bear's head sticking out. His gaze travelled on to the fjord.

'Get the spears,' he said. 'We will go on a hunt. If we cannot have bear, maybe we will eat seal.'

He took all the men except Jones; Nadya, on her insistence, provided the replacement. They scrambled down through the snow to the fjord. The surface had been frozen completely by the blizzard; there was no sound or sight of running water anywhere.

After they had been ten minutes or so on the ice, Josef called:

'Hi, Captain! Maybe the seals have gone south for the winter? Maybe they are sitting on the beaches of the Mediterranean Sea?'

'Maybe,' Olsen said. 'Keep looking, all the same.'

Stefan said in a puzzled voice: 'What is this thing?'

He was looking at an opening in the snow. Just below there was a hole ringed with ice. Olsen came over and began to brush the snow away with his gauntlet. He revealed a flat-topped, hollow dome. It rose about six inches from the surface of the ice and was some two feet in diameter.

'They have not gone to Cannes after all,' Olsen said. 'This is a breathing hole. The seal keeps this open all winter, breaking the ice as he comes up for air.'

'So we wait for him,' Josef said, 'and stick him with the spear when he comes up?'

'There will be several holes round here,' Olsen said. 'If we search we will find them. Then one of us stands at each of the holes round about, stamping, making noises; and one stands quietly at the middle hole, with a spear. A score of years ago I was told of this, at Scoresby, by an Eskimo. I think he knew his business. I bought a pair of seal-skin trousers from him, and they are still good.'

It took them half an hour to locate another four holes. Olsen gave Josef the spear and the central position. The others stood by their holes and made as much noise as they could by stamping and kicking the ice.

It was an hour before they abandoned the task as hopeless. Dusk was deepening; it would soon be night.

Josef said: 'I was right at the start. They are sitting on the beaches, taking buns from the Princess of Monaco.'

'They had been there,' Olsen said, 'today. Otherwise the domes would have frozen over.'

'They are not here now,' Mouritzen said.

With barely restrained anger, Olsen said: 'It was worth trying. Did you have a better suggestion?'

Mouritzen said: 'Even an Olsen must fail sometimes. You are offended too easily, Erik.'

They plodded in silence back to the tent. It began snowing when they were half-way there – powder-fine, drifting snow. It was less palpable than the earlier snow, and more penetrating. It seemed to sift right through their clothes to lie, cold and wet and uncomfortable, against the skin. They struggled back into the tent and took their outer garments off, feeling miserable and depressed. Olsen turned on his side away from the others and lay in silence. Even at supper time, his speech was curt and monosyllabic. When Josef spoke to him, he ignored him.

Chapter Twelve

All night and all the next day the snow drifted down. During the day, in addition to maintaining the paths, they cleared most of the snow off the tent itself, packing it high on either side so that the tent lay between tall, white walls. It gave their position a gloomy air of permanence which was in grim contrast with their dwindling supplies of food. The meat and chocolate had long been eaten. They were living chiefly on biscuits and oats, and the store of these was almost gone. They also cut steps leading up to the top surface of the snow.

In the early morning of the following day, Olsen went outside to inspect. The snow was still coming down, and he thought the wind was higher again. There was no prospect of improvement, and unless some improvement did come soon their position was likely to be desperate. The weather would clear in time, but by then few or none of them might be strong enough to continue the trek towards Scoresby.

Yet there was nothing else to do but wait. Olsen crawled back into the tent. 'Not yet,' he said, when someone put the usual question, 'maybe it will clear later.' He made little attempt to put conviction into his voice; for all of them, hope had become a nebulous, far-off thing.

It was close on ten when Stefan needed to go out; he had to climb over his father and Olsen to get to the nearest exit point. When he opened up the flap, he said: 'It is more light.' He put his head outside and then pulled it in again.

'The snow has stopped!'

The others wasted no time in getting their boots on and following him. Olsen saw Stefan's figure on the upper level, outlined against a sky that was grey-blue and powdered with stars. He climbed the steps to join him.

The view was impressive, and heartening. In the south-east, the last of the clouds lay above the peaks of the Stauning Alps, their undersides flushed salmon red from the sun that had not yet risen. The rest of the sky was clear, with a pale full moon and stars that faded and began to flicker towards extinction as the light slowly advanced. To the south, across the mouth of the fjord, there were hills with the dawn glow over them. The air was very clear and, despite the wind that still howled over the snowy crest behind them, there was a feeling of stillness everywhere.

Mouritzen, joining Olsen, said:

'That looks good.'

'Three days ago it would have looked better.' Mouritzen glanced at him. 'It is easier to lie still and starve,' Olsen said, 'than to march and starve.'

Josef, standing some yards from them, called:

'Captain, you have the glasses? What is that – across the ice, at the foot of the hills?' Olsen put up his binoculars and swung them in a small arc in the direction of Josef's pointing. Josef said: 'I am silly, maybe, yet it looks like smoke.'

Olsen took the glasses away. His face was controlled apart from a twitching at the corner of his mouth.

'Smoke,' he said. The word was non-committal; it could have indicated a despairing and contemptuous denial. Then he gave the glasses to Mouritzen. 'The most easterly point of land,' he said. 'By the first dip.'

The scene came in focus. Folds and slopes of snow, all white, blank, and there, at one point, a smudge of brown that curled against it, and thinned out and was lost.

Mouritzen said foolishly: 'It is smoke. Then someone has lit a fire there?'

'A hunting hut,' Olsen said. 'They are placed at intervals along the trail. Someone – a scout or a trapper – has been snowed up there, as we have been.'

'And by the time we can reach it, he is likely to be gone. Should we send up a flare?'

Olsen shook his head. 'We are over thirty kilometres away. And there are only two flares left.'

'Then if we reach the hut,' Mouritzen said slowly, 'we only profit by having better shelter than the tent.'

'The huts have stores of food,' Olsen said, 'and fuel. Some have wireless transmitters.' He studied the distant view through the field-glasses again, as though reluctant to believe what he had seen. He was smiling when he turned back to Mouritzen. 'Our luck turns with the weather.'

'Over thirty kilometres – we cannot do that in one day.'

'With the sledge, not even twenty – we must go slowly with the sick woman. But a couple, travelling light, can reach the hut by nightfall. If there is a transmitter, they can call Scoresby for help – perhaps get a nurse for Mrs Jones. In any case they can bring food back to us along the trail – if we walk today we will be in poor shape tomorrow.'

'A couple? Who?'

'You and Thorsen.'

'I would rather stay with the main party.'

'We will look after Mary and Annabel. The child is hungry. Bring food to her.'

Preparations for departure were undertaken in a cheerful mood, although most of them were surprised at the physical weakness revealed by their exertions. Packing, as a result of this, took longer than had been expected. Olsen said:

'It is better for you two to start at once. You will not have much time to spare in reaching the hut.'

Thorsen had roped round the typewriter case. He put it on the sledge. He grinned at Jones, who was standing near him. In a low voice, he said:

'Look after our typewriter, Mr Jones. It would be a pity to lose it now.'

There was a tremor in the snow, a few yards from the spot where the sledge stood; it was not strong, but they all felt it.

'What is that?' Stefan asked uneasily.

The tremor was repeated, more positively. The snow heaved volcanically, and split. A furry brown head lifted, and a large brown body unwound after it. Nadya ran across, slipping and plunging in the loose snow.

'Katerina! So you are a faithful bear still – you found another bed but you did not go far.' She put her arms round the bear's neck. 'You do not desert me.'

Olsen eyed the bear speculatively while the others crowded round. Nadya caught his eye. She hesitated for a moment and then went to him.

'We will also go on the advance party, Katerina and I.'

Olsen said: 'They cannot be delayed.'

'We will not delay them,' Nadya said. 'We are ready now. She does not have her harness to put on since we have stolen her rations. There may be food for her at the hut. And you will not be tempted to go bear-hunting if you are hungry tonight.'

'Two are enough in the advance party,' Olsen said. 'We need you to help with the sledge.'

'Then let Niels or Jorgen stay behind. We are going.'

Olsen shrugged. 'As you please.'

'Shall I stay?' Mouritzen asked.

'No, you go. You can leave Jorgen, if you want to.'

Mouritzen glanced from Nadya to Mary. 'I need Jorgen.'

Nadya said: 'Then we go à trois – à quatre, with Katerina. That makes two couples.' She grinned. 'Katerina and I will chaperone each other.'

They carried no food and no blankets. Reaching the hut that day was vitally essential; it was only when they were well out on the ice that it occurred to Mouritzen that they had only Olsen's word for it that the plume of smoke necessarily implied a cabin. It might come from a fire laid in the open. If there were trappers who had been snowed up like them, they also might have been in a tent. When they reached the spot there might be nothing but cold ashes and a depression in the snow.

Whether his doubts were reasonable or not, there was no point in dwelling on them. They were committed to the enterprise, and it had to be carried through with the minimum of delay. He set a fast pace. He had thought he might have to chivvy Nadya on or, in extremity, to abandon her to be picked up by the main party, but she kept up with him cheerfully and, it seemed, almost effortlessly. It was Thorsen who had to be bullied and who, even so, tended to fall behind. The bear followed Nadya, keeping three or four paces behind her, as though on a lead.

They walked into the sunrise. The wind dropped, and soon they were quite hot from their exertions. The sun itself, even when fully clear of the horizon, gave little warmth. It barely cleared the hills and almost immediately began to sink back below them.

Hunger was something that came in waves: on the crests it was a gnawing pain, in the troughs no more than a dull, nauseous ache. They rested for a time, about one o'clock in the afternoon, and Nadya chewed snow. The ice was quite flat there, and not far away there were signs of the domed seal-holes. Once Mouritzen saw a small jet of water spurt up, presumably as a seal came up to breathe. He was tempted to try hunting them again; the spears had been left behind but he and Thorsen both had knives. Or he could stun it, perhaps, with a shot from the flare-pistol – Olsen had given it to him so that he could signal when they reached the hut.

Hunger sank back into nausea, and he realized the absurdity of his speculations. He stood up.

'It is time to move on.'

Thorsen objected, but Nadya moved off even before he did. They were now in the middle of the fjord estuary. There had been no further sign of smoke from the headland towards which they were moving. The contours, too, seemed different as they got nearer. It was important that they should get into that region while there was still a reasonable light.

They got clear of the ice before three. In front of them the ground stretched up in quite a steep slope towards the point where, as well as Mouritzen could judge, they had seen smoke in the morning. Thorsen objected again when they started up that way.

'We should go round,' he said. 'The smoke was coming over from behind the hill. Up there the hill curves round to the south. That will be the way the trail goes.'

'We will go straight,' Mouritzen said. 'If we turn away, we may get lost.'

Thorsen gasped. 'We are wasting what little strength we have left.'

'You waste more by talking.'

But as they forced their way upwards, Mouritzen began to think that Thorsen's view might have been the right one. A sledging trail would keep to the lowest possible level, and the hut, if there were a hut, must be visible from it. His parenthetic doubt clutched at him again, with a surer, more vicious grip. They were finding themselves stumbling into drifts of loose snow, from which extrication was difficult and exhausting; and the light was fading.

Nadya showed the least sign of flagging. Gradually she was taking the lead. Ten or twelve paces ahead of the others, she paused and called to them mockingly to come on.

She set off again before they were up to her. In front, Mouritzen saw, there was a slight depression in the surface of the snow. When he first saw her legs sink into it he thought she was in another drift. Then, with a soft echoing roar, several square yards of the surface collapsed. A cloud of fine snow lifted and hung briefly in the air. There was no sign of Nadya.

Mouritzen called to Thorsen, and made his way forward, warily. He stopped at the edge of the crevasse, and looked down. Where the snow had slipped the brown face of the frozen earth was exposed. There was a steep slope down to a ledge, about twenty feet below. Just below the ledge, Nadya was lying in snow.

'Nadya!' he called. 'Are you all right?'

'Yes.' Her voice echoed up from the cleft. 'Only shaken a little.'

'If you can reach the ledge,' he said, 'I think it is possible to climb up the slope.'

She said: 'I have tried. It is too high, and when I stretch up, this snow goes down. See.'

Her hand reached up, and clawed at the side.

'It went more,' Nadya said.

The movement had been imperceptible from above, but

158

Mouritzen now saw something which, since his gaze had been concentrated on Nadya, he had not seen earlier: not many feet from her there was a gap in the snow, and below the gap a drop of ungaugeable depth. She lay on a bridge of snow, perilously spanning a crevasse much deeper than either of them had thought. A sudden movement, a transfer of weight from one point to another, might well send the whole lot cascading down.

He called urgently: 'Do not move! Lie still – quite still.'

Katerina was padding up and down beside the crevasse, aimless and bewildered. The vibration, he realized, could start the snow moving. He shooed at the bear to make her go away but she paid no attention to him. She looked down in a puzzled fashion to where Nadya lay. When she started padding back along the edge Mouritzen, in desperation, unhooked the flare pistol and fired it past her. The rocket streaked over the snow and Katerina, with a howl of fear, fled from it.

Thorsen had come up. Mouritzen said to him:

'Move gently. There is nothing under her but a few feet of snow wedged between the sides of the crevasse.'

'So?' Thorsen gazed down. 'She is unlucky, our Nadya.'

'If we had a rope ... The only other thing is for us to get down to that ledge. I think we can get a hand to her from there. But we will have to go carefully. Some of those boulders look as though they might be loose.'

Thorsen continued to stare into the crevasse. Nadya called up:

'It is still sinking.'

'We must lose no time,' Mouritzen said. 'I will go first. You come after me, by the same route.'

He eased himself backwards over the edge and felt for footholds as he made his way down. The slope was steeper than he had expected and twice he had to stop and change direction. The second time, he called to Thorsen:

'You can start coming now.'

Thorsen stood there, unmoving. He did not reply. Perhaps he was scared of heights, Mouritzen thought. It might be possible to get Nadya and pull her clear without him, anyway.

The ledge was about three feet wide and had an irregular downward slope. Mouritzen knelt and tried to reach down to Nadya, but there were several inches between their stretching fingers. He would have to lie on the ledge and reach down; but for that he would need Thorsen with him as an anchor.

He called, sharply, urgently: 'Jorgen! I need you down here. You will not find it difficult.'

Thorsen said: 'It is strange how one finds a pleasure by accident.'

'For God's sake! What are you talking about? I'm telling you to come down.'

'I want to talk to Nadya,' Thorsen said, 'not you. But you can listen, if you like. I am not ashamed any longer.'

'What are you not ashamed of?' Mouritzen felt a cold weight of concern on his mind, but he did not want to look closely at it. 'Come down now.'

'In Dieppe,' Thorsen said, 'you pulled my hair, and the tears came to my eyes, as though I were a baby, and ran down my cheeks. On the *Kreya*, you held me down and slapped me and poured whisky into my mouth and all over my clothes. I think maybe you are sorry now, little Nadya.'

Mouritzen said: 'It is no time to talk like this, Jorgen. It is dangerous, I tell you. Help first, and make complaints afterwards.'

'Nadya,' Thorsen said, 'say you are sorry – beg for your life.'

Nadya said: 'You're mad.'

'Some of these stones are loose,' Thorsen said. 'Niels was right about that. This one.' A boulder, a couple of feet across, jutted out from the edge of the cleft; Thorsen put his foot on it and rocked it. 'I can kick you into Hell, little Nadya, and not even hurt my foot.'

Mouritzen whispered to Nadya: 'Yes, he is mad. And there is no shame in pandering to a maniac. Say you are sorry. Quickly.'

There was a moment's pause. Then Nadya said in a clear, unstrained voice:

'I am sorry, Jorgen. I was wrong to act as I did.'

'Better,' Thorsen said. 'And if I help you, you will behave differently? You will kiss me nicely and offer me your body?'

'Yes,' Nadya said, 'I will do that. Come down and help.'

Thorsen laughed. 'I am not coming down!'

Getting her on to the ledge, Mouritzen thought, would relieve the immediate peril; after that, they would have to see what could be done. He had put the remaining flare into the pistol while Thorsen was talking: it might be necessary to use it. He lay flat along the ledge, excruciatingly aware of the outward slope which inclined his body towards the drop below, and stretched down his right hand. He felt Nadya grip his wrist, as Thorsen spoke again.

'I do not want your body. This is what I want. Do not try to pull her up yet, Niels, or my foot will jerk against this stone. You think I am a fool, but you are wrong. I always work out consequences before I do things. Once you are up here with me, what is the saying sorry worth? The same as the promise – nothing!'

Mouritzen felt the cold of the frozen earth against his face. He dared not move.

'I was always bullied,' Thorsen said. 'At home, at school – all my life. Always there were Nadyas, the strong ones, the clever ones, who tormented me and laughed at me. I was ashamed to admit this before, but I am not ashamed now. Because this is worth all of it – this makes up for everything.'

If he could reach the flare pistol with his free hand, Mouritzen thought . . . But it was almost impossible to aim it, prone as he was. It was short range, but from this position, with his left hand . . . He craned his head, racking the muscles of his neck, to look up at Thorsen. He stood at the top of the slope, his legs braced apart.

'If there was any human pity in you,' Thorsen said, 'you would feel sorry for me. But in your kind there is not pity, and that is why you deserve none. You also, Mouritzen – the big man, the man who can get into any bed he chooses. How do you like the bed you have now? How . . .'

He broke off and Mouritzen saw him whirl round to look behind him. He shouted something indistinguishable. He moved back, as though to avoid a blow, and his foot scattered snow into the crevasse. He cried out again, this time for help, in Danish. Mouritzen thought he would recover himself, but then his body was black against the dark blue sky as he hurtled down. Mouritzen closed his eyes and tightened his hold on Nadya. He heard her cry something also, but what she said was swallowed up in the sound of a mass of snow shifting, falling.

He hung on as the echoes died away, conscious only of the rough ledge beneath him and the extra weight on his arm. But it could not be Nadya's full weight. He said:

'Nadya! How is it with you?'

She said: 'I have a toe hold. If you stick tight, I think I can get up.'

The weight increased. He felt his body pulling sideways towards the cleft, and forced himself downwards, anchoring himself with all his strength. There was a moment's almost unendurable strain and she scrambled up over him. She helped to pull him upright. They sat side by side on the ledge, panting.

'I don't know how you did that,' Mouritzen said.

'I work the trapeze, remember,' She rubbed her shoulder. 'He hit me as he fell.'

Mouritzen looked over the edge. The mass of snow had fallen, and he could see they were on an overhang. The drop below them was fifty of sixty feet, with rocks at the bottom. It was just possible to see a figure splayed out on the rocks, to see that it did not move and, from the disposition of the limbs, was unlikely to move again.

'Something frightened him,' Mouritzen said. 'What?'

'Maybe Katerina?'

'He was not frightened of Katerina.'

'Whatever it was, we must get up there. You first. I will catch you if you fall.'

It was not an easy climb. Mouritzen, tired and hungry, his muscles aching from the recent experience, found it taxed him to the limit. Nadya came up after him quite easily. She stood up, looking around.

'What is it?'

'Katerina. You frightened her away.' She cupped her hands round her mouth and called: 'Katerina!'

'It is more important to find the hut,' Mouritzen said. 'Katerina can wait till morning. We do not know how this rift lies under the show. So I think we go downwards and to the left. Down across that ridge.'

Beyond the ridge the ground dropped sharply; to the left there was the surface of the fjord which they had crossed earlier. Nadya was looking to the right. She cried happily:

'There she is, my true one, my faithful bear. Katerina!'

Katerina's large brown shape was conspicuous, even in the dusk, against the snow: she was shambling unhurriedly towards them. Mouritzen looked back towards the fjord. Something was moving in that direction also – something still larger, but less easily seen, white against white. He knew now what had come up behind Thorsen and scared him into falling.

'I go to meet her,' Nadya said, 'My Katerina.'

Mouritzen remembered something he had once read some-where: that the polar bear never normally sees an animal that does not run from him, and that, for this reason, a man who stands his ground, or advances towards the bear, may scare it into retreat. The one thing deadly is to seem to run.

He said to Nadya: 'Stand still. Don't move!'

She was already running. The two bears were closing to meet each other, and Nadya was between them. The white bear began to lope forward at a faster pace; for all its great bulk and height, overshadowing Mouritzen's own, it travelled easily, lightly. Mouritzen lifted the flare pistol. When the bear was level with him and about ten yards away, he fired.

The bear checked, and he thought he had hit it. It roared, with shock or pain or anger, and then went on. Nadya had got to Katerina. She stood watching, in apparent fascination, as the polar bear came towards them. When it was a few paces away, Katerina moved forward. The roaring had stopped. The two animals closed on each other in silence.

This was the time to get away. Mouritzen called to Nadya:

'This way! We will escape while they are fighting.'

But instead of coming towards him, she threw herself against the flank of the polar bear, her hands grappling for its neck.

'You silly bitch!' Mouritzen said.

He pulled his knife free as he ran. Katerina had gone down under the white bear; Nadya, as well as he could see, had her arms round its neck trying to pull it off. A stretch of white, furry back was exposed. Mouritzen threw himself at it, stabbing wildly.

He felt the bear roll back against him and wrenched the knife free to plunge it in again. His actions were unplanned, directed only by random instinct. He remembered a time at school when he had tackled a bully in much this fashion, though without a knife. The bully had lived to bully again, and Mouritzen's nose had never been the same.

This time he was more fortunate. He stabbed a third time, as wildly, and felt the large, furry body shudder and grow limp. Mouritzen lay with the snow stinging his face, savouring the fact that he was still alive. After a moment, he said:

'Nadya, help me to pull it off.'

His legs were trapped underneath; she helped to lift the bear's body slightly and he heaved himself free. He saw that she was crying, that tears were pouring down her cheeks.

'We are all right now,' Mouritzen said.

'Katerina,' she said.

Mouritzen stood up. On the other side of the polar bear, Katerina was lying, half on her back and half on her side. Her head was thrown back and her throat torn and bloody. Blood stained the snow between the two bears, the streams joining and mingling.

'She was a good bear,' Mouritzen said.

Nadya knelt down beside the dead animal. She put her face to Katerina's and kissed the nose that was already cold. After she had knelt there a few moments, she stood up.

'We must find the hut,' she said. 'It is getting late.'

They went on in silence. Mouritzen himself was in poor shape – the dead weight of tiredness had fallen back on him and each successive moment cost him greater effort – and Nadya was now in as bad a state. They staggered down the slope, at times reeling against each other, slipping and sliding in the snow. Mouritzen fell once – Nadya a number of times. He had to help her up, to urge her to make an effort. Overhead the stars were coming out. If they did not find food and shelter soon they would have no hope of surviving the night.

Nadya slipped and went down again. He tried to lift her, but he could not. She murmured something about resting and he said something equally incoherent about the importance of moving on. It was a futile argument: the conclusive point was Nadya's inability to get up, and his to make her. In the end he slumped beside her on the snow. A little rest, he thought – a few minutes, a night, eternity . . .

He looked up at the stars and then along the slope down which they had come. A world with too much white in it. All white. Except the darker patch up there. They must have come past it, not seeing it, their eyes fixed on their stumbling feet. Dark, upright, regular against Nature's lavish curves . . .

'The hut!' he said. 'Back there. We almost missed it.'

It was strange how, with an accession of hope and purpose, strength flooded back into exhausted limbs. The door of the hut had a heavy, old-fashioned fastener, such as Mouritzen had not seen since childhood in the country. There was a porch, with pegs for clothes and a rack for boots and skis, leading into the one main room. Doors at either end only opened on a pantry and the latrine. The room was snug, with small windows and a pot-bellied iron stove in the centre. It was sparsely furnished: there were two truckle beds, with half a dozen blankets stacked on each, a large cooking pot, a zinc bath for melting snow, and a picture calendar on the wall. The picture was of Copenhagen's little mermaid.

The stove had been made ready for lighting, and there was a box of matches on top of it. Mouritzen struck one, and watched paper flare into orange flame. He lit the hanging paraffin lamp also, then he followed Nadya to the pantry.

Cans were stacked in neat rows; sacks, and frozen hunks of meat, hung from hooks in the ceiling.

'Supper,' Mouritzen said. 'Tonight we will eat, Nadya – really eat, not nibble a biscuit or chew dry oats. Tonight we will have a banquet.'

'And I will be your servant,' she said, 'just tonight. Go and rest. I will prepare the food.'

Mouritzen bent and picked up a bottle.

'We will live a king and queen,' he said. 'Schnapps! No liqueur glasses? Then we must drink from the bottle.'

'There are a couple of enamel mugs.' Nadya pointed. 'On the rack. With the tin plates, and the knives and forks.'

'Two knives, three forks,' Mouritzen said, 'and five spoons! Here is culture. And a mug for you and a mug for me.'

Warningly, Nadya said: 'We have had nothing to eat for eight hours, and little then. It is better to keep the Schnapps until later.'

'But a little,' Mouritzen said, '– one small measure. We drink to being alive. Skol!'

When he went back to the stove, it was well alight; flames roared noisily up the metal chimney. Mouritzen went outside, filled the bath with snow, and brought it back to rest on the stove's flat top. The hut, as he came back into it, felt already warm. It had, of course, been lived in during the blizzard; the stove would only have been out for a few hours. He drew one of the beds up nearer to the source of warmth and stretched out to take his ease. Almost at once he succumbed to drowsiness. Nadya came in and bustled about with the cooking. Mouritzen half opened his eyes, and closed them again.

She had to shake him to wake him up.

'Supper is ready,' she said, 'your Majesty. Stew. I do not know what the meat it.'

Mouritzen sat upright. 'It does not matter what kind of meat it is,' he said. 'I can eat anything tonight.'

It was inclined to be tough, and had a distinctly fishy flavour: Mouritzen guessed it was seal meat. But it was rich and nourishing, and there was plenty of it. Afterwards Nadya produced a can of pineapple and Mouritzen laced the syrup with *akvavit*. The banquet closed with coffee and more drinks. They were both happy and replete, and a little bit drunk. The stove was beginning to flow a cherry red. Nadya had put the bath, still half full of water, back on top of if; steam was beginning to rise from it.

'Help me to lift this off,' Nadya said. 'Be careful. The handles are very hot.'

'Washing the dishes can wait till morning.'

'This is a different washing. It is more than a week since my body was clean, and I found soap out there in the pantry.' He helped her to put the bath down beside the stove. She looked at him. Her voice matter-of-fact, she said: 'There is only one room and we have no screen. So while I wash myself you must lie down and look the other way. Is it agreed?'

Anticipation, excitement, stirred like a feather on his nerve-ends.

'Agreed,' he said.

He did not turn round until the splash and trickle of water told him that she was washing. He rolled over slowly, careful to make no noise. Nadya was kneeling in the bath, rubbing her wet limbs with a piece of yellow soap. The light from the paraffin lamp and the glow of the stove threw gleams of rose and gold on her glistening flesh. Her body, when she reached up to soap her back, was a splendid arc, bearing the lesser but equally magnificent arcs of her breasts.

He said: 'You are lovelier than ever, Nadya.'

She turned to look at him, untroubled and unashamed.

'It was agreed that you do not look.'

'Did you think I would keep my word?'

She moved her head slowly. 'No.'

Mouritzen got up and walked towards her. He put his hands on her neck, beneath her ears, and looked down at her.

'In all the wide world,' he said, 'wherever a man looks at a woman, there is none who looks at one more beautiful than you.'

'Only looks?' she asked.

His hands reached farther down, clutched the wet, slippery skin. He knelt down beside the bath and kissed her.

'You are washed,' he said. 'Come, I will dry you.'

Looking at him, she shook her head. 'I have only started washing and I will not hurry it. And there is no towel: I must sit close by the stove and let the heat dry me.'

'Then I will watch you, with what patience I can.'

'No, you must not watch. I will tell you what you must do. You must drink some more Schnapps and go back to bed and rest quietly until I come – and this time you must not look round. Those are my conditions.'

'And you will come to me then?'

She nodded. 'I promise.'

Mouritzen drank the Schnapps and lay once more on the bed, his head looking away from the stove and the light. He pulled a couple of blankets roughly over him. The bed would not have seemed comfortable right after the *Kreya* but now it represented luxury and ease – there was a three-part biscuit mattress, and wire springs. He lay in a haze of fullness and intoxication, pleasantly, not urgently expectant.

He awoke to find Nadya pulling the blankets up over him. He tried to sit up and she pressed him down.

He said, with disappointment: 'You have put all your clothes on.'

Nadya smiled. 'I left my pyjamas on the *Kreya*. Lie still. I will tuck you in.'

'I don't want you to tuck me in.'

'What you want we are both too tired to have.'

'I'm not too tired.'

'Then I am. Lie still. Go back to sleep.'

'No.'

'You will, because I say you will.' She pulled another blanket over him and tucked it deftly underneath. Suddenly Mouritzen felt like a child being put to bed by his mother: a child who has been mildly naughty but knows he is forgiven. It would be futile to demand any more; better to resign himself to the simple warmth and comfort of the bed. And he was tired, so very tired.

Nadya stayed for a moment, looking at him. She smiled curiously.

'You belong to Mary,' she said. 'I have given you back to her. But I do not think she will thank me.'

Chapter Thirteen

The rear party had no easy time of it. Although she made every effort to conceal it, Sheila was clearly in pain, and made worse by every jolt of the sledge. They camped for the night on the ice, about half-way across the fjord, and shared out the meagre rations. They had watched for the flare in the southern sky – the sign that the advance party had reached the hut – but it had not come. They had no assurance of reaching refuge even by the following evening, and by then there would not be as much as a biscuit left for them to eat. Perhaps, Olsen thought, they could go after the seals again; but there was no reason to expect better luck. None of them was skilled, either in hunting or the use of weapons, and none had much strength left. If they did not find the hut tomorrow, they were finished. He wondered what had happened to Mouritzen and the others – probably the same that must soon happen to them. He shrugged. If one died, one died, and there were worse places to die than in this cold, white, empty world.

But while an ember of hope remained, he would not resign himself to death. The next morning he had them up and breaking camp while the stars were still large in a near-black sky. They pushed on towards the darkness out of which, for a short time, the sun would rise. Slowly it lightened in front of them.

It was Mary who first glimpsed the figure approaching. She called out gladly:

'Look! It must be them.'

'Two,' Olsen said, 'not three. But I think you are right.'

One of the figures waved. The sun was half risen and the arm semaphored for an instant against its disc.

Mary said: 'I know it's Niels.'

Mama Simanyi said: 'And that is Nadya – the red hood, see.'

As they approached, Mary ran forward. Mouritzen embraced her. They stood locked together; Nadya came forward to the sledge and threw down the sack she had carried over her shoulder.

'We took turns to carry it,' she said. 'Biscuits, cans of meat, some chocolate. This is for a snack, unless you are not hungry?'

Olsen said: 'We are not hungry, and it is not yet lunch time, but we accept because it would be impolite to say no. In fact, we will eat at once.'

When Mouritzen came back with Mary, Nadya and Mama Simanyi were already sharing out the food. Mouritzen took Annabel from Josef and tossed her up in the air.

'Then you found the hut?' Olsen said to him. 'How far is it?'

'Eight kilometres, I guess.'

'We looked for the flares last night, but saw nothing.'

Mouritzen tossed him the empty pistol. 'We used them in bear-fighting.'

'Bear-fighting?' Olsen looked round, conscious of an absence. 'Katerina?'

'And another.'

'Is there wireless at the hut?' Mouritzen made a gesture of negation. 'And Jorgen? Did you leave him there?'

Mouritzen said slowly: 'Jorgen is dead.'

'How?'

Mouritzen told them the story. They ate the biscuits, covered with corned beef, while they listened. With the exception of a commentary of sighs and cluckings by Mama Simanyi, no one said anything.

'So we stumbled on the hut,' Mouritzen finished. 'We were lucky there. And we found a stove ready to light, food, bed, blankets. And Schnapps! But I do not want to run things so close another time.'

Mary said: 'In the hut – there were only the two of you then?'

There was reluctance in her voice, but also a deep-seated need. He looked at her. He tried to disguise his guilt and embarrassment; he knew he was not succeeding.

'Yes. That was lucky also. There are two beds.'

'Are there?'

'You will see that.'

He had over-explained. Reading her face he saw that she thought him guilty; and guilty in act as well as intent. Her features had fallen too easily into lines of disappointment and mistrust: the lines were not new, and they made her ugly. He was glad that Annabel had wandered out of immediate earshot and was climbing an ice hillock.

Nadya spoke before Mouritzen could think of any protestation that would not protest too much. She said to her mother:

'It was cosy in the hut, with the stove; so warm that I had a bath. There is only a small tin bath, but it was big enough to bath myself in. I found soap. Now I feel clean at last.'

'Do you call it clean?' Mary said. 'And is it clean to do that sort of thing with a man you know is to be married to another woman? It would take a big bath to clean the like of you.'

Nadya moved forward until she was quite close to Mary. She was smiling slightly. She said softly:

'Are you not grateful? I brought you food. And I brought you back your man.'

'You can keep him. I don't want him, soiled from you.'

'You suspect too much,' Nadya said, 'too quickly. It will not be a good marriage if you think he is in bed with another woman each time you turn your back.'

'Take him! Marry him yourself. That's what you want, isn't it?'

Nadya was silent for a moment. She said:

'He is a good man. He saved my life twice. He was in great danger. He deserves a woman who will be glad of him and who will still love him, even if he sleeps with me when he is tired and happy to be still alive, and a little drunk. But he did not sleep with me. We did not make love together. He is not soiled from me.'

'You're a good liar,' Mary said bitterly, 'but he's not. He leaves you to answer, and there is guilt in his face. Take him. You are two of a kind.'

Nadya was preparing for a new rejoinder, but Olsen spoke first.

'That's enough,' he said. His voice was not loud, but cold and decisive. He turned to Mary. 'One half-hour ago I was thinking we will all die tonight – of cold, of hunger. Now death stands off a little. But a little only.' His arm made a sweep across the frozen waste of ice. 'There is no room here for jealousies, infidelities. Our purpose is to survive and to reach safety. When we are at Scoresby there is time for your quarrels and kisses. Not before. Understood?'

Mary said: 'I'm sorry.'

Olsen continued to look at her for a moment.

'So,' he said. He turned to the others. 'The meal is over. We march.'

They reached the hut soon after half past three, with the shadows thickening over the snow. Mouritzen and Nadya had left the fire burning in the stove; the atmosphere was warm and welcoming. After so long a time in which there had been no warmth in the world except the warmth of their bodies huddled together, they knelt around the glowing metal and stretched their hands forward to it like worshippers. Mama Simanyi bustled around, fixing the supper.

Sheila had been put on one of the beds. Jones sat beside her. He said:

'Is that better?'

She nodded. 'I'd forgotten there could be such comfort.'

'Tonight you must eat something. It will be hot.' He looked at her anxiously. 'You will eat something, won't you?'

'I'll try.'

'More than try.' He pressed her hand. 'Everything's going to be all right now.' He leaned forward. 'I'll tell you something,' he said softly. 'Thorsen guessed about us – and he found the money.'

She looked at him. 'I wondered.'

'He was going to blackmail us. He talked of taking half, or more.'

She nodded, but only slightly, as though the movement taxed her strength. 'I see.'

'But he's dead, and we're safe. Now we're going to be all right.'

'Yes,' she said. 'We're going to be all right.' Her hand moved beneath his. 'I do love you.'

'Just eat your supper,' he said, 'and get well and strong.'

But when the food came, she only ate a couple of mouthfuls. Despite his coaxing, she could eat no more.

She said: 'It's rest I want most. I haven't been able to rest properly before. Perhaps in the morning I'll be hungry.'

The others finished their food, and the Schnapps bottle went round.

'A toast,' Josef said, 'to Captain Olsen, who has led his crew across the frozen seas.'

Olsen shook his head. 'Too early,' he said. 'We are not yet in harbour. I give you a better toast: to the men who built this cabin here, and put in it food and refreshment for the traveller.'

'I'll drink to that,' Josef said. He paused. 'Who pays for this?'

Olsen shrugged. 'The Government, the company – does it matter? Maybe they will send us a bill. And if they do, maybe we will pay it.'

Mama Simanyi said to Mary: 'The little one is tired. A full belly after so long makes her sleepy. There is still a bed free. You and she must have it. If we push it against the wall, you can both sleep there.'

'You have it,' Mary said. 'We'll be all right on the floor.'

'No, no, you must have the bed! We insist.'

Mary said: 'But we don't want it.' Her voice had an edge and she looked at the bed with loathing. 'I would rather sleep on the floor.'

Mama Simanyi read the look. 'You do not speak just for yourself. There is Annabel.'

'She will be better on the floor, too.'

Mama Simanyi came closer to Mary. She took her wrists in her hands, lifted them up and together, and shook her. The shaking was unobtrusive but thorough. She said:

171

'Pride is good, but not too much. And a woman who deprives her child for the sake of her pride is – is wicked. The little Annabel has had ten nights sleeping out on ice. She needs comfort. If she is my child, I will put her to sleep on a whore's bed if there is no other.'

Mary turned her face away, Mama Simanyi drew her closer, but gently this time. She said:

'You love the child. I know you would not hurt her. Come, we put her to bed together. And if you like it better, you lie on the floor beside her.'

Mary drew a sobbing breath against her. She said:

'I wish I could help it. I don't want to... It's just...'

'I know,' Mama Simanyi said. 'Now let it rest. You will let me help you put Annabel to bed?'

Mary blinked her eyes. She nodded.

'Yes, please.'

'Come, my little one,' Mama Simanyi said. 'Innocence can sleep any place; but a soft bed is best.'

In the morning, after breakfast, the women were clearing things up. Josef put on his outer clothes and warmed his boots by the stove.

'Get your boots, Stefan,' he said. 'We take a walk, eh?'

Olsen said: 'A walk? Where?'

'To find Katerina, and the polar bear. We will get two good skins.'

'By now,' Olsen said, 'they will have been torn to shreds. Even here there are plenty of scavengers.'

'We will see,' Josef said. 'Maybe there is something worth saving.'

Olsen shook his head. 'Anyway, there is no time. We set out at once. There is the sledge to pack.'

Josef looked round the hut. 'We are snug here,' he objected. 'We could stay a little time.'

'No. There is still a long way to Scoresby. We must get there while the weather stays good. We start at once, and travel fast.'

Jones said: 'You will have to leave us, Captain.'

Olsen went and stood by Sheila's bed. He said:

'You did not eat breakfast, Mrs Jones.'

'I wasn't hungry.'

He studied her face. 'You want to stay here – you and your husband?'

Her voice was faint. 'I can't go on. Really and truly. And you'll get on faster without me.'

He nodded. 'Yes. It is best, I think. You will rest here, and we will send help back from Scoresby. You will be stronger then, and there will be a proper sledge, with dogs to pull it. Meanwhile there is food here and fuel for the stove.'

Mary had been listening. She said:

'You will travel better without Annabel and me, too.' Her glance touched and left Mouritzen. 'We'll stay here as well.'

'No.'

'Why not?'

Olsen turned and walked away from the bed. Mary followed him. 'Why not?' she insisted.

In a low voice, he said: 'For one thing, not enough food.'

She said triumphantly: 'But it's the same whether we go with you or stay – we still have to eat.'

He made an impatient gesture. 'These huts – they are designed for one, maybe two travellers, caught by the blizzards. We are locusts by comparison. And when we go, we strip things more. It is five days to Scoresby – maybe more if the weather turns bad. Maybe a lot more. We will leave very little here.' He nodded towards Jones, sitting on the bed. 'Barely enough.'

'But if you leave enough for two, surely you can leave enough for me and the child as well – especially as you'll have two less mouths to feed on the way?'

'We will not leave enough for two,' Olsen said. He spoke slowly and quietly, his eyes on the couple at the other side of the room. 'Only enough for one. That is another thing, Mrs Jones is dying.'

In horror, Mary said: 'No!' Olsen looked at her. 'But we must do something.'

'There is nothing to do. Death is with her now.' He touched Mary's arm. 'Yes, there is one thing we can do. We can leave her to die alone with her husband. That is the way she wishes it, I think.'

Chapter Fourteen

Jones watched them set off, looking out of the little window in front of the hut. Mouritzen and Josef were hauling the sledge, with Annabel perched on top. They moved fast and to the south. In the dim morning light it was not long before they had disappeared from view. Then he turned back to Sheila.

She said: 'They've gone?'

'Yes.'

'You're not sorry – that you didn't go with them?'

'And leave you?'

'I would have been all right. I could manage for myself.' She looked anxious and tried to sit up. 'You could still go after them. You could . . .'

He pressed her back. She had not as much strength as a child. He said:

'Don't be silly. I'm better off here, aren't I? No trudging across the snow, taking turns to heave a sledge – all we have to do is sit quietly until they send help back to us.'

She half smiled. 'I suppose so.'

He said: 'And we're together – and we're alone. This is our real honeymoon.'

'It was supposed to be South America.'

'This is better. Don't you think so?'

There was pain in her face. 'I wish I could – give you pleasure.'

'That can wait. This is enough.'

She shook her head weakly. 'No. But thank you for making do with it.' She sighed. 'I feel like an old woman.'

'You look like a child.'

'An old woman,' she repeated. 'As though the story were all over. Did we have a good life together?'

'We will have.'

'Three children,' she said, '– the two girls, and then the boy. Ralph. I'd always wanted that name for a boy. I called him after my first sweetheart. You weren't jealous, were you? He had blonde hair and blue eyes and he was younger than I was. He was five and I was six.'

Jones said: 'No, I wasn't jealous.'

'I think you always liked the girls best. Madelaine, anyway. Fathers always do fall in love with their eldest daughters, don't they? And she was always so beautiful. Anyway, she's married now – they're both married. You have to put up with just me again.'

He smiled. 'Confidentially, I'm not too sorry. The last few years they were a bit of a strain – jazz and boy friends and clothes and gossip and giggles. I'm getting too old for that kind of life.'

'Well, there's still Ralph. But of course, he's away at the university most of the time. He's doing very well, isn't he? He must get the brilliance from you.'

'I was never brilliant. I wasn't even clever.'

'I think you were.'

'You always had too high an opinion of me.'

She said slowly: 'I always loved you. All that time, all those long years. Spring and summer, autumn and winter, again and again, and loving you more all the time. There's nothing better than that.'

'No more than I loved you.'

Her lips moved in a little smile. 'I'm not going to argue. I love you too much even to say I love you more than you love me.'

'We'll let it rest equal.'

She closed her eyes and, after a few minutes, he thought she had gone to sleep. He went to the window again and looked out. It was still dark, but less dark than it had been. There were the marks of the sledge and the footsteps leading away; but nothing else to show that life had even come to this barren white waste, or would ever come.

When he looked back, Sheila's eyes were open. As he went to her he saw the tears welling there and brimming on to her cheeks.

'Don't cry,' he said. 'There's nothing to cry for. Everything's going to be wonderful.'

'I know,' she said. She closed her eyes again. 'I know.'

They were encouraged by the fact that the going was better than at any previous time. They were on snow, with no more ridges and barriers of ice over which the sledge would have to be manhandled, and the snow itself was firm and close-packed. There was no longer the need to protect the sick woman from jolts; when they did come Annabel squealed with pleasure. And they themselves were refreshed by the food and warmth and comparative comfort of the previous night's stay.

The weather stayed fine as they tramped through the brief day and on into the new twilight. The wind was still from the north-west, and so a supporting one. At night they put up the tent in the protecting lee of a rocky rib of the hills. Once again they had to do without artificial warmth or the means to heat their food; but at least the food was sufficient to remove hunger.

Except for Mary, they formed a cheerful company. Mouritzen had made one or two attempts to come to terms, but she had unequivocally rejected them. Josef and Mama Simanyi had found themselves, although more gently, as firmly excluded. Mary was isolated from the others by her own choice. Apart from the necessities of communication, she spoke only to Annabel; but Annabel herself continued to chatter to all of them.

On the second day, with Olsen and Stefan pulling the sledge, Mouritzen watched Mary trudging along beside it. Annabel, from her perch on top, was chatting to Josef on the other side. Nadya and Mama Simanyi were bringing up the rear, about ten yards behind, and Nadya was laughing at something. Mary's loneliness was pathetic, and made more so by their situation: in this empty, frozen land, human relations were thrown into higher, starker relief, and her isolation stood out.

He called to her softly: 'Mary.'

There was no answer; she did not look round. He said more loudly:

'Mary!'

This time she did turn slightly to look at him. Her face was blank and unregarding, almost like the face of a blind person. Then, without saying anything, she turned from him again.

Mouritzen moved up to walk beside Olsen.

Olsen said: 'Then she will still not talk to you?'

He spoke in Danish, as they commonly did when alone together but not when, as now, there were foreigners within earshot. In the same language, Mouritzen said:

'She will not even look at me.'

'You are lucky,' Olsen said. 'You might not have found out her temperament until after you had married her.'

Mouritzen protested: 'She had justification.'

'Justification? For what? For slapping your face – maybe even for deciding you would be no good as a husband. Not for behaving like a sulky child.'

'Life has not been easy for her.'

'The little love-child?' Mouritzen looked quickly at him. 'Thorsen told me. The Customs Officer told him the passenger list was wrong, since it showed her as a married woman.'

'That was not what happened. He pried, as usual.'

Olsen nodded. 'That does not surprise me. He is no loss to Denmark. But to return to your little Irish woman – there have been plenty of women who have found themselves caught with a baby and no husband.'

'She is virtuous,' Mouritzen said. 'As you have said, she is also Irish.'

'The gloomy Dane and the Irish puritan. Maybe you are both well out of it.'

Mouritzen was silent for a moment. He said:

'You see people objectively, Erik.'

Olsen said, with satisfaction: 'Yes. There is no trick in it. It is not difficult to do so.'

'For you, perhaps not. You look through a glass wall.'

'I can touch also.'

'You do not touch what counts. And without that touching one does not know anything. To see a man or a woman objectively is to see nothing but an object.'

'You think there is more than that to see?'

'If one sees rightly.'

'That comes from being in love, Niels.' Olsen smiled. 'A state of fever and self-delusion.'

'You have never been in that state?'

'No, but I have observed it.'

'What kind of a doctor would you have made,' Mouritzen asked, 'having such contempt for your fellow-men?'

'A good one,' Olsen said. 'To cure a man, one does not need to love him. A surgeon does not operate on his own son.'

'Son? Or wife?'

'Or wife.'

Mouritzen laughed. 'You see motives in others, Erik, but you have them too. They go a long way back.'

In English, Olsen said: 'Halt! Time to change horses.' He stepped out of the harness and handed it to Mouritzen. 'You can pull and brood at the same time. Maybe it will help both.'

On the fourth day they travelled by the side of a frozen fjord, which broadened out until it was about a mile wide. Olsen found its appearance disconcerting; his recollection of the geography of the district was imprecise, but he had not expected to encounter such extensive ice again before reaching the Sound, and there the ice would be before them and twenty miles wide at least. He was forced to recall that his attempts at navigation had been conducted under considerable difficulties, which might have rendered them unreliable. The immediate chilling suspicion which occurred to him was that what he had confidently assumed to be King Oscar's Fjord might in fact have been Scoresby Sound – that he might have turned his party southwards when only a short distance farther to the east – perhaps no more than an hour's journey – they would have found the Settlement. If that were so, then they were heading now into unknown southern territory. The only other village, Angmagssalik, was over five hundred miles from Scoresby. They would have no hope of reaching it.

Providing he could be certain of that, the obvious thing to do would be to retrace their steps: their reserves of food and strength might just be enough to get them there. That was if the weather stayed good, and there were signs that it might be breaking. For the first time since the blizzard, clouds had appeared in the sky and the wind – now at their backs but one they would have to face if they turned north – had risen again.

It was a complex problem, but it did not occur to him to consult Mouritzen over it. Olsen decided he would press on for the remainder of that day at least. Something might appear which would make the decision easier. Whatever happened it would be his decision.

The sun rose and sank in a deeper welter of crimson than usual, and after it had gone the afterglow lit the southern clouds with a bloody red. Mouritzen and Stefan were pulling the sledge, with Mary and Mama Simanyi walking beside it. Olsen, Josef and Nadya were forty or fifty yards in the lead, setting the pace. The wind howled over the snow and across the ice to their right.

Unexpectedly, Mama Simanyi sank to the ground. Mouritzen checked the sledge but she waved him on.

'It is nothing,' she said. 'You go on. Mary will help me and we will catch you up.'

'What is it?' Mary said. 'Is it your foot?'

Mama Simanyi smiled. 'It is only that I want to talk. Let them go on a little.'

Mary said stifly: 'I don't think there's anything to talk about.'

She began to walk on. Mama Simanyi said:

'Stay. Please stay for an old woman.'

She hesitated, and then came back. The sledge pushed on away from them across the snow. Mama Simanyi said:

'You make yourself sad for nothing. I do not like to see you sad. Not Niels either.'

'Nothing?'

'You think he and Nadya made love together when they were alone in the hut that night. But you are wrong. It did not happen.'

'She gloated over it,' Mary said, 'and I saw his face. It would be too late for them to try denying it now.'

'She is naughty, my Nadya,' Mama Simanyi said. 'And she is young so she does not know what is tease and what is torment. She saw that you were jealous – that is why she talked as she did.'

'I know you're trying to help, but I don't think it helps to lie to people, even for their own good.'

'I am not lying.'

'Then Nadya is to you.'

'That neither. I talked with her this morning. She is a great liar, but I am her mother – I know when she tells the truth.'

Mary said: 'There was guilt in Niels' face.'

'Do you read a man's face so well?' She let the question, with all its implications, hang between them for a few moments. She went on: 'You had shown you suspected him. You both knew what there had once been between him and Nadya, and Nadya was saying things that would make you think they had happened again. What could poor Niels say? If he denied, it would be worse. No wonder he looked guilty.'

They tramped on in silence; they were a couple of hundred yards behind the sledge.

'It was thinking,' Mary said, 'that if he could betray me at a time like that – with Annabel and me lying out there, cold and hungry, on the ice...'

Mama Simanyi shook her head. 'Is it any better when you lie in a warm bed and well fed? But nothing happened. I tell you that, for certain. Nothing happened.'

There was silence again. The wind howled on a higher, harsher note. Mary turned round to look in the direction from which they had come. She said sharply:

'What's that?'

It looked like a belt of fog, covering the hills – a high, grey wall reaching up to the grey, twilit sky. But the wall was moving. As they watched, features were blotted out of the landscape in a steady and swift obliteration. It was not until it had almost reached them that they understood what it was, and a minute later they were blinded by the driving fury of the snow.

'Keep together!' Mama Simanyi said. 'We must try to keep straight, so we find the others.'

For a short time they were able to follow the tracks of the sledge; then the snow filled them. They tried to carry on in a straight line, but it was hard to know if they were succeeding. They could see for a few yards in front of them, no more. They were in a world without dimensions, a world of wind and snow and bitter cold.

'We will call to them,' Mama Simanyi said. 'Maybe they will hear us.'

They called, straining their voices against the wind, but only the wind answered. Probably they could be heard for not much farther than they could see. They staggered on, calling from time to time, but with increasingly less hope of being heard. Time was passing.

'If we went straight,' Mama Simanyi said, 'we must find them by now. So we are not straight. Too much to the right, I think. We try to the left?'

'Once we start wandering . . .'

'What else can we do? If we stop, then we die.'

They turned to the left, trying to count their paces so they would know how far they had gone from their original course. They found nothing, and the snow, coming from the side, lashed them more viciously. It was still more bitter when they turned into it, in case they had overshot the others. Now, despite what she had said, it was Mama Simanyi who wanted to call a halt.

'We rest a little – just a little, maybe. Then we will be stronger.'

Mary urged her on. 'We mustn't stop. You know that.'

After they had gone a little farther, she collapsed again. She said: 'You go on.'

'Not without you.'

'You have Annabel to think of.'

Mary pulled the older woman to her feet and, putting her arm round her, persuaded her to go on. She fell again, and the coaxing and lifting had to be repeated. They could no longer, Mary felt, go against the wind. They turned and had the blizzard at their backs. It made things a little easier, but not much. And they were lost now, truly lost.

When Mama Simanyi fell again, Mary stood over her for a moment, trying to summon up the strength to help her to her feet. Then she collapsed beside her.

'You – go on,' Mama Simanyi said.

But what point was there in going on, when for all she knew they might be heading directly away from the others? Mary huddled against the other woman, hoping to shelter her. She thought of Annabel. Niels would look after her. Niels would . . .

It snaked across their bodies and had almost gone before she realized what it was and, desperately, reached for it. She caught the rope, but had no power to do anything but hold it against the tug from somewhere out in the blizzard. She did not have to hold it long; almost at once a figure appeared out of the whirling snow. He reached down, and she saw it was Mouritzen. She lifted to him and their two chilled faces met.

'We walk back along the rope,' he said. 'The other end is at the sledge.'

'Annabel?'

'She is all right. Can you walk? I will carry Mama.'

She nodded. 'I can walk.'

'The rope,' he said. He looked at her. 'Three metres less and I could not have found you.'

She sighed. 'I knew you would look after Annabel.'

'Why not?' He put his face to hers again. 'She is our daughter.'

Day by day he had watched her grow weaker. From time to time he tried to persuade her to eat something; she would take a mouthful or two at his urging, but this was known by both of them – although it was never stated – to be a token only, a sign of companionship and love.

Strangely, it was not a sad time. From minute to minute, hour to hour, they were happy together, and they looked no farther ahead. Even after he had realized that she was dying, and knew that she knew this too, there seemed to be no constraint between them. Only once, when he got hot water and washed her, he saw her thin white body, lying without movement, as a corpse; and fear savaged him. But he looked up to her face, and saw her smiling. He dared not look at the future, and so he did not look. In the present they were both serenely happy.

In the afternoon he went to the window and looked out. He came back to his customary seat on the side of her bed. She looked at him in inquiry.

'The wind's getting up,' he said. 'Blowing snow up from the fjord in places. I'm glad we're not out there in a tent.'

'We're lucky,' she said.

'Very lucky. Are you comfortable? Shall I prop you up?'

'I'm all right.'

She hesitated, and then said something. Her voice was weak and he did not catch the words. He bent down to her.

'What was that?'

'Perhaps it's silly.'

'Tell me.'

'That.' She pointed feebly. The typewriter case was lying by the foot of the other bed. 'I don't . . .'

He thought he knew what she meant. 'Don't like seeing it? I'll put it out of sight.'

She said, speaking quickly and with more strength:

'I don't want that to be with us when I die.'

It was a breach of their unspoken agreement and should have been appalling; but neither was appalled by it. He offered no protestation. He simply said:

'I'll take it outside. Will that be better?'

She nodded. 'You can bring it in again, afterwards. It will be quite safe, won't it? There's no one to take it.'

'Wait for me.' It had its significance; he bent and kissed her. 'I won't be long.'

He had thought at first merely of carrying the case out and burying it in the snow; it would be easy enough to mark the spot so that he could find it when he wanted to. She had said: 'You can bring it in again, afterwards.' And she would be lying there, white and unmoving, and this time she would not smile. He found himself saying, as though to that dead body, 'It was for you – there's no point in it otherwise,' and knew that it was true. It was she who had given him hope and redeemed him from failure; he had willingly lied and cheated and stolen for their future together, and now the future was over and done with.

There was only the present, and no room in it for anything but the two of them. No room, certainly, for what he was carrying in the typewriter case.

He climbed up the slope behind the hut; he had gone up there the first day they had been left alone, and found the torn carcases of the two bears, and looked down at the still sprawled figure of Thorsen at the bottom of the ravine. He decided he would throw it down there. Thorsen had wanted it: he could have it. Then he could go back to the hut and tell Sheila; it made no essential difference but he wanted her to know that it had only been for her, and had no meaning without her.

The carcases were stripped to the bones now, and the bones had been crunched and scattered. There were marks of animals in the snow: probably wolves. When it happened, he would not put her outside. He would let the fire go out, and let the cold creep in, and lie there beside her. He brushed away the sick feeling of fear that this thought gave him. The present was not yet over.

Although it was hard to be sure from this height, he thought that Thorsen's body had so far escaped the scavengers. He leaned over and dropped the case. It bounced on the side of the ledge and broke open and spilled its bundles of paper out on to the rocks below. He watched them scatter on to the snow and then turned away.

Almost at once he saw the grey cloud sweeping across the surface of the fjord. It moved faster than he had expected; in a minute or two he felt the sharper bite of the wind and then the cold, burning harshness of the teeming snow. He let it turn him away from his previous route. If he went over the next ridge, he thought, there would be some protection from the storm and he could beat his way down to the other side of the hut.

He knew he was lost quite soon. Just beyond the ridge he plunged into deeper, softer snow, and by the time he fought his way clear he had lost all sense of direction. The blizzard which, smothering and blinding and freezing, surrounded him, was from the north, and he had a hazy idea that he must struggle across it and down, but the slope of the land here was confusingly different. He plunged again into a drift, and was tempted by the warmth and softness. But he remembered that it was important to keep going; and Sheila, in the hut, was waiting for him.

At least, he thought with relief, he no longer had the case to carry. He was travelling light, as Sheila was. There was nothing now to tie them, or hold them back.

His face had been first cold and then numb. Now, somehow, he felt warmth on it. He tried to look up, to see if in some incredible fashion the sun was shining. Nothing to hold us back, he thought... we can go anywhere we like... to the island she dreamed of... the great golden sun, the warm waters – the feasting and the singing and the dancing ...

In the hut Sheila waited, feeling the tiredness spread farther and more deeply into her body. She tried to speak when it reached her throat and was at first distressed when the words would not come. But it did not matter. When Henry came back he would talk and she would listen. She found a heaviness lying on her eyelids, too, dragging them down despite her efforts to keep them open. That did not matter, either. He would sit beside her and hold her hand, and the touch would be enough.

The wind outside howled more fiercely; she hoped he would come back before he got too cold. But perhaps he had not been long; perhaps the dragging tiredness dragged time out as well. When he came back it would be like that – seconds stretched into minutes, hours, years even.

The wind rattled the door and she saw it open, and saw him stand there, smiling at her. His body was framed against bright sunshine, and as he came forward the sunshine poured in behind him, making the small room swim with light.

'I waited for you,' she said; and closed her eyes again.

Olsen had seen the storm coming up in time for him and Josef and Nadya to get back to the sledge before it engulfed them all. With Stefan and Josef he fought to get the tent unpacked and erected, while Nadya and Mouritzen, with the aid of the longest rope, made a continuous searching arc for the other two. The wind was too strong for them. In the end they had to compromise with a shelter formed by a canvas stretched from the top of the sledge. They huddled underneath this, keeping close together for warmth. At the beginning the freezing wind blew in through all the open chinks, but as the blizzard continued, snow piled up round them and gave them some protection. For the time being they were safe.

As to the rest, much depended on the duration of the blizzard. If it lasted over three days, as the first had done, there was no hope of their surviving it. It was impossible to get at the food, or the blankets. Even in the shelter of the snow, cold would seep in. Already Olsen's feet were numb with the beginning of frost-bite. Without food their bodies could not fight for long against the Arctic chill. Some of them might survive the night: he doubted if the child would.

This land of ice and snow and bitter winds had defeated them:

the effort had been good but now it was drawing to its end. Olsen felt no resentment; rather he felt respect for an adversary that fought so fiercely and relentlessly, and fought, at the same time, with such a wild and burning beauty. Whether one conquered it or was conquered by it, it was a good land, a clean and savage place.

He could see the luminous face of his watch when he pulled his hand from inside his jacket; he had crossed his arms in front of him and tucked the hands in to protect them. The hours ticked by towards the moment when defeat would be made final. When, after the blizzard had been blowing for over four hours, the wind sounded stronger than ever, he abandoned the half-protected hope of an abatement sufficient to let them get the tent up. The cold was in his legs and at his back. He found himself dozing, and no longer struggled to remain awake.

Silence woke him; a surrounding silence in which the breathing of the others was loud, even harsh. He was bitterly cold. Blinking, he saw that it was nine o'clock by his watch. He did not know how long he had slept: it might be morning.

He was at the most exposed end, which made it easier for him to get out without disturbing anyone. He pushed his way out through the snow into a night of clear, still brilliance.

There was no moon, but the stars were intensely big and bright, and all across the northern sky hung curtains and rays and arcs of light. As he watched, they changed; shifting, pulsating, dimming and bursting out into new and more splendid forms. A cluster of rays seemed to be slowly spinning on a central axis. High up in the sky there was a corona, such as he had sometimes seen around the moon, but in its centre there were only stars.

He could wake them, and they could put up the tent. In the morning, unless the blizzard returned, they could set out again. In which direction? It was probably safer to go back. If they could get to the hut they would have shelter and warmth and they could try trapping for food. The chances were not good but better, probably, than to continue trekking south now that he had lost his confidence that they were on the right trail.

Olsen felt a deep weariness of spirit. They depended on him, but they meant nothing to him, and there was nothing he could do for them. Between one desperate chance and another, what balance could one hold? More days, perhaps weeks, but in the end there was no difference. He looked at the mound from which he had crawled. It was very like a grave.

He began to walk away, not knowing why he did so, content to stride through the snow under this sky which gleamed in saffron and pink and green. He walked to the south, to the still untrodden land. This was the slope along which they had been advancing when he had seen the storm coming up from behind them. Now he walked alone, untroubled, forgetful of everything but the vast purity of the snow, and the lights which seemed to hang no more than a few hundred feet above his head.

There was a howling in the distance, but of an animal, not of the wind. A wolf, perhaps. The thought gave him no anxiety. Another howled, and another. They were like dogs, he thought, howling at the bright sky as dogs howl at the moonlight.

Like dogs ... His stride lengthened. He breasted the ridge and stared. In front of him stretched the broad, ice-bound reaches of a bay. Then to his left ...

Here and there brighter, yellower lights were pricked out against the snow. The nearer ones showed the squares of window frames and he could even see the shapes of the houses. That was where the dogs were howling, the huskies sleeping out in the snow. It was the Settlement. Olsen stood staring at it for several moments and then slowly, almost reluctantly, turned back towards the distant mound in the snow.

Cold and numb and tired and hungry as she was, Annabel could still feel the excitement and wonder of it – to be perched on Mouritzen's broad shoulders as he strode through the snow, the sky overhead lit with all manner of fireworks ... a bonfire night, only wider and stranger, and with the snow, to which she had grown accustomed, once more magical. It was like Christmas, and the grown-ups were all happy, and they were going to some place where there would be fires and hot food and beds.

Her mother and Mouritzen dropped behind the rest. She urged him on, pummelling his head with her small fists as she had done before. But he paid no attention. They were talking quietly together, in the way grown-ups did talk, with the words making sense and yet not meaning anything.

Mary said: 'You don't have to go through with it, Niels.'

He laughed. 'Are we talking of torture?'

'It might turn into that.'

'I am happy to take the chance.'

'You've seen how I can be – jealous and vindictive and unjust. I gave you no chance to tell me I was wrong. I just believed the worst of you.'

He was silent. Then he said: 'Not unjust.'

'What else?'

'Nothing happened,' he said. 'That is quite true. But that was because of Nadya – she did not permit it.' He paused. 'I had to tell you this, Mary.'

In a flat voice she said: 'Yes.'

There was silence. Annabel said:

'Come on, slowcoach! They're leaving us behind.'

Mouritzen jerked his shoulders, and she squealed with pleasure.

'They won't leave us behind,' Mouritzen said. 'We will catch up. You wait and see.'

'I suppose I ought to be grateful?' Mary said. 'To someone like her.' She laughed bitterly. 'She said that, didn't she? She told me she'd brought my man back to me.'

'She is not bad. You must judge her hardly.'

'She loves you. You know that, don't you? Why don't you marry Nadya, Niels?'

Annabel said: 'He can't, Mamma. He's going to marry you. He said so.'

Mouritzen jogged her again. 'That is right.' To Mary, he said: 'A man can desire many women. He only loves one. And her he loves truly. Even if she is jealous. Even if she is jealous and scolds him some time when he is not to blame. He still loves her.'

'But there will be times,' she said, 'when he is to blame. Won't there? Other Nadyas.'

'I hope not. That does not happen often – a time like that was. And you can keep close watch on me. I will not complain. If you wish, you may set a chain on my neck.'

'A chain on your neck!' Annabel echoed. She shouted with laughter. 'You would look funny!'

'It wouldn't do any good,' Mary said. She paused. 'It doesn't matter. What you say about loving is true. Even if he is weak, even if he makes love to other women, she still loves him truly.'

'He will not,' Mouritzen said with great firmness. 'He gains strength from love and will be weak no longer.'

Mary said warningly: 'And don't you ever dare quote what I've just said against me.'

Mouritzen laughed, and Annabel felt his head vibrate against her. She began to pummel him again.

'Come on. We aren't catching up. Do be quick!'

'Now we make a sprint,' Mouritzen said. He caught Mary's hand with his. 'Come – we will all run together through the snow!'

There would be difficulties, Olsen realized. At close on forty a man could not give up a career and start afresh without difficulties. Hardships, also. He would forfeit the pension. He smiled, thinking of this. And to do what? He did not even know.

But if now, why not twenty years ago? He knew the answer to that: he had been too young, too confident, too deeply buried still in all the illusions of human commerce. The twenty years had not been wasted. A man came to know himself and to know where truth and beauty lay.

The Simanyis were laughing and joking together, their voices harsh against the cold, still air. Josef clapped a hand against his back.

'You are too silent, Captain. Cheer up! Soon you will be home.'

Olsen looked up at the sky. He said:

'I am home already.'